HIDDEN AMONG US

Other books by Katy Moran:

Bloodline
Bloodline Rising
Spirit Hunter
Dangerous to Know

HIDDEN AMONG US

KATY MORAN

WALKER
BOOKS

First published in 2013 by Walker Books Ltd
87 Vauxhall Walk, London SE11 5HJ

2 4 6 8 10 9 7 5 3 1

Text © 2013 Katy Moran
Cover illustration © 2013 Alejandro Colucci

The right of Katy Moran to be identified as author of this
work has been asserted by her in accordance with the
Copyright, Designs and Patents Act 1988

This book has been typeset in Bembo

Printed and bound by CPI Group (UK) Ltd, Croydon CR0 4YY

British Library Cataloguing in Publication Data:
a catalogue record for this book is
available from the British Library

ISBN 978-1-4063-8546-5

www.walker.co.uk

MIX
Paper from
responsible sources
FSC® C020471

For

Delilah Wells

"I met a lady in the meads,
Full beautiful – a faery's child,
Her hair was long, her foot was light,
And her eyes were wild."
From "La Belle Dame Sans Merci", by John Keats

PART ONE
THE COVENANT

1

Rafe

I'm building a tower.

The red and yellow bricks are smooth in my hands, and the fire is making them warm. Rain bashes at the window. It's getting dark but Mum says it's not the night. The radio is playing. Mum has gone out to the barn to get wood. She's cross because the roof is leaking and our firewood keeps getting wet. Most days since we came to live here I sit in the wheelbarrow and go with Mum, but today I was making my tower and I said no.

So now I'm on my own. It's Uncle Miles's house, but we never see him. Dad says he's like a ghost. Lissy doesn't count because she's a baby. A few weeks ago, she wasn't even here at all. She was just nobody.

The scream comes blasting out of nowhere.

Lissy, upstairs. It's not her usual crying. Something else. Something bad.

I'm scared so much it hurts in my belly but I get up anyway, leaving the tower of bricks by the fire. The hall is cold. It's full of the screaming from upstairs.

"Lissy!" I shout. "Lissy, it's OK!"

What am I going to do?

I'm running up the stairs now because it sounds so bad, that screaming, like someone's hurting her, or she's scared—

And she stops when I'm halfway up the stairs. The scream stops. Our house is quiet again, just the radio in the kitchen. And me. Like it was before she got here, before she was born.

"Lissy?" I call, but she doesn't answer because she is just a baby. She can't do anything.

I run. Up the stairs, along the hall. The curtains are open and I can see Lissy's baby basket on the big bed. Rain is rushing down the window.

Maybe that's it: she's gone back to sleep, really quickly.

I feel sick now but I keep going, walking slowly across the stripey rug till I reach the bed and stand there looking into Lissy's basket.

She's gone. My baby sister has gone.

There's just a tangled blanket. And a pile of dead leaves, all brown and broken. Where did they come from? A leaf jumps like it has come alive, and the biggest spider ever crawls across the sheet where Lissy lay.

I can hear screaming again but this time it's me.

2

Miriam

She's been gone for over three weeks. My baby. If we'd left the Reach when Adam wanted to, when I was still pregnant, would they still have found us? It's all my fault.

Will writing this down even help?

It's two o'clock in the morning now, but it was only just past midnight when I left Adam and Rafe sleeping together in the big double bed. I couldn't stand lying there in the dark, wanting to turn back time.

I've let everyone down.

I knew sleep would never come. I went downstairs; I pushed open the great oak front door and stepped outside into the darkness. Miles once told me this door was made over seven hundred years ago, but there are parts of the house which belong to a time before that. Hopesay Reach is an old, old place. It remembers everything.

Miles took away all our protection, and they came.

The cold was breathtaking, but I deserve to suffer. I've got to find Lissy, whatever the cost. I dropped to my knees on the front lawn – whitened with a late frost, a killing frost that will blast every last blossom from the fruit trees.

All I could hear was her sharp cry echoing inside my head.

She needs me; I can't help her.

I begged.

It was all I could do, my only option. I begged them for mercy, in a jumbled mix of French and English that probably didn't even make sense.

"Je veux mon bébé," I whispered to the cold, cold ground. *"I'll do anything. Bring her back and I'll do whatever you want."*

I would have torn open the earth to find her; I leaned forwards ripping the grass with white-cold hands. I broke the ground, tearing a fingernail from its root. Exquisite pain shot up my hand and through my arm, but it was nothing compared to losing Lissy. My mouth opened wide but the scream was silent, and that's when it happened. I never thought they'd listen.

One did.

A voice whispered through the darkness. *"Miriam—"*

I scrambled up, breathing hard. The frozen grass burnt my bare feet. The yew tree on the lawn was shaking: branches twisted and whipped by a sudden violent wind. The waters of the lake shivered. The yew is older than Hopesay Reach itself, older than the village church, they say, and it must have weathered a million storms. But that wind sent two of its branches crashing to the ground. My hair was torn and twisted; I remember the nightgown flapping against my legs.

I looked up. A ragged black shape passed across the silver face of the moon. It circled in the sky, wheeling above me, wings spread. I didn't know what it was — some kind of bird of prey, a falcon? It dropped hard and fast like a stone. But when the bird landed, there was no falcon, just a tall boy with tangled red hair.

Despite my agony and fear, I'm still breathless at the wonder of it, three hours later in the grey light of dawn.

He was one of the Hidden. There was a smear of blood across his cheek; so beautiful I couldn't take my eyes away, not for a second. There was something familiar about him, even then. I felt like I'd seen him before.

"Miriam." He spoke quietly. He knew my name. I didn't know his, not then, but I saw the fear and hesitancy in his eyes. "I hear your voice in the rain." He shrugged: an odd, fluid and wholly inhuman movement that always betrays his kind to those who know, and I do. "I come against my father's word."

I'll admit a jolt of fear knocked through me when he spoke. *My father?*

"Please," I whispered, "please help me. I can't bear to be without her. Please bring Lissy back. She'll die. She'll die without me. Won't she?"

"You ask me to do what has been forbidden."

Tears streamed down my face and I asked if she was still alive.

"Of course." He sounded incredulous, as if I'd said something stupid, but how could the Hidden know how to look after a baby? They can't have their own children, not any more.

It's why they took mine.

"Why don't you come with me?" he said, so gentle and beguiling.

15

"I'll take you to her."

I looked back at the house. "My little boy." I shook my head. "I can't come with you. Not to stay. I can't leave him. He's only four."

It's true what the fairy tales say: a man follows his beloved into the fairy hill. When he steps out into the light of day, it is not the next morning. A thousand million mornings have come and gone as he danced with the Hidden, with the fairies, the fee, the elves, the Sidhe, whatever you choose to call them. In the end, it is all the same. He dissolves into dust. I couldn't risk that, finding Lissy but leaving Rafe without a mother.

"Please don't cry. Lissy belongs to us now." He sighed, as if upset by the difficulty I was causing, my inability to accept she was gone.

"But she's my baby," I whispered. He wasn't going to help me. I turned away, and all I wanted to do was lie down on the frozen ground and die.

"Wait." He laid one cold hand on my arm. "Then we'll make a covenant: you can borrow her."

"What do you mean?" My voice was cracked, desperate. Even after all these years, there are still a few English words I don't recognize. "What's a covenant?"

"An agreement. A deal." He shrugged again. "I'll bring Lissy to you, and no matter how far from here you run, in fourteen years you must return to Hopesay, where our worlds meet. Bring her home to the Reach. Don't fail me, Miriam, I'm trusting you."

I told him fourteen years wasn't enough. We *could* run.

16

We could hide. "What if I don't bring her back?"

He smiled. "You will. Don't try to cheat me, Miriam."

I tried to interrupt, but he spoke again, and what he said and did will freeze my blood and bones till the day I die.

The boy reached out and softly blew on his outstretched fingertips. As I watched, a tangle of briar roses appeared from nothing, cupped right there in the palm of his hand, fresh green leaves and petals stained pink like the sky at sunset, still flecked with dew.

"With this gift, I curse thee, Miriam Harker," he whispered. "Hear this. Unless one of the Hidden willingly gives up their own life in exchange for Lissy, in fourteen years any mortal child born from your body will die if you don't bring Lissy home to my father." He smiled, as if he'd just made a joke and he was waiting for me to laugh.

I watched, breathless with horror. The green leaves twined about his fingers were starting to wither, turn brown. The petals began to curl up, yellowing.

"So don't try to shut the Gateway, Miriam," he said, gently; "and don't cheat."

The briar roses shrank to nothing but a withered stick, then a small heap of dust in his palm, which he let fall to the frozen ground.

"Just promise you'll bring her back." I couldn't believe what I'd just seen. My whole body tingled with fear. Yes, and wonder, too.

The boy nodded. "My word is my bond. Do you believe in a god, Miriam? Some enormous mind who made the very earth we stand on? A force that shapes the world and makes

17

sense of it, something kind and good and merciful?"

His question stunned me; I thought it might be some kind of trick. Twenty-five years of church-going prompted me to find an answer, even though in truth I'm not sure there is one. "Of course I believe in God."

"Good," he said, quietly, "because only such a thing will now save me from my father's rage. I'll come back with the sun, and bring her."

Before I could speak again, he was gone. Simply gone, leaving nothing but a whirlwind of green summer leaves. As I watched, they withered and turned brown, just as the briar roses had done, landing on the frosty earth.

And now I'm scared. So, so scared. Fourteen years isn't enough.

I have to find a way of unravelling that curse, of cheating him – them. The Hidden.

His father.

I won't let them have Lissy. I won't let her go.

PART TWO
THE CHEAT

3

Rafe

Fourteen years later

"Yes?" The librarian barely looked up from his computer; I got a prime view of his greasy thinning hair. I showed my Reader's Pass: he had no choice but to help commit my crime. He wouldn't know that until afterwards, though.

I handed over my request, written on a sheet of paper with the school letterhead. All I could do was hope that and the forged letter from the Head of History would be enough to impress the librarian. My heart rate accelerated.

When the librarian looked up, his expression was blank, all trace of emotion ironed from his face. "You do realize that we advise all researchers to inform us of their needs up to two hours before—"

I shrugged, carefully. Could he sense my panic? "Sorry."

The librarian glanced down at his computer screen. "What you've asked for is restricted access, anyway."

Frozen sweat spread across my back, between my shoulder blades. I tugged the counterfeit letter out of my back pocket and handed it over. My tormentor glanced at it, sighed, and at last, he got up out of his seat.

"If you'd like to follow me, sir." Extremely sarcastic with the *sir*.

But inside I was punching the air. I'd done it. First stage complete. Now I just had to finish the job.

Stealing a priceless manuscript from one of the most famous institutions in the world.

I walked after the librarian, keeping my eyes on the back of his shirt. The faint dark sweat mark between his shoulders. Wrinkled trousers. Past rows of long dark wooden tables, walls lined with bookshelves – a chubby woman with glasses, head down. Some idiot in a tie-dyed t-shirt. So this was where all those awkward losers ended up: the ones who, unlike me, never learned to disguise their intelligence.

One step at a time.

The sheaf of yellowish paper was fragile – almost brittle – between my fingers. A jumble of black lettering.

I must have looked surprised because the librarian said, "It's more of an obscure journal than a book." He gave me a grey-lipped smile. "According to my records, this issue hasn't been touched since 1917. Congratulations – in a few moments you'll be the only living person on earth to know what the author knew."

The only living person on earth. It was hot and stuffy in there but I felt cold, all the same. I would be sharing secrets with the dead.

"The Reading Room closes in two hours. Of course, you're free to make notes. I'm sure I don't need to point out to a young man from *your* school that annotating the manuscript itself is strictly forbidden." One last sarcastic smile, and the librarian was gone.

I chose a seat furthest from the information desk and put on the latex gloves he'd given me, horribly slippery against my skin. I glanced down, allowing myself a look. The words flew out at me, stark and terrifying, releasing a wave of memories I wish I could have surgically removed. It's still so clear after fourteen years. *My parents both crying, led away by policemen. The empty baby basket, and—*

I forced myself to make sense of the letters on the page.

It is well known they take children, for what purpose only God can tell—

This was it. I'd found it. No time to read on. I had to get this over with. Get out of there.

I had no bag except a library-branded clear plastic carrier; my stuff was all waiting in the locker room downstairs, according to the strict regulations. That was OK. That was just fine. I didn't need a bag. I picked up the manuscript, leaning back in my chair. Everyone else was busy reading. The tie-dyed guy stared off into space but towards the door, well away from me.

Now. I had to do it now.

After fourteen years I was going to know for sure who they were. Why they took my sister. And if they were coming back.

Just as I was about to hide the journal, I saw that someone else had broken the rules, too.

There was writing in the bottom margin. Brown ink, sloping old-fashioned letters – no one writes like that any more: a hundred years old at least.

They will kill you—

Then I felt true cold fear, all right: an ice-cold hand taking hold of my guts and twisting.

What was it supposed to mean? *Who?*

I slid the manuscript down between my tucked-in shirt and my skin and walked out of the Reading Room, through the British Library café — black smoked glass everywhere like some kind of low-grade club in Shoreditch — out past the lobby and down a flight of steps into the wild mad roar of the Euston Road: four insane lanes of lorries, cars, double-decker buses and lycra-wearing cyclists gambling with death. A bit like me.

And all this time, Lissy was running for her life and she didn't even know it.

4

Joe

The house loomed up behind me, all rain-slick stone and glittering windows. Daylight was fading now, and the air felt like damp cold hands on my skin.

Out in the courtyard, Connie was crouched down by a puddle, bare feet in the water, bright red shorts and legs streaked with mud. Her hair was pinned back with a load of shiny clips that stood out bright against the grey evening; they were decorated with red plastic cherries, an orange pineapple. The overgrown cobblestones shone with wet.

"Connie!" I called. "Your mam's looking for you."

She turned and smiled, a jumble of white teeth. "All right. In a minute, Joe. Don't worry about Mum. She's just in a massive stress because of Lissy." Connie reminded me of a puppy, loud and enthusiastic. "We were on our way to pick Lissy up when she texted and said she'd got on the train instead. I couldn't believe it! We had to drive all the way here without her!"

"It's not like she robbed a bank." I was sort of intrigued by Connie's sister and I'd not even met her yet.

"Mum was sooo cross." By the look of it, Connie was half enjoying the scandal and half terrified by her sister's crimes. Catching a train didn't seem like a big deal to me, but I didn't know the full story then. "Anyway," she said, "have you met my friend?"

"What are you on about? There's no one here." I followed Connie's gaze over to the tangle of undergrowth on the far side of the courtyard.

I'd been wrong: we weren't alone.

There was this tall lass standing among the rain-drenched nettles and cow parsley. A wave of shock shot through my body. How could I not have seen her before? Long white hair coiled around her shoulders, even though she looked only a couple of years older than me, sixteen or so maybe. She smiled at us, just watching. She didn't seem fussed about the rain or even seem to notice it, even though it was falling so heavily now her face was dripping.

She never took her eyes off me.

"Isn't she beautiful?" Connie said. "She said she's a princess, and I believe her." She laughed, like she knew it sounded daft.

The girl smiled at me again. My heart was hammering like a bloody train. There was something about her. She wasn't just pretty. It was more than that – I couldn't take my eyes off her, either. She looked amused and a bit thoughtful, and I'd got this bad feeling she was working out how to get one over on me. A bit like a cat teasing a mouse.

"Come inside, Connie," I said again, deliberately looking away from the white-haired girl. The yard had gone very quiet. When me and Dad arrived, he'd pointed out a fledgling blackbird nosediving from the branches of an apple tree, and you could hear birdsong everywhere. Now it was silent, as if they'd all been switched off.

Which was creepy, to be honest.

"Come on!" I hissed at Connie, and she looked up, surprised at the panic in my voice. I was pretty surprised too – I just wanted to get away from that girl, and I couldn't have said why if you'd paid me.

"All right, keep your hair on." Connie got up, looking down at her soaked clothes, her mud-streaked legs, smiling. "Mum's going to kill me – these shorts are new!" She ran over to the door, shivering theatrically and waving at the white-haired girl, who lifted one hand but said nothing. I turned back, screwing up the courage to tell her to get lost, but there was no one there. She'd gone. Just disappeared.

Lost in the rain.

I must've imagined the silence before, because now the yard was full of birdsong again – chattering starlings, even a cuckoo.

I followed Connie inside, walking quicker than I needed to, and as we came in I saw how thick the walls were here – nearly two feet of ancient stone. Were all medieval houses built like nuclear bunkers? Connie skipped off down the corridor leaving wet footprints on flagstones worn smooth by centuries of human traffic. I locked the back door behind us, just in case. The girl may have gone but what if she'd got mates nearby, looking for trouble?

Call me suspicious but you don't just hang around in other people's gardens.

That's when I saw it: a patch of bare grey stone left in paint the colour of curdled milk, just above the door frame. It was the shape of a cross, as if a crucifix had hung there for years and years, since long before the walls were painted.

Whatever the reason, the cross was gone now. Dad had said the house was really ancient, that it used to be a priory hundreds of years ago till Henry the Eighth closed down all the monasteries. *It's probably haunted,* I told myself. *Headless monks and all that stuff.* Then I told myself not to be an idiot, and wondered again what I was going to do with myself for a whole week. There was no TV: even the radio didn't work. What did Miriam's stepbrother *do* here all the time? Dad said he didn't even have a job, and muttered something about inherited money. So far, the only sign of his existence was a battered old estate car parked on the drive and a dusty bottle of champagne in the fridge with half an inch left in the bottom, which made Miriam tut and shake her head. *Don't worry about Miles,* she told me and Dad. *He's a bit eccentric. More like bloody rude,* I thought, but I'd the sense not to say it.

We'd only just arrived. I was bored out of my brain already.

Connie had left the kitchen door open – I could hear her chatting to Dad – but there was another door off the stone-flagged corridor. This one looked much newer, with peeling white paint, glass panels and a pitted, tarnished brass handle. I pushed it open, thinking that maybe I could kill a couple of hours exploring the house – it was big enough: a great rambling sprawly place, all black and white timbers, windows in odd places, and gloomy panelled rooms. I didn't fancy reading, and I'd broken a guitar string so couldn't even do any practice till we'd found the nearest music shop.

I found myself in an old lean-to built against the side of the original house. There was a battered, stained table with a jackknife on it, and a dirty sink with a load of manky feathers blocking the plughole. Someone had been gutting pheasants by the look of it – illegally shot, because it wouldn't be the shooting season for another few months. They were still breeding. *Grandad wouldn't approve,* I thought. He was retired now but still read *Modern Gamekeeping* every month. I looked around the room, feeling uneasy. There was a lot here Grandad wouldn't like: next to a pair of mud-spattered boots, a wooden cabinet leaned drunkenly by the cobwebby window, the door swinging open. I went over and shut it, turning the rusty key. What about Connie? You'd have to be brain-dead leaving a gun cabinet unlocked, especially with a kid in the house. It made me feel nervy, like the Reach was a dangerous place. Hanging on the wall beside it was a collection of what looked like torture instruments, all springs and horrible steel jaws. Gin traps, designed to catch and mutilate poachers. Grandad had one in his shed. *Evil things,* he'd once told me. *They'll maim a man for life, not to mention the kiddies that used to get trapped in them by mistake. It's a good thing they were banned.*

I couldn't help shivering, like someone had just dropped a handful of snow down my back. Unsecured shotguns, illegal traps. *It's not safe here.* I wanted to turn round, go into the kitchen and find Dad. Get back in our car and just drive away.

"What do you think you're doing?" A harsh, upper-class voice: angry.

I spun around, feeling really guilty, like I was a trespasser, not just an unwilling guest. The stranger was wearing a battered old jacket patched with gaffer tape, and had a soggy roll-up hanging out the corner of his mouth. He looked older than my dad, grey-haired and pale as cheese, but there was something hawkish and dangerous about him. His fingers were covered in blood. *Christ.*

"What do you want?" he snapped. "This is a private house."

So this was Miriam's stepbrother, the bloke who owned this place: Miles, a stupid posh-sounding name. What a charmer.

"I'm here with Miriam."

He frowned and lit a match, holding it to the end of his roll-up, watching me all the time. His eyes were a weird shade of pearly grey, like the sky just after it's pissed it down. He blew out a cloud of rank smoke.

"You're not Rafe. Not her boy." His nostrils widened like he was sniffing the air, and I couldn't help thinking of Grandad's cocker, Meg, when she got on a scent. OK on a dog, a creepy look on a *person.*

I shook my head. "No." Hadn't Miriam explained *anything?* Talk about bloody awkward.

He took another draw on his fag, obviously losing interest. "Stay out of here. It's dangerous. The Reach isn't a safe place. She shouldn't have brought you here." He gave me a long, searching look, then turned and took an old shotgun from the cabinet, not even seeming to notice that I'd shut the door, turned that rusty key in the lock. It should've had a proper combination, a padlock. Shouldering the gun, he turned and went out the garden door, letting it slam shut. I stood watching rain hammer against the window, thinking about the empty fridge. It was like he never went to the shops, but just lived on scrawny old birds from the woods.

I don't mind admitting I wanted to go home. That I was even a bit scared.

5

Lissy

I was the only one left in the carriage; the train pushed slowly westwards after the fourth and last change, no more waiting at platforms. I leaned against the window, hugging my arms around my knees, feet up on a seat peppered with the shiny slate-coloured remains of other people's chewing gum. Outside, shadowy hillsides climbed up and up. It was well past eight o'clock; the sky had turned grey, streaked with a crazy fluorescent pink.

I watched the sunset fade over rising hills, wondering what Mum would say when I called from a station more than a hundred miles away from where I was meant to meet her, hours ago. I didn't have a sensible explanation. I've been a prisoner all my life. I had to escape at some point. It was surprisingly easy. Most of the girls on our Year Nine Shakespeare field trip were being coached back to school ready to get picked up by their parents in the usual end-of-term madness. A few, like Alice and me, were waiting to be collected from the railway station in Stratford-Upon-Avon.

"Cover for me," I'd whispered to Alice when Mrs Venables' back was turned. "Please."

It was so easy. I went into the station, crossed over to the west-bound platform, and climbed onto a waiting train. I texted Mum, telling her I was OK, what time I'd get into Hopesay Edge station, and asking her to please pick me up – as if all this was completely normal, not my biggest ever act of rebellion.

I replied to a frantic message from Alice, reassuring her that I hadn't gone mad, then switched off my phone with a glorious sense of freedom. I had committed an unforgivable act of disobedience and stupidity. Mum and Connie must have been almost at Stratford in the car by the time I texted. They'd made a completely pointless detour there on the way from our house in Oxfordshire to Hopesay Edge, hours and hours long, only to find me gone. Yes, there would be consequences, big ones, but I didn't have to face them yet. When the inspector came, I bought a ticket heading west, knowing that would take me in the right direction. He told me when and where to change trains. I was doing OK.

I could look after myself.

I was alone. Safe, even if only for a few hours.

Alone, I can be myself without attracting the wrong kind of attention. I can read *Anna Karenina*, untranslated, and no one will know or care that I've never been taught Russian. No one will touch my hand or arm and give me that *look*, saying, *Oh, my God, Lissy, you're so cold.*

It was good to be free for a few hours, not pretending to be like everyone else.

I had to show Mum I could do this or I would be a prisoner for ever.

I stared out of the window as the train slowed down again; I was so tired and my head felt foggy. I never sleep well after the dream, and last night the dream had returned, but I couldn't think about that now because it was my stop, time to move. I pushed away the memory of falling, got up, grabbed my bag, ran along the carriage to the doors, thinking, *That was close; I nearly didn't notice.* But I'd done it, I'd come all the way here on my own without messing up. Like an adult. For the first time ever, I was coming back to the place I was born. I literally did make my entrance at Hopesay Reach on the kitchen floor. It only took half an hour, and the ambulance arrived just in time to get Mum to hospital, who was bleeding so badly she nearly died. Which is probably one of the reasons why she wants to ruin my life.

Maybe now I'll find out why we never visit Hopesay, why Mum never sees her stepbrother, I thought. *Maybe she'll finally tell us what the big secret is.*

I've invented so many different explanations over the years, I'm convinced the real one couldn't possibly surprise me: *Uncle Miles is deformed and refuses to see anyone. Uncle Miles has got leprosy and his face has gone rotten.* That bright idea came when we were doing Medieval England in Year Five. *Uncle Miles has gone mad like Mr Rochester's wife in* Jane Eyre. Or — a more recent notion — *Uncle Miles was Mum's secret boyfriend and Dad found out.* It was Alice who thought of that one. All these years to puzzle over this mystery and my best friend came up with the likeliest story.

Isn't that a bit gross, though? Alice had screwed up her nose as if she could smell something bad. *Brother and sister together? Eugh!*

Uncle Miles isn't Mum's real brother, I'd explained for the tenth time. *He's her stepbrother. It's not the same.*

Alice could be very stupid sometimes.

The train didn't stop.

It just crept on through the station, slow but still going. Frantic, I pressed the black rubber button by the doors but they stayed stubbornly shut. The train picked up speed again. I'd missed the station. I gripped the handle of my bag, trying to ignore the horrible burning prickling at the backs of my eyes.

I'd made a huge mistake.

Don't cry, I told myself, fiercely. *Don't be such an idiot. It's fine. All I have to do is get off at the next station and phone Mum. It'll only be a few miles. It's not my fault the train didn't stop. She's going to be furious anyway.*

But when I took my phone out of my pocket, there was no signal. I had to push away the panicky feeling that the train was going to keep moving till it got to the Welsh sea. At last the train did stop. I leapt off onto the platform, bag banging into my legs as I stumbled. The station was in almost complete darkness; there was just a circle of orangey light spread by the lamp standing next to a bench. Somebody was sitting there. Waiting. A man or a boy, hooded.

I could hear my heart beating now, blood pounding. It was stupid of me to be so ridiculously terrified of a man on a bench. I glanced down at my phone again. Still no signal. Hardly any at the house. What kind of place was this?

35

Like going on holiday to another century. I ran into the station building – just a silent ticket office and a bare-bricked waiting room with a few plastic seats. No lights on anywhere at all. Nobody there; no phone. OK. It would be OK. I'd just have to walk down into the town, or village – wherever it was. I could get help. But outside the ticket office there was nothing except a dark, tree-lined country road, shadowy houses just visible in the distance. Not even a single streetlight. I stopped, glancing back at the station. I was kidding myself, trying to put off the moment where I'd have to start walking, ask a stranger for help, which would all somehow make this more serious, even more proof that I wasn't capable of doing anything for myself.

What have you done, you idiot? I thought.

And then, from out of the shadows, somebody spoke.

"You seem afraid. Are you all right?" A smooth, light voice.

My heart raced off again. I could smell this person, I realized. Musty. Clothes left in the washing machine too long. Dry hot dust, too, and the faint mouldy scent of last autumn's dried leaves. There was something else, as well: sweet and cloying. I just hugged my bag to my chest. Children are always told not to speak to strangers, but I wasn't a child. I was fourteen. Seven and seven again: a fairy tale age, magic. In the near distance, I could hear a car. I was all right. Completely safe.

He stepped forwards so I could see him. And then there was nothing I could do but stare.

He was beautiful: high, arching cheekbones like a model,

36

a wide hood shadowing his face. What was he wearing? It looked like a *cloak*, fastened at the neck with a gold brooch which seemed to shift and change even as I watched; first just a dry leaf caught in the folds of heavy woollen fabric, now glinting gold. Black eyebrows like flicks of ink, a ragged coil of red hair escaping from the hood: weird colouring. He was very tall, looking down at me. I hadn't noticed that while he was sitting on the bench. It must have been his clothes that smelt, I thought. Woolly and ragged, kind of hippy-ish.

I couldn't stop staring. He looked so incredibly strange, yet there it was: a quick hot spark of recognition. I felt sure I'd seen him somewhere before. Known him.

"Well?" said the boy. "Can I be of help?"

Of course, my face immediately went idiot red, burning. That car was coming closer, closer. It shot past and then, a few yards further on, it stopped and the driver started to turn, inching slowly around in the narrow road.

Now I was really scared.

"I – I missed my stop," I said, and regretted it instantly. What a stupid thing to do, telling this stranger that I was lost and alone in some one-horse town in the middle of nowhere. But somehow the words had just slipped out, as if he'd pulled them from between my lips like fish on a line.

"Hopesay Edge?" he said, watching with polite disinterest as the car finished turning and inched back along the lane towards us. "A request stop only, I collect." He smiled, so utterly gorgeous that I was shocked by it, almost insulted, like someone had just slapped me in the face. No one has the right to be that beautiful. It wasn't fair. "You have to really *want* to go to Hopesay, Lissy," he said, quietly, almost whispering. "Do you?"

I just stood there, frozen. I looked up the lane after the car. And when I turned back, the stranger had gone.

He knew my name.

6

Joe

Trees hung over the lane; it was like being in a tunnel, down some kind of pit. It started to rain and Dad flicked on the windscreen wipers. Connie had gone up to bed with a temperature in the end, and we'd been sent out to collect the AWOL elder daughter. The official reason was that Connie might wake up and want her mam. Unofficially, I could tell Dad thought Miriam was too wired to drive properly.

It sounds stupid but I went cold thinking about that lass in the yard. Wondering if I should've told Dad or even Miriam about her, white hair against the black of her cloak. But what harm could she have done? It's not like I'd seen some bloke hanging around with a wrecking bar and a ladder. She was just a girl. Miriam was on edge anyway. Her hand had been shaking when she'd poured the tea earlier. Dad had taken the pot from her, put an arm round her shoulder.

"Don't worry, love," he'd said. "Lissy's going to be here soon. She's a clever girl – she can manage a train journey, and it's not really that surprising she's switched off her phone. You'll sort it out between you."

Excuse me while I puke. And now we were lost – great.

I peered at the unfamiliar name on the sign post ahead. "We must've missed the turn-off for the station." I glanced at the map. "This isn't Hopesay Edge – it's the next village on."

"What was *that*?" Dad slowed the car right down.

"Dad, why are you stopping?" I glanced down at the road atlas on my lap again: on the way out here, our SATNAV had given up on the tangle of tiny lanes not long after passing the last major town, sending us round in circles till Dad had chucked it in the boot. We were on our own. "We're nowhere near."

"I know." Dad eased the car into a crawl, reversing carefully round the corner, craning his neck to get a look out of the back window. "But I'm pretty sure that was Connie's sister I saw by the road back there. She must've got off at the wrong stop—" He wound down his window, leaning out. "Lissy?" he said. "Are you all right?"

And there was this incredibly tall girl at the side of the road, red hair lit up by our headlights like she was burning. She turned to look at Dad, mouthing his name.

I saw it straight away. In her eyes. Something beyond the reach of school and homework and normal boring life. She didn't care about any of it and you could tell.

She looked terrified and I wanted to help her.

I wanted to tell her that everything was going to be all right.

I don't know what I was thinking. Looking at her *did* something to me, made me feel crazy and reckless, like I'd do anything to help her.

I didn't like it.

7

Lissy

The stranger had just *disappeared*. Had Nick even seen him?

My heart was still thundering like I'd run a hundred miles. *He knew my name—*

"Lissy?" Nick said, again. He turned, and I realized there was a boy in the front passenger seat, eyes fixed down at a road atlas open on his lap. Nick's son. Mum had told me about him when she'd first written about Nick. *Other news, darling, is that I've met someone nice.* "This isn't Hopesay, is it, Joe?"

The boy glanced up, looking at me as if I were the biggest loser on earth. I just had time to notice shortish, ragged hair, a worn-out jacket. Boring.

"No, Dad," he said, turning back to the road atlas. "Definitely not."

"It was a request stop," I said, heart still thundering. "I didn't realize I had to tell them to stop the train." *You imagined it,* I told myself fiercely. *That boy didn't really say your name.*

Nick got out of the car, came round to my side and opened the back door to let me in. My hands were actually starting to sweat. *Calm down,* I told myself. *Jesus.* It was starting to rain, a silver mist of tiny drops spreading across the car window.

Nick turned to look at me, releasing the handbrake, ready to drive off. "Are you OK, Lissy?" he said, gently. "Your mam's been pretty worried. So have your teachers."

I took a deep breath. I couldn't be angry with Nick. He was just too nice. "I wanted to get the train instead." My voice sounded very small. Small, young and stupid. "Where's Mum and Connie?"

Nick frowned again, obviously wondering if I'd gone stark raving mad but too tactful to ask. "Back at the house – Connie's not feeling well so I said I'd come and pick you up." Mum and Nick hadn't been together that long, only about nine months or so, but Nick always spoke to me like an adult. Now he sounded disappointed and sad at the same time, like I'd let him down: in a way, it was worse than Mum yelling at me.

Cold unease crept over me. Connie was never ill. She just didn't seem to get bugs and viruses like other kids. And taking that train had seemed like a good idea at the time, but now I was moments away from facing up to Mum it seemed like the stupidest thing I'd ever done. She was going to freak out. Completely. I'd psyched myself up to meet her at Hopesay Edge station, just the two of us, but now I'd have to wait till we got back to the house with everyone there. What would she do? What would she say? It was torture. If she'd met me at the station, she could have killed me in private. Now Joe and Nick would be our audience. Great.

"First left after this village, Dad," Joe said from the front. And that was it – we just drove off.

They hadn't even seen the boy I was talking to, I realized.

The car smelled of Nick's tobacco; inside it was littered with service station coffee cups and empty crisp packets. A guitar in an old leather case sat in the seat next to me. It was all so different: Mum's people carrier is always immaculate, the vanilla smell of air freshener. *I'm in the wrong life*, I thought, staring at the battered guitar case. *I shouldn't be in this car.*

When Nick stopped at a garage I leaned back in my seat, shutting my eyes, breathing in the smell of old pipe-smoke and the faint oily scent of diesel. All I could see was the boy from the station looking back at me, eyes like puddles of black ink. Where had he gone?

It was as if the boy had never been there. How could Joe and Nick not have noticed me talking to him? Why hadn't they mentioned it? Looking out of the window, I watched the dark trees as we drove away from the lit-up forecourt, a menacing tangle of knotted branches looming out of the darkness.

"Right down this lane," Joe said in the front, breaking the spell. "We're here, this is it." I wished he'd shut up; I was worried about Connie and terrified about confronting Mum, but at the same time my stomach was fluttering with sheer excitement. As we turned into a long, tree-lined drive, a sort of friendly familiarity washed over me, like driving on the left-hand side of the road after being in France for two weeks and finally seeing the same old English petrol station chains on the motorway.

I climbed out of the car onto rain-swept gravel that scrunched beneath my feet before Joe and Nick had even undone their seatbelts. I breathed in chilly night air, harsh with the faint tang of woodsmoke. I turned to look at the place where I was born. An overgrown lawn swept away towards a long, low house: ancient grey stone at one end, the rest black and white timber like a picture-postcard cottage. A forest of chimneys rose up from jumbled rooftops and small, odd-shaped windows glittered in the moonlight. The front door was enormous – arched and wooden, like you see in churches. *This is my place*, I thought, which was totally irrational. *This is where I belong: an ancient house surrounded by trees, waiting just for me in a puddle of silvery moonlight.* For a moment, I didn't even care what Mum was going to say.

I must have been standing there like I'd forgotten how to move, because Nick and Joe edged politely past. Joe reached for the plastic doorbell and I remember thinking how out of place it looked. There was a faint lighter patch on the wood where you could see an old-fashioned knocker had once hung. The door swung open before Joe had the chance to ring.

Mum had heard the car. My throat felt dry. I tried to swallow but couldn't. She was going to go mad. What if she started screaming at me in front of everyone? What if she *cried*?

Inside, we burst into a bubble of light and colour. Mum and Nick were both talking at once. The hallway was painted blood red, and thick wooden beams criss-crossed the ceiling. I looked over my shoulder and noticed a darker patch in the paint just above the door. It was the shape of a crucifix, like a cross had hung there for years as the blood red faded around it, and it had only been taken down quite recently. Nick and

Joe were backing quickly away through the door at the end of the hallway.

"*Lissy!*" Mum turned to me, and it was then I saw that she didn't look furious, more frightened. Tears beaded in her eyes. *Oh, no.* "You caught the train all the way on your own?" She was speaking in French – always a sign she'd lost control. "Why on earth did you do that? For God's sake, Lissy! Anything could have happened. You could—"

"Well it didn't, did it?" I said, deliberately replying in English. Our worst arguments are always in French, for some reason. "I should have asked but I knew you'd say no. I just wanted to come on my own, OK? I'm not a baby any more, I wanted you to—"

"Never, ever do *anything* like this again! I knew I should never have let you go on that school trip!" Mum roared at me, her voice deep and bloody. She'd totally lost control; I'd expected it to be bad but not like this. "You can't do these things, you can't!"

I stood in the shadowy hallway a moment – frozen – then turned and slammed out of the door.

Hot angry thoughts skittered around in my head. *She's going to keep me a prisoner the rest of my life. What's wrong with her? What's wrong with me?*

I ran down the drive, tripped on a tree root hidden in the gravel. Fell.

Stupid, stupid, stupid! What did you expect? Had I really thought that taking the train on my own without permission would make her *less* overprotective? No, I'd just had enough, that was all. The only girl in my year not allowed to walk

45

into town on Saturdays. The only girl not allowed on the Easter trip to Rome. *There will only be two teachers,* Mum had said. *It's not safe.* Always watched, monitored, like a laboratory rat. Not allowed, never allowed. One rule for Rafe, another for me. For God's sake, soon even *Connie* would have more freedom than I did.

And why? She would never say. Refused to even discuss it. I'd shown her now, though.

I heard Mum shouting after me as I picked myself up, palms burning, knees scalded even through my jeans, half winded from the fall. Tears scorched my face. I was glad no one could see them.

Stay out a few moments to cool off, I told myself. But at the back of my mind I was thinking, *And let her worry. Just let her.*

I flew out of the gate, heard it banging behind me, banging open and shut in the wind. Mum was still shouting for me, but I ignored her. Rain slammed into my face. *When did the weather get so bad?* It had been barely even spitting at the station, and now this. I stalked off down the twisting, tree-lined lane. Would she follow? I glanced back over my shoulder; the gate and the house were already out of sight. I walked on. *Just around the next corner,* I told myself. *Then go back. That'll teach her.* I was soaking already; rain dripped down the back of my neck, slithering between my shoulder blades. So cold. May is supposed to be a time of magic, it's like the earth takes a deep breath as springtime turns into summer. Not this year.

I turned the corner and saw I wasn't alone.

Moonlight glinted off the plastic sides of a bus shelter

cowering against the hedge. There was someone waiting inside, slouching on the metal seat. He got to his feet, left the bus shelter, walked towards me.

I froze, thinking, *Murderer, rapist, mugger?* And then immediately, *Don't be such an idiot, maybe he's lost and wants to ask for directions.*

It was that boy from the station, hood up against the rain.

My heart was racing again, a mixture of panic and – something else. Excitement.

"Come on," he said. "We're going to be late. I waited."

8

Rafe

I took the Tube. It was rush hour so I changed at Oxford Circus in a hot sweating ocean of people. Hundreds of bodies pressed up together, the stale-coffee breath of strangers in my face, sickening. And all the time my heart was racing like I'd sprinted a mile.

I hadn't checked the Reading Room for CCTV.

Even now the police might be following me, tracking down the manuscript hidden in my shirt, light and tickling against my skin. There was no way of explaining this. I would be arrested.

I wanted so much to read it.

I scanned the carriage: too many people with tired faces, sweaty clothes. And *there they were*: pressed against the window I caught sight of a policeman stepping into the next carriage, a flash of fluorescent yellow jacket.

They were coming. I was trapped. I looked down at my rucksack, staring at the black plastic buckles, concentrating on boring detail to block the panic. That feeling I was going to vomit.

Bond Street, Marble Arch, Lancaster Gate. Queensway.

The train spewed passengers onto the platform and there it was again: fluorescent yellow among dark suits, drab work clothes.

The policeman stepped off the train, moving down the platform in a rush of commuters.

Not for me. Of course not. I couldn't help smiling as we pulled away, back into the black tunnel. I was a step ahead. But for how long? Sooner or later, someone would notice the journal was missing. If they hadn't already.

Still no time to stop, no time to look. Even now that librarian could be starting to panic, to make telephone calls, raise the alarm. Notting Hill Gate. At last. I allowed myself to be swept along with everyone else up the escalator, through the ticket barrier. Rushing to get home no faster than anyone else.

It wasn't my home, Dad and Elena's house, just free parking. I didn't even knock on the door, just went straight for the line of cars squeezed as close to the kerb as possible. I felt in my pocket for the car keys. Still there. Sliding the manuscript carefully out of my shirt, I laid it face-down on the passenger seat, hidden beneath my rucksack. At least I couldn't sweat on it there and blur the writing. So precious it could only be touched with gloves. Just sitting on the passenger seat in my car.

I started the engine and reached for the steering wheel, saw my hands were shaking. I pulled out into our road, leather steering wheel hot to the touch.

London traffic at eight o'clock on a Friday evening is hell but I'm a good driver with a functioning sense of direction.

It took almost an hour to reach the furthest edges of town, slipping up back streets. I didn't notice the car until I was waiting at traffic lights, trying to remember Dad's shortcut onto the Westway. A grey Alfa Romeo, waiting behind the van who'd been tailgating me: nondescript but very fast. The same Alfa Romeo that had overtaken me earlier, I was sure. Now it was behind me again.

"Don't be paranoid," I said aloud. "No one's following. Why would anyone be following?"

Because of the manuscript. Because of that message in brown ink: They will kill you.

Rubbish. Shut up. It's just a stupid old journal from the library archives that—

That I've stolen.

It was Friday night. *Everyone* was leaving town, heading west. So what if I'd seen the same car twice? It was hardly a miracle.

I pulled out onto the motorway. Now I was moving along in fast traffic and driving into a wide summer sky, I could see sense: even if the librarian *had* realized what I'd done (which he must have, by now), it would be hours before the police responded to a report of theft on a Friday night in central London. I could relax. There wasn't a chance they'd trace me here, not so quickly. Especially not after the precautions I'd taken. I might have used the school's name as leverage, but my own remained out of the equation.

For now.

It was a fairly transparent trick, and I just hoped it would work. For a few days at least.

Once I'd been on the motorway an hour, I felt safe

enough to stop and look. Finally.

The service station streamed with people: businessmen in suit trousers and crumpled shirts, people escaping London for the weekend, carloads of families leaving for half-term. I got a gritty espresso from a chain outlet inside and sat in the car with the manuscript in my hands again at last.

The librarian had been right, of course. It *was* a journal; I should have expected that after finding the title on their database: *Facts Concerning Concealment of a Hidden Race 5*. Five was the issue number. There had been no record of issues one to four, no mention of anything that might have come afterwards. It was dated May 1820. *1820*. So old.

I waited before opening it again, ancient paper fragile beneath my fingertips, savouring the single word "facts", after a lifetime of trawling through websites produced by pathetic delusional hippies about elves and fairies and crystal pathways.

Because none of that comes even close to the truth about what happened fourteen years ago.

I started to read.

It is well known they take children, for what purpose God alone can tell. Bewitched by their whispered promises, grown men and women have left the civilized world, never again returning to their families and friends. I have ridden every inch of this island and only once did I hear of such a Creature facing Justice.

I turned the page, hardly even breathing. I'd found it at last. Evidence. A shadow of proof.

In the parish records of Hopesay village it is written that in the Year of Our Lord 1707 a young child, one Philippa de Conway, was snatched from her bed. Fitzwilliam de Conway's men captured one known to be Elven and held her fast in the Gaol. It is recorded that the Creature screamed out most horribly when the iron fetters touched her skin—

Elven? So this was just more stupid fantasy. Elves and fairies and aliens. I felt like hurling the manuscript out of the window, letting it blow across the motorway. I'd risked everything for this and it was pointless. But somehow I couldn't quite stop reading; the story so exactly mirrored my own. Lissy's own.

And de Conway, Philippa de Conway. She must be related to Miles. Dad hated him so much he had to be involved in this one way or another. That wasn't the only disturbing thing. *Iron*. Mentioned on almost every website about the paranormal, definitely in every book I'd ever read about witches, fairies, elves, all of that bull.

Which was why last summer in a remote French village, I escaped Dad and Elena for the afternoon and I went to the blacksmith.

I asked him to forge me an iron knife.

The blacksmith's southern accent was so strong I couldn't understand what he said when I came to take my knife away. Probably for the best. I've carried it in my pocket ever since, a sharp blade held safe in a leather case, a smooth wooden hilt.

Yes, it's paranoid and bizarre to keep an iron knife in my pocket, but whenever I think of just throwing the stupid thing away, I remember the empty bed, that spider jerking across the still-warm sheet. I was so young, but I can still see it all so clearly.

You can't be too careful.

It's also paranoid and completely crazy to steal a manuscript from the British Library, I reminded myself. *But that hasn't stopped you.*

I knew all this was becoming an obsession, unhealthy and peculiar. I knew that, this time, I had in all likelihood gone too far. Sometimes overstepping the mark is the only viable option.

I looked down again, found my place in the cramped columns of text.

Descending into the Gaol when the hour came for the Creature to appear before the child's distraught father, who was the magistrate, de Conway's men found nothing in her cell but a heap of dead winter leaves.

I shut my eyes, pushing away the memory. Not just of looking down at the empty basket, the brown decaying leaves, that spider, but of the fear. Feeling more scared than I'd ever known. Because even then I *knew* they were so powerful—

Philippa de Conway was never returned to her parents, alive or dead. If the Elven put period to her Existence, she was not given a Christian burial and her poor soul wanders yet. In truth, her father Sir de Conway disappeared only a matter of days after the Elven

Creature, and indeed there are some who believe it was nothing but a case of Infanticide, the guilty Parent running from Justice. Of course, in Hopesay itself the people say their lord followed his Child into the Halls of the Hidden, searching for her.

This was it. I shut my eyes, weak with relief. Relief that I hadn't somehow imagined everything because that would mean I was crazy. Wouldn't it?

The memory rose up again like something dead and rotting floating on water.

Walking step by step across Mum and Dad's room. The silence, that thick, relentless silence after all the screaming. Reaching the baby basket. Looking inside, and...

Just keep on reading. I turned back to the journal, forcing myself to focus.

Depend on it: should knowledge of the crimes committed by this Race reach the population of this island, no longer disguised as foolish fireside tales designed to haunt the sleep of children, yes, if all were to learn the Truth, there would be an Uprising. We might think ourselves safe now the Gateway is closed, thanks to the perspicacity of de Conway's grandson, but it will only take a single mistake to open it, a lone moment of weakness, of human error, and the Creatures will once more have the power to hunt Christian men and women, to take their prey home—

An uprising. I tried and failed to imagine the newspaper headlines if everyone knew. Because they *are* here: this Gateway or whatever it is has already been opened, God knows how or when. They're Hidden, but here among us all the time. I know because I've seen them. My eyes travelled to the bottom margin of the page, to those words scrawled in brown ink.

They will kill you—

Even though it was hot in the car at nine in the evening, I felt cold when I read that.

When I drove back onto the motorway, I saw the grey Alfa Romeo again. Two cars back. Waiting, like a buzzard hanging in the air, waiting to fall through the sky, claws open and ready to drop.

9

Lissy

The boy smiled at me, waiting by the rain-swept bus stop. I could see the moon in his eyes, reflected.

"I – I'm sorry—" I started to tell him he'd got the wrong person, made a mistake, but it was as if my head had been sucked clean as a cracked egg. All I could do was look at his face, not asking myself any of the questions I should have done. He'd mistaken me. He must have done. He was acting like we knew each other: that he really had been waiting for me.

"When you got off the train, I knew you must be coming too." What was he talking about now? Coming where? The boy reached out and I found myself taking his hand. His skin felt oddly cool yet so familiar. *It's cold out here*, I told myself. *Cold and wet.* Now we were walking together, side by side. He was taller than me. Much. Well, I knew how that felt. I tower above all the girls in my year. His face looked so young.

What are you doing, you idiot? I thought. *You don't know who he is.*

"I've got to get back," I said; "they'll be wondering where I am." That was an understatement.

The boy didn't seem to hear. He stopped a moment,

staring at the hedge, then pulled me towards it. "Through here," he said. "There's a gap."

It's not as if he's some creepy old man. He's just a boy. He can't be much older than me. Maybe sixteen at most. The thought blew through my head faster than a leaf in a gale, and disappeared. He stepped lightly over a nettle-filled ditch, still holding my hand, and he didn't even have to ask me to follow. Hoping like mad I wasn't going to make an idiot of myself and fall into the nettles, I leapt after him, thinking, *Why not? Just why not?* He took my other arm, steadying me, smiling into my face as I landed, crouching against the hedge.

"That was well done. You're getting wet. Wear this." The boy shrugged out of his cloak and hung it around my shoulders with a flash of gold as he fastened the leaf-brooch. The cloak was heavy. The smell of it caught at the back of my throat and for a minute I couldn't think about anything else. It was disgusting and delicious at the same time, just like a fairground – a mixture of hot salty sweat, wet dog and something deep and sweet, like burnt candyfloss. It was an animal smell, burning and alive. I'd thought the soaked wool would be wet on the inside too, damp and cold, but it wasn't. Instead I felt a lot warmer.

"But—" I looked at the boy, unable to hide my shock. His hair was now free from the cloak's hood, a great sweep of bright red hair, snaking down past his shoulders, redder than mine, redder than the sun as it sinks away behind the hills. "Won't you get wet?" I finished, stupidly.

He smiled. "It doesn't matter. We're late. We must hurry. The dark time is already here." He was walking on now;

I scurried along, trying to keep up. The cloak flapped around my ankles, dragging in the long grass. I'd changed out of my school uniform on the train and had my biker boots on, luckily. The ground really was getting muddy, though; it was much harder to move.

I tried one last time to make the boy understand. "I'm not who you think I am." But he didn't seem to hear. He'd let go of my hand now; I was half running to keep up. He seemed to be heading for a clump of trees at the far end of the field. It sounds ridiculous but I knew all the time that this was crazy. Mum would be going mad, calling the police, probably. *I* was mad for just going off with this boy. All the same, I followed him.

Serves her right, I told myself. *I've only been a few minutes. I'll go back soon.*

Then the boy started running, really running, reaching back to take my hand, and I stopped thinking at all, his hand in mine. His skin still felt too cold, and for a tiny second I shuddered as if I'd just touched a frog. One last sensible thought came and went: *He really could be a murderer.* Yet I was running, too, legs burning, lungs tearing.

The boy let me slow down when we reached the trees. Dark branches brushed my face, touched the back of my neck. I could hear music now. Now it all made sense: he was heading to one of those illegal outdoor parties. Old people moaning in the local newspaper afterwards. The police. A jolt of excitement shot through me. But as we got closer, still hand in hand, I realized the music wasn't right. It was live, for a start: scratchy wild violin-type music — folky, the kind of stuff Nick listens to – a sort of flute or pipe, all mixed with something watery and silverish that might have been a harp. A *harp*? And the drums. A crashing, exciting roar of sound.

It can't have been much later than nine o'clock, but everyone was dancing, lithe figures moving among the trees. Fires blazed, fire was everywhere, hanging in lanterns from branches, flickering piles of flame dotted about, casting long shadows.

He turned and spoke to me again but I couldn't hear, just saw his lips moving, eyes like smudges of coal. So pale. And I danced with him. The music got inside me, the drumming. I had no time to worry about tripping over or looking stupid. He was holding me, leading the dance as the heavy cloak flew out around my legs. All the time I just kept thinking, *I can't believe this is happening.* Everyone was gorgeous: laughing, smiling.

I don't know how long it was before I realized what was wrong with the rest of the dancers. There were so many of us, moving and swaying between the trees, whirling, stamping, heads thrown back, teeth shining in the firelight. The others were so tall and slender. It wasn't right, like seeing a whole load of catwalk models all together. There's a girl at school whose older sister is a model, Rebecca Dawlish. Rebecca stands out because she looks so different: pale and very thin, but here they were in the woods, these people, *all* looking like that. They had so much hair, and the smell: sugary-smokey, stale. I was noticing it more and more. As if none of them had washed in years. Years and years. Everything that had felt so exciting and wonderful now looked ragged and dirty.

It wasn't just that, either. No one spoke to us or even looked in our direction. It was like we weren't really there, nothing but a pair of shadows dancing among the dancers.

I had the strangest feeling of being cut off and deliberately ignored, just like at school with Tasha Bennett and her plastic friends. No matter how many times Alice tries to persuade me it's because they're jealous – *You're* stunning, *Lissy* – being given the cold shoulder still makes me cringe. I'm used to it.

Now it was like that here in the woods with a load of people I'd never even met. *Great*, I thought. *Clearly my natural charm at work once again. Why does this always happen to me?*

"What's wrong?" The boy smiled at me, lightly holding both my hands, leaning back a little as if to see me properly. "Come, have a drink." There was something strangely old-fashioned about the way he spoke. I couldn't help looking at his hard, sharp teeth, bright in the flickering glow of a lantern hanging from a tree, a metal cup of fire.

"I – I can't—" I pulled my hands out of the boy's grip, trying to ignore the coolness of his skin. *Not right*, something deep in my brain screamed at me. *Not right, not right. Run.*

"Oh, stay," the boy whispered, leaning closer. There was something ragged and desperate in his voice. "Please. It's only just begun." I felt his breath on my face: a warm, sweet smell that made me feel dizzy and terrified at the same time. "Please," he whispered again; his eyes were so dark but I saw fear in them: real dread.

It's all right, I wanted to say. *Don't be afraid. I'll help you—*

Suddenly I thought of Mum. She would be frantic. What was I doing here with these people I'd never met before in my life? Wasn't I in enough trouble already?

And in that second I knew that if I wanted to leave, I would have to run.

Shrugging out of his cloak, I turned and scrambled away. Suddenly, I was visible. They were all looking at me. I ran, bumping into dancers, tangled in the woolly, smokey folds of their clothes, touched by their cold pale hands, ignoring the whispering music of their voices beneath the pounding drums, the bright high pipes.

As I reached the clearing's edge and started running through the trees, I sensed another shift in the mood, felt the heat of their eyes on me, all of them at once. A pack of beasts turning to look as one. I don't know how to explain it but somehow a deep ancient part of me knew that if they chose, these tall strange people, then I would be hunted.

Some part of me that remembered how it felt to be prey.

10

Joe

"Nick!" Miriam came into the sitting room with red eyes like she'd been crying. I wished I wasn't there. "Lissy's run off— I've got to find a torch, I'll have to go after her and it's dark now—"

"I'll help you find her, I've got a torch in the car. She can't have gone far." Dad turned to me, looking really worried. "Joe, you stay here in case she comes back. Listen out for Connie, too."

We were in the middle of the countryside, not a war zone. Fair enough to mind Connie but Miriam was acting like Lissy was four, not fourteen.

I watched Miriam follow Dad into the kitchen. She'd better not try treating me like a bloody four year old. I'd already decided the only way to survive this holiday would be to keep my head down and hope Dad didn't decide to marry Miriam or anything stupid like that. I could do without a stepmother who thought that taking a train on your own was potentially lethal. I sighed. I'm not the world's most intuitive person but that was blatantly the real reason we were all at Hopesay Reach. Dad and Miriam were serious. *The next thing I know,*

I thought, *they'll be telling everyone they're moving in together.*

I went to stand by the fire; it was warm against my back and I was relieved to get five minutes' peace and quiet. I was starting to feel claustrophobic, penned in. When I'm with Dad, normally it's just me and him. Now there were all these hysterical women everywhere. And somewhere in the house or out in the woods, *he* was hanging around. Miles. Probably down the nearest pub – he had the lairy and unpredictable look of the seasoned piss-head about him. I'd been back to check on the gun cabinet. Miles might've told me to stay out of there but he could jog on. You don't leave shotguns lying around for anyone to pick up. The cabinet was locked again now, but he'd disappeared again, leaving just those vicious steel traps hanging on the wall.

Great.

I kicked a burning log with the toe of my boot, watching the flames flare up. Miriam had told me this was the oldest room in the house, that the fire in here had never gone out for centuries, lit each morning from last night's embers, even in the middle of summer. On either side of the fireplace, set back into the ancient, thick wall, there were two long narrow stones left unplastered and one lying across the top of them, like a mini Stonehenge. It was as if the original priory had been built right around some kind of monument. They did that in the old days, though, didn't they? Put churches and stuff on pagan sites, encouraging people to forget about their old beliefs. I'd read about stuff like that. I'd never heard of a church being built right over a stone circle though, kind of like *absorbing* it.

Weird.

The door swung open, slow on its hinges.

Miriam's panic was infectious, because I got a jolt of pure fear then, hoping it wouldn't be Miles, all drunk and scary.

It was Connie, standing there in her pyjamas. *Of course,* I told myself. *Don't be stupid.*

Even I could see she didn't look great. Her face was sickly pale except for two bright red patches on her cheeks. When she gazed around the sitting room her eyes were weird and unfocused, with dark purple shadows underneath.

"Mum? I want Mum. And Lissy. Why hasn't Lissy come to see me? I heard her come in." Connie's voice sounded scratchy, like her throat was really sore.

"I think they just went out to – get something." I'm a crap liar. "Do you want a drink of water or anything?"

"Juice." Connie stared at me. "Apple juice, please. My head really hurts. Where's Lissy?"

I wasn't about to tell Connie that her sister was lost. I went into the kitchen looking for the fridge and as I turned around I heard this huge thud. I spun around and Connie was slumped on the floor, right in the doorway.

Oh, no.

What was I supposed to do? What if she was *dead*?

Don't be daft. One step at a time.

I put the apple juice down on the table. Shut the fridge. Walked over and knelt down beside her. Her chest was moving. So she was alive. Of course. I put a hand on her forehead and it was burning hot. Oh, no.

"Connie?" I tried to sound calm.

She let out this little whimper. "I don't feel very well.

64

I want my mum." She started crying but without making a sound, tears trailing down her face.

"OK, don't worry. Your mam's going to be back any second, all right? Can you get up?"

She just lay there, shaking her head and crying. "My legs hurt."

So I picked her up. She was heavier than I expected but she kind of clung to me like a monkey. I edged up the stairs, terrified I was going to drop her over the banisters or something. I didn't even know which was her room and had to do this kind of shuffling dance along the corridor till at last I found it, just off Dad and Miriam's room. She got heavier every second. I let her roll out of my arms into the middle of a big double bed and covered her up with the duvet, heart pounding. Outside, rain hammered the window.

"I want Mummy," Connie whispered, tears still rolling down her face. "I don't feel very well. Don't go away, Joe."

She really trusted me to help her, like I was the adult.

"It's OK, I'll stay," I said. "She'll be here in a minute."

I didn't have a clue what to do next.

11

Lissy

I ran, and as I left the trees behind I could still feel the chill of the boy's touch on the palm of my hand. I smashed through that long wet grass, gasping, half sobbing, terrified, heart burning a hole through my chest. What was that sound, that yearning dark howl throbbing up through the ground beneath my feet? Closer, it was coming closer.

I remembered: realizing. Frost-pinched fingers, horses and hounds gathering outside the Whitaker Arms after Christmas; the Boxing Day hunt—

Dogs. No, *hounds*.

Hounds, chasing me across a field in the dark, thirsting for blood: there was hunger in their song. I ran as fast and mindless as a beast, full of white-hot fear. At last I reached the hedge, panting, still sobbing, lungs on fire in my chest. This time, I slipped down the bank and up to my ankles in freezing cold water. Why was it so cold here?

As soon as I hit the water, the terrible song of the hounds disappeared, as if someone had just switched them off. Gasping, I hauled myself out, gripping stringy wet plants that slid between my fingers. All I could hear now was the distant hum of a car on the road, and Mum.

And was that laughter? *Faint but unmistakable laughter.*

She was standing in the middle of the lane; when she saw me she started running.

"Lissy, Lissy!" Mum's voice was ragged with panic. She wasn't even wearing a coat. Raindrops hung in her hair like tiny pearls.

"*Maman,* Mum!" We clashed together into a clumsy hug, both sobbing. Hounds. Those tall strange people in the woods. What would I tell her? Nothing. Nothing, of course.

Take notice of your breathing, Miss Coder always tells us in yoga – and I did, balancing myself, breathing in and out. It was OK. Everything was going to be fine. I'd just met some strange people, and that was all. She didn't need to know about any of it.

"Oh, my God, Lissy." Mum held me so close I could hardly breathe. "Please don't— I couldn't bear it if anything happened to you." I felt her tears running down my neck and she was shaking. "Your teachers really wanted you to go on that Shakespeare trip, but I didn't want you to, not now, it was the worst possible time but they—" She started sobbing again, and I wished I'd never even set foot on that stupid train. I'd ruined my one chance of independence.

"I just want to be like other girls," I said. "Why can't you let me be like everyone else?"

Mum just stared at me, unable to speak, silent tears streaming down her face.

This isn't right, I thought, hugging her, patting her back.

I don't blame her for being angry but this is not normal: she's not even furious — she's just really, really scared.

I was the one comforting my mother, rather than the other way round. I didn't like it.

"It's OK," I said. "It's going to be all right, Mum."

Mum pulled away to look at my face as if she couldn't believe I was really there, making an obvious effort to get a grip and take control of the situation. "Nick's right: you got here in one piece. That's the most important thing."

Whoever the boy was, he had gone and so had his friends. So had the dogs. I shivered, walking slowly beside Mum, back across the rain-swept yard, trying to ignore the little voice at the back of my mind saying, *Not whoever he was. Whatever.*

By the time we reached the house my hands were burning, a deep fiery pain that brought tears to my eyes. When we got into the hall I glanced down at my palms when Mum wasn't looking. They were blistered raw. Nettle stings. Those weeds I'd grabbed hold off, pulling myself out of the ditch, panicking — they were stinging nettles.

I hadn't even noticed.

12

Joe

At dinner, they all made out nothing had happened.

Miriam attacked me with an embarrassing hug for being "such a star" with Connie (now finally asleep and dosed with paracetamol). Dad heated up spaghetti Bolognese and Miriam produced a lemon tart.

"I'm sorry Miles isn't here," Miriam said, glancing out the window. What was the matter with her? She was permanently distracted. "He had plans already – something long-standing I think."

Yeah right. A long-standing plan to visit the pub, more like.

So I didn't say anything about the white-haired girl. Again. There was a moment when I could have, when Miriam and Lissy were both upstairs, and it would've been easy to bring it up with Dad as he stirred Bolognese sauce on the stove.

But I kept her to myself. Miriam was crazy enough. And a skinny lass like that: all scrawny and pale. She couldn't do any harm. Connie was safe inside now, so what did it matter?

It didn't.

Lissy helped out with plates and cutlery, moving around

the kitchen without speaking a word. Her red hair had got wet in the rain.

"Your favourite, Joe," Dad said, when we started on the lemon tart. Silence. He gave me a look but I didn't know what to say, and he let it go.

Lissy sat staring down at her plate, holding onto a silver fork; her fingers were so long and ice-white. A strand of dark red hair clung to her neck, sending drips of rain water sliding down towards her collarbone.

She looked up at me. Oh, shit. Her eyes were really dark, and when she glanced sideways into the light I saw they were blue, almost black, like sky before the light goes. Most people my age, we're all in the same boat: coursework, funny stuff that happened at school, the cretins you have to put up with every day, late for the bus. But there was something about Lissy I didn't *recognize*. Like she was above all that. Or didn't care.

Maybe it was because she went to some posh boarding school. Our lives were pretty different, after all.

For a second, we stared at each other.

I got the message clear enough: *Leave me alone.*

I was about to make an excuse and escape to my room, but Lissy got in there first.

"Sweetheart," Miriam said, "your hair's soaked. I don't want you coming down with something as well. I'm going to check on Connie; I'll get you a towel. You should have a nice bath. That's one good thing about this place: there's plenty of hot water."

She was gabbling. Filling the silence.

"I'll go," Lissy said. "I want a shower anyway; I'll check on Connie."

Without looking at me again, she got up and left.

I felt like I'd been punched.

13

Lissy

Upstairs, I opened every single door till I found Connie.

She was sleeping in a room that led directly off Mum and Nick's. Connie looked very small lying in a double bed. My little sister. A bottle of Calpol sat on the mantelpiece, the plastic spoon already rinsed and laid neatly beside it. Boring Joe, hero of the hour. Helping the sick child while Mum and Nick chased up and down the lane after me. Well, let him have his fifteen minutes of glory. Joe didn't look the type to find it anywhere else. Connie had pushed the covers away and was in my old pyjamas: pink and white striped, thick cotton. I remember wearing them one Christmas, Dad helping me unwrap my first ever new bike, not just a hand-me-down from Rafe.

"We'll go on a bike ride together, Tinkerbell," he'd said. Dad's the only person ever allowed to call me that ridiculous nickname; I hadn't heard anyone say it for nearly a year.

Forget about him. I was furious with myself for thinking about Dad. *He's forgotten about you. Think about something else. Poor Connie.*

Connie's hair was spread out over the pillow, thick and

fair like Rafe's. Easter was only a few weeks back really, but Connie looked different, slightly older with her fringe grown out. My eyes started to burn and tears slipped down my face. For years, it had been just me, Mum and Connie. Rafe away at school. Dad gone. Now I'd gone, too, and Connie was changing just like everything else. I watched her a moment then went over to the window and shut it.

I wasn't taking any chances. I couldn't help smiling at myself. I was just as bad as Mum: overprotective. At least I had a reason, though. Mum didn't.

I escaped into the spidery bathroom and stood under the shower till my skin was pink and hot and my fingertips started to wrinkle. Then, wearing pyjamas (well, stripey thermal leggings and a Bob Dylan t-shirt), I took my pile of clothes downstairs, trying not to breathe in that mouldy sweet smokiness.

I was about to push open the sitting room door when I heard Nick say, "Look, it's not my place to interfere, but don't you think it might help to ease up on Lissy a bit? Give her a bit of freedom? She's not stupid; she doesn't even seem that naïve. You can't protect her for ever."

Go Nick, I thought.

"You don't understand," Mum said. "I couldn't expect you to. Nick, there's no *time*—"

"I know what happened," Nick went on, "but sooner or later she'll have to protect herself."

"Stop it," Mum said. What were they talking about? *I know what happened?*

"You can't go back and change anything now," Nick said, quietly. "Miriam, you've got to tell her or she'll start to hate you."

What?

I waited for Mum to speak, breathless. But then I heard the kitchen door opening, and Nick said, "Night, Joe."

The stupid idiot had gone into the sitting room from the kitchen, interrupting.

Tell me what? What was Mum supposed to tell me?

I opened the door and let Joe past, looking away. I needn't have bothered. He stepped past, deliberately not looking at me. Loser.

Mum and Nick were sitting on one of the battered sofas, drinking red wine, firelight casting flickery shadows on the dark panelled walls. Mum looked up sharply when I came in.

"What's that smell?" Mum said, giving me a very strange look.

My clothes. For a minute it was almost like she *knew*—

She frowned. She had gone completely white, like she was going to throw up or pass out. "Lissy, did you *meet* anyone on that train?"

I thought my heart was going to literally stop right then and there. I gripped the bundle of clothes even tighter. "No," I said. "Of course not. I'm not stupid. I didn't speak to anyone except the ticket inspector. Is there a washing machine?" I'd already decided that if there wasn't, my jeans and jumper would go straight into the bin. Mum was still staring at me like she was trying to read my mind. "There wasn't anywhere to wash clothes at the youth hostel," I added, which was true.

"I haven't got anything clean for tomorrow."

"It's in the lean-to — in the corridor outside the kitchen. You must be turning over a new leaf." Mum turned to Nick, forcing a smile. "At home, she lets her laundry pile up for weeks." She'd obviously decided my crimes were going to be swept under the carpet. For now. Till it suited her to bring it all up again. Did she know I'd overheard?

At least she wasn't on the warpath any more.

I'd have to get Mum on her own in the morning, try to make her talk. I was actually quite excited. Maybe everything *would* be different now, not because of my solo train ride, but because Nick made her see sense. At last I'd be like the other girls, going into town on Saturdays to buy cookies and earrings.

Maybe my life was about to change.

I put my jeans, t-shirt and jumper on a hot cycle with far too much washing powder. I wanted to boil and bleach that horrible exciting stink out of existence. I wanted to wash away the woods, the dancing, the woodsmoke. And the boy.

Those hounds.

Had I imagined them chasing me, that terrible bloody howling? Where could they have come from at that time of the evening? A hunting pack that someone had released by mistake — or even maliciously? Perhaps there were just a couple of lost pet dogs out, and being alone in the dark had made them sound louder, more scary. There had to be a proper explanation. What had Nick meant when he said one day I'd have to protect myself? Probably nothing. It's what happens to everyone in the end, after all. Ultimately, we're all on our own.

I couldn't wait.

14

Rafe

I pulled over into the slow lane behind a cement lorry that everyone else was overtaking. The dark grey Alfa Romeo was still two cars back. I glanced at the clock on the dashboard. I'd been driving for almost two hours and it was there almost every time I checked my mirrors.

You can't be the only person driving from London to the Welsh Borders. Is this really such a big deal? Even so, my heart hammered and my back was damp with sweat again, shirt sticking to the skin. My body knew I was being chased even as I tried to reason with myself.

There was an easy way of finding out for sure.

Keeping my eyes on the road, trying not to swerve, I reached around and pulled the road atlas out of the seat pocket behind me. Holding the steering wheel steady with my knees, I found the right page, scanning the network of A-roads that led west, mentally listing the towns I'd need to head past.

Come on, I thought, *catch me if you can.*

I left the motorway at the next exit and went twice around the roundabout before peeling off towards the town centre. I was buzzing with the thrill of it. I probably should have been scared but I was in control now; it was exciting.

I hit roadworks on some kind of ring road and had to sit there, waiting, watching, crawling along. I glanced in my mirror again.

There it was. Three cars behind me now but still there, all the same. The Alfa Romeo. And I was stuck in a queue as these brain-dead corporate lemmings commuted home from work, just waiting. A target.

A target? What do you think they're going to do, shoot you? You're in suburbia, not an American cop show.

I still didn't like it, though. I yanked the map from the passenger seat, looking at all the roads out of town. Took the first turning I could, a backstreet through a maze of identical new houses. It wasn't marked on the map but at least I was heading in the right direction.

The Alfa Romeo had gone, too.

Idiot, I told myself, slaloming through artificially winding streets. *There's such a thing as paranoia.*

I wasn't really being followed, of course not. That kind of thing just doesn't happen, I told myself. I headed west again, following the rising moon as it shone over a horizon of modern executive homes, then endless DIY warehouses, tile shops, garden centres. I found my A-road again just as the traffic finally started easing and the second-hand car salesrooms and take-away shops thinned out more and more till I was driving along surrounded by dark fields, the road to myself.

Not completely to myself.

A pair of headlights appeared in my mirrors. I knew, I just

knew, before the car even got close enough.

When it did, I was sure. They were still following me. There could be no question about it now. The Alfa Romeo hung back, not on my tail but not overtaking either. Like they were taunting me.

It was strange but now I felt calm, driving steadily, resisting the urge to go too fast. It was a winding road; I didn't want to end up in a ditch. After all, perhaps that was their intention. Instead, I considered my options, watching the headlights in my mirrors, bright like a pair of silver moons.

Why were they chasing me? It could only be because of the journal. If I was honest, I'd known I would be followed, *sensed* it would happen. The question was what to do next.

I could drive faster. Push the car as hard as it would go.

Or try to lose them in the winding mass of back roads and small towns leading west. There was a junction up ahead anyway. A chance.

It took me only a few seconds to decide. I stopped, suddenly. The car swerved; I eased the brakes. Changed down two gears, pulling into a lay-by. The stink of burning clutch filled the air. Dad would murder me if he knew.

The Alfa Romeo shot past. Its windows were blacked out but I wished I could see the faces inside.

I sat back, allowing myself a second of relief, heart beating hard and fast.

Who were they? It was just a journal about elves and goddamned fairies from the British Library.

Stop it, I thought, *stop lying to yourself.* Because I knew the truth, and whoever had written that thing was right.

They're here. All the time. They do whatever they like and no one stops them.

If everyone knew what I did, there would be an uprising.

What you've asked for is restricted access. I shut my eyes, seeing the librarian's blank expression. Perhaps there was some kind of alert when anyone asked for it. A trap. Making sure anyone who got to the truth was silenced.

They come and go like shadows. They take children, leaving nothing but dead leaves. They don't *age*. Always the same.

There has to be a reason no one knows they're here. Why no one ever talks about it. Not seriously.

And then I saw headlights again, coming straight towards me this time. I waited, every muscle in my body screaming at me to run. I waited as the Alfa Romeo U-turned right in the middle of the road and pulled into the lay-by behind me. I waited as the doors opened, both doors. Two people got out, a couple of men in suits. I watched them walk closer, closer till I could see their faces in my wing mirror — boring, nothing to talk about, one had grey hair, another was younger. Closer.

Closer.

I stamped on the accelerator and sprang away from the lay-by, shooting up through the gears till I hit eighty-five miles an hour; knowing they surely must be running back to their car — who, who were they? — I took the junction at sixty, nearly hit a signpost on the corner, took control again, breathing hard, and floored the accelerator again driving west as hard and as fast as I could, taking every corner, dodging, twisting, turning.

Hunted.

15

Lissy

I stood by the bedroom window, wrapped in a nylon seventies bedspread, watching rain flooding across the glass, hammering the lawn outside, pouring from the branches of that yew tree, splashing into the weed-choked lake.

Who were they?

There was a small crack in the top left-hand corner of the window that someone had tried to seal with brown parcel tape, and a cold breeze snaked around the room. I pulled the bedspread tighter around my shoulders. *They were just having a party in the woods, students or something,* I told myself angrily. *Don't be so stupid. He thought you were someone else, that's all.*

I knew I was lying to myself.

I went to draw the heavy velvet curtains and that's when I noticed it: a darker patch in the cream paint, just above the window. I looked closer. It was in the shape of a small cross. A crucifix had once hung in this room, just like downstairs by the front door. Now it was gone.

Cold, irrational fear shot through my body as I drew the curtains, half afraid I might *see* something outside. I stumbled across the room, tripping on the bedspread, and scrambled into bed. I lay there listening to the rain, and I slept with the light on. I should have known the dream would come: it always does when I'm feeling even more trapped, more hemmed in than usual, or sometimes just upset and confused. The dream has always been with me, like a birthmark on my skin, a visitor who arrives in the hours of darkness.

The dream says a lot about me.

It starts, as usual, with the clear limitless light of a blue sky on a hot day. And the sky is all around me, air rushing past my face, between my outstretched fingers, into my wide-open screaming mouth, because I'm falling. I look down and watch the ground coming closer every second, the patchwork of green fields and darker smears of woodland, the glittering trail of a river, cars inching along a motorway, the grey sprawl of a town staining the beauty of it all—

I'm falling and I'm going to die.

Then that physical sensation across my back: muscles stretching, lengthening, something *unfurling*. I squeeze my eyes tight shut. And the lift, that incredible lift, warm air beneath, pushing me up, higher and higher. I want to open my eyes again, to look down and see those fields and forests, that ugly town, but I know what will happen if I do. I soar, wind rushing past my face, and when I can stand it no longer, I open my eyes and—

And I wake. It's always the same. Just at the moment I can't resist the urge to look, I'm jerked out of sleep, away from the dream. Back to the ordinary world: our dorm at school, Alice muttering in her sleep, bundled in the bed beside mine, or in the back seat of my dad's car, even a train carriage, wherever I might have fallen asleep. The usual feeling of flat disappointment washed over me: one day, *one day,* I would defeat my waking body. I would open my eyes still in the dream and *see*—

Disappointment was chased away by fear. I was cold all over, every inch of my skin tingling.

I sat up in bed again, leaning back against the pillows, the bedside lamp still on. Yellow electric light filled the room. Still half asleep, I stared at the dark brown curtains looped back against the wall. Someone had opened them, come in. Mum? Why would she do that in the middle of the night? The rain had eased, but the window glittered with trails of water. I glanced at my watch. It wasn't even quite two in the morning. Not her, then. So who had opened the curtains?

I became aware of a presence – just on the edge of my vision – and snatching the bedspread in both hands I whipped around, heart hammering, mouth dry.

The boy sat on the end of my bed, smiling, rain-wet red hair spilling around his shoulders, black eyes shining like wet pebbles, cloak spread out around him. I watched him breathe, the smooth rise and fall of his chest; he watched me, smiling all the time. It was so quiet. All I could do was stare at him.

"Why did you run?" asked the boy.

When I spoke, my mouth was so dry with terror I could hardly spit out the words. "Because I wasn't meant to be there. My mum—"

"But I invited you." I could tell he was angry, now, his eyes flashing. "You were my guest. There was no need to show me discourtesy."

"I don't even know your name." In the back of my mind, I screamed, *Why aren't you shouting for help?* But I couldn't. At last I managed to ask, "Who are you?"

He laughed — a strange, silvery sound. I knew he would never tell me his name.

"What do you want?" I forced each word out between lips frozen with fear.

"What do I *want*?" His voice was incredulous, mocking. "Listen to me. We have watched for so long. We saw them crawl out of hot seas when the sun was still young. We were there when they came down from the trees and began to hunt. We guided their hands like mothers with young as they first began to mix colours and paint their dreams on the walls of caves. We watched in awe as they multiplied and spread across the earth." He reached out and cupped my chin in his hand. I flinched, drawing in a sharp breath. "Do you not see, Lissy, that there are too *many* of them?"

For a second, we stared at each other, and I looked into his black shining eyes.

He was talking about the human race. Which meant, which must mean, that he was *something else*—

He was the first to look away. "Your time's up," he whispered. "I gave you as much as I could. I have suffered enough for you, Lissy Harker. I've been alone among my own kind, despised by my closest kin, all for you."

And the curtains blew, filled tight and round like the sails on a boat, flapping and snapping in the wind before dropping back to hang against the wall, now still.

When I turned back to face the boy, he had gone.

I just heard his voice, whispering in the shadows. "Come dance with us. Come dance."

I leaned back against my pillows, grabbing one of them and clutching it against my chest. My breath came in short gasps as if I'd been running in freezing fog. He was gone, as if he'd never been there. As if I'd imagined the whole thing. Which I had, of course. All that weird stuff about people evolving and spreading across the earth like a *virus* or something—

Your time's up? What was that supposed to mean? It sounded like a threat.

He really did know my name.

"A dream," I said aloud. "It was definitely just a dream."

And, then, I heard a noise in the house. Downstairs. A great bright smashing noise – breaking glass. It hadn't been a dream. He was still here. I wanted to scream but I couldn't, I couldn't make a sound; it was so horrible wanting to shriek and nothing coming out but a weak gasp. I waited a moment, expecting to hear movement down the corridor, where Mum and Nick's room was. They were the adults. They should have been responsible for making sure everything was all right. But I waited and waited and no sound came until I heard the soft squeak of bedsprings coming from the room right next door to me.

Where Joe was sleeping. Not sleeping but moving: he was getting out of bed. Did he hear the boy, then, as well? Did he know?

I heard the floorboards creak slightly, footfalls one after the other. No hesitation.

Is he brave, I wondered, *or just completely unimaginative?*

I suppressed a wave of pure irritation. Boring Joe, getting in the way again. Obviously his fifteen minutes of glory weren't enough. Now he was playing heroes again.

I heard the latch click as Joe turned his bedroom door handle, listened as he stepped out into the corridor. The stairs creaked one by one. Downstairs, right beneath my bed, it seemed, a chair shrieked across the kitchen floor. Still Joe kept on going.

The boy had come here because of me. I remembered his flashing gunmetal eyes. I remembered the strength in his cold hands as we danced. It was nothing to do with Joe. I followed out of fear rather than courage, knowing how awful it would be if something bad happened to Nick's son and it was my fault. And there was Connie. The boy had got into my room. What was to stop him getting into hers?

I swung my legs out of bed, ran to the door and across the landing, cold in my stripey leggings and t-shirt. Joe had put the light on, thank God. I snatched a folded blanket from a chair on the landing, wrapping it around my shoulders as I went down the stairs.

I paused outside the kitchen, watching my own hand reach for the speckled brass door handle. I opened it, went in. It was empty, dark. The other door was slightly ajar, letting in a chink of light. I stepped into the corridor. The heavy back door was still firmly shut, but there was another door slightly open, glass panelled, much newer.

Joe stood alone in a shabby lean-to leading off the kitchen, wearing a pair of faded tracksuit bottoms and brown desert boots. His pale shoulder blades stood out like wings and he had terrible bed-head. Holding a plastic broom, he turned to face me, hair standing up in crazy spikes. I met his eyes, determined not to look embarrassed by the fact he wasn't wearing a t-shirt. There was a lingering smell of cigarettes.

"Are you all right?" Joe said, very calm. He had more of a Yorkshire accent than Nick; it was a shock, I hadn't noticed it much the evening before but between the two of us alone in the night, his words fell like hard stones, blunt and strange.

I tried not to think about my dream, the red-headed boy sitting on the end of my bed. How could I explain that to someone I'd only just met? Joe would think I was crazy and maybe he'd be right.

"I – I heard something."

The door behind Joe was missing a pane of glass. I looked down and saw broken shards swept into a pile.

"My dad locked up: someone's broken in," he said. "They must've smashed the glass in the outside door and reached through to turn the handle."

He didn't look scared but he must have been.

"My mum's stepbrother? Miles?"

Joe shook his head. "Wouldn't he have keys?"

I stepped around the table to get a closer look and Joe said, quietly, "Wait. There might still be some on the floor. Listen, I had a look out the front. There's another car on the drive. Is it your brother's?"

I just turned and walked back into the kitchen, following that faint reek of tobacco. Joe came after me. The door to the sitting room was still ajar. I pushed it open and there he was, sprawling on one of the battered red sofas like a fallen angel. Asleep.

Rafe.

Not the boy, but just my brother. Making an entrance, as usual. "Yes," I said. "Yes, that's him."

Joe frowned. "Nice of him to clear up. Your sister could have trodden in that."

I turned, looking at Joe properly for the first time. "Rafe never clears up."

"What an idiot," Joe said, as if talking to himself. He reached past the sofa, took a newspaper off the pile on the coffee table to wrap the glass in, and went back to the kitchen. I didn't know what to say; I'd never heard anyone call Rafe an idiot before.

I didn't follow, just went back upstairs to bed. I sat there, leaning against the pillows as I'd done hours before, waiting to fall asleep. I shivered, imagining the boy walking through the kitchen in the dark, opening the landing door, climbing the stairs up to my room. Waiting till I woke. But that didn't make sense. Nick had locked the house.

If Rafe had needed to break a pane of glass to get in, I wondered, how did the boy reach my room?

It was a dream, I told myself again. *It didn't really happen. This just proves it.*

But in the back of my mind, I saw the boy walking across the dark shadowy garden outside. Pausing in the rain. Waiting just a tiny second, then leaping high, high into the air with big bright animal strength, like a leopard, landing in a crouch on my bedroom windowsill.

No, no, no, I told myself furiously. *Don't be so ridiculous. He didn't come. You dreamed it.*

I remembered the feel of his breath on my face, the faint scent of it, sweet and exciting. *Can you dream something like that?*

16

Lissy

By eight o'clock, I had dragged myself out of bed. Every scrap of my body ached and my head felt fuzzy, the room cold and gloomy. I grabbed the clothes I'd washed the day before, now tumbled-dried and left in a neat pile by my bag. Mum's way of trying to make peace: old jeans, a polka-dot top, my favourite grey jumper with holes in the cuffs. I hooked my thumbs through the holes, trying not to think about him.

We watched in awe as they multiplied and spread across the earth— What was that supposed to mean?

I was hoping to be first down. I couldn't do much about the shattered window, but if Connie stepped on broken glass Mum would go over the edge. Connie's never been one of those children who gets up super early, and anyway, I reasoned, she'd had a temperature; I'd go up to her room with my coffee and we could sit together. She still loved being read to, and I knew she'd have a huge bag of books with her, largely featuring princesses, dragons and, more recently, the occasional vampire. The worst thing about school was missing Connie. But when I reached the kitchen Joe was already there, standing awkwardly by the radiator. He was wearing jeans now and thankfully a t-shirt as well. I glanced at the table. The bottle of Calpol from Connie's room sat next to a half-drunk cup of coffee, and one of Mum's silk scarves had been left on the worktop near the cooker like seaweed washed up on a beach.

Something was wrong.

"What's going on?" I said.

Joe opened his mouth to answer but Rafe came in, still in last night's clothes. Looking at my brother when you haven't really seen him for a while is like being hit in the stomach with a football. Shining hair, bright as honey, golden skin, eyes like melted chocolate. *I want to eat him*, I once overheard Alice's mother saying to one of her friends.

He never gets up before twelve in the holidays.

"Where's Mum?" I asked. "What's happened?"

Rafe looked me up and down. I instantly felt very stupid. What had I done now? *Don't*, I told myself. *Don't let him make you feel bad.*

"Just tell me," I said.

"Mum did try and wake you, Lissy." Rafe looked at me with faint disgust as if I'd done something unforgivable. Something else. "Didn't you hear the ambulance?"

An ambulance. Cold panic shot through me. "It's Connie, isn't it? What's wrong?" Connie had gone to hospital and I'd slept through the whole thing. I could have gone with them. I should have been there.

"How weird you didn't wake up," Rafe said, quietly. "They think it's meningitis. There was a rash. It means she's got blood poisoning. That's what they're really worried about."

I didn't know much about meningitis other than that you could die from it. Especially children.

"Connie—" I started to cry. "Is she going to be all right?"

Rafe just turned and went out of the room, leaving me with Joe, who I'd met precisely ten hours earlier. For a moment, we just stood staring at each other, unable to speak.

"Don't worry," Joe said at last. "She'll be OK."

"You don't know that!" I snapped, and ran out of the kitchen, letting the broken door slam behind me.

Stepping into my mud-caked boots and grabbing Mum's waterproof from the back of a chair, I ran out into the yard, calling her on my phone. Nothing. No network coverage. Even if she'd tried to text me, I wouldn't know.

"Why don't you just work, you stupid thing!" Like an idiot, I threw my mobile across the yard, watching it skid across the moss-covered cobblestones.

I couldn't stay near that place a moment longer. It wasn't safe. Houses are meant to keep things out, not allow them in when all the doors and windows are shut. But bad dreams and sickness move like smoke, seeping through tiny cracks. Getting in and breaking loose. You can't hide from them.

Now Connie was gone.

I walked along the lane, head down against the rain. My boots were still wet from the night before so my feet were freezing, as if summer had given up and died. *It's going to be OK*, I told myself again and again. *She's gone to hospital. Doctors know what they're doing. She'll be fine. They'll look after her.* I thought of Mum rushing into my room, shaking me, trying to wake me, but I'd stayed awake so late I was too deeply asleep. What if Connie had wanted me to come with them?

What if I never see her again?

A shiver slid down my back.

"Look, you should just watch out."

I turned around and Joe was standing there, wearing a cagoule that had been repaired with black shiny tape. His hair was already soaking wet. Rain dripped into his eyes. He'd followed me. Not Rafe. Even now Rafe was going to make me suffer, more than a year later. I would never be forgiven.

"What do you want?" I shouted at Joe. Couldn't he see I just wanted to be on my own?

"Running away in the rain – that's not exactly going to help anyone, is it, you daft cow," Joe snapped.

I turned away, facing the hedge, not wanting him to see me crying. The rain hammered down, dripping off the hood of my waterproof.

"Listen," Joe said. "I found a mobile outside the house."

I took it without looking at him, embarrassed. Had he heard me shouting, seen me throw it across the yard?

"We've run out of milk," he went on. "I'm going to the village."

I didn't answer, just carried on walking, and he walked behind me. Neither of us said a word; what was there to say? I didn't know the first thing about him. The lane was dark, even at eight thirty in the morning. Trees met overhead in a great green arch, keeping out what little daylight there was. Rain splashed through the leaves. After a while we passed a pub. The lights weren't on inside, but behind the leaded windows I could just see people moving about: silent, ghostly. I shivered, unable to shake the feeling they were watching us.

Where was Connie now? I pictured her lying small and pale on a hospital trolley, being rushed down a corridor. What did they do when you had meningitis, anyway? Would she have to have injections, a drip: needles stabbed into the back of her hand? Connie hates needles.

All I could do was keep on walking. If I stood still, I wanted to scream.

Hopesay Edge was nothing more than a few rain-battered stone cottages, a war memorial, and, weirdly, a butcher's shop with skinned red carcasses already hanging up in the window. The lights were on inside, even though a sign on the door said it was closed. I couldn't see any other shops at all. Finally, as we were crossing a sodden village green, Joe suddenly peeled to the left and started walking towards the church.

Oh, no. A mixture of panic and outrage bubbled up in my belly. *What on earth is he doing in there?* If he had some kind of religion obsession, this wasn't the time or place to indulge it.

Joe stepped into the porch and hauled open the big door. Finally, I noticed an advertising board standing just outside. On one side a news headline read LOCAL MAN WINS PIG, which would have made me laugh at any other time. On the other side, there was a fluorescent orange sign with "Village Shop" written in black marker. So I followed Joe inside. Even the porch had that churchy smell – slightly damp, old books. At first, everything inside looked normal – dark wooden pews and an altar, a noticeboard with pictures of disciples scribbled all over by Sunday School children. But just by the great stone font, there were tables with groceries laid out for sale: jars of jam and honey, loaves of bread in a basket, tins of tomatoes, packets of toothpaste, stacks of loo roll, kitchen sponges, bottles of shower gel, tea bags, coffee.

Joe was crouching down by a small fridge plugged in next to the tables – a long grey extension lead snaked off into a stack of plastic chairs. I checked my phone again. It was still working and there was one tiny bar of signal. I could phone Mum. At last.

I called her, holding the phone hard against my ear as rain dripped off the hood of my waterproof. Straight to voicemail. And just as I was leaving a message, the phone beeped. A text. I read it, not daring to breathe. *Boo in intensive care, ward C3. Try not to worry. Best people looking after her. Will try call soon, bad reception.* I scrolled down. It had only come half an hour earlier. Why hadn't I tried to call Mum from the landline at the Reach instead of storming out like an idiot?

This can't be happening. There was nothing I could do now but wait. I was useless.

Hot tears leaked slowly down my face. I brushed them away with one hand. *Let her be OK,* I whispered, feeling like an idiot. *Please, God, please let Connie be OK.* I only go to chapel at school because they make us but I would have tried anything. I stared at the font, a pool of holy water cupped in ancient stone. How many babies had been christened in this place over hundreds of years, had holy water tipped onto their heads, crying as the devil was driven out? How many had died before they grew up?

I thought of Connie lying silent and still in her hospital bed, drips and lines coming out of her small arms.

I'll do anything to save you, I thought.

It was my fault: I knew that. If Mum and Dad were still together, Connie wouldn't be in hospital now. Everything is connected, like an endless row of dominoes. If somebody pushes the first domino, they all fall, one after another. That day had led step by step to this one; I'd picked up the birthday card poking out of Dad's laptop case, glanced at the artistic black and white photograph of some mountains, then looked inside, read the message.

"Dad, who's Elena?"

Mum turning to stare, mouth half open. "Adam? What's she talking about?"

Dad frowning at me. I could see it in his eyes: Elena was meant to be a secret. Now she wasn't.

If I hadn't made that mistake, the infection in Connie's body, in her blood, would have found another home.

All because of my stupid fat mouth. No matter how many times Alice or anyone else tried to reason with me, I knew it was my fault Mum and Dad had split up. Alice had said it so many times I lost count: *Seriously, Lissy, your dad must have wanted to be caught. Why else would he keep a birthday card from his secret girlfriend in his laptop bag and then ask you to get his charger? Come on, you're being stupid about it!*

The truth was, in the split second before I'd spoken, I *knew* that Elena was meant to be a secret. And it wasn't fair. Mum deserved to know. Rafe has hated me ever since.

He blamed me.

Connie was so ill? Making up silly stories: no one could be that old. "Do we need anything else?"

—A boy I'd met at the station and then followed into the woods.

A woman had appeared behind the table now, waiting with Joe's stuff in a plastic bag. She had long dyed blonde hair and wore those crushed-velvet hippy clothes you see in shops that sell incense and crystals. Both she and Joe were looking at me expectantly, waiting for an answer.

"No. Only milk." I was about to go and wait for Joe outside when I realized the shop-woman was staring at me from behind her rimless glasses. Her eyes were round and jelly-ish, like enormous frogspawn. Her skin was pale, too, as if she never saw daylight. I shivered: looking at her more closely was like turning over a rock and finding a shuddering mass of worms.

"You're staying at the Reach, then?" The shopkeeper's voice was light and breathy, fairy-like. It might have suited an eight-year-old girl. Coming from a woman older than Mum, it just sounded scary.

"Yeah." Joe turned to leave, obviously not wanting to chat as he picked up the blue plastic bag. "Cheers."

He took a few steps towards the door, but the shopkeeper kept her eyes on me, just staring. Half smiling. "Tell Miles Conway that Virgie Creed sends her regards," she said. "Tell him I said to take care of himself." She gave me a horrible knowing look, like we were in a conspiracy together. "We used to step out together, Miles and I, before his head was turned."

Oh, my God. She was Miles's *ex-girlfriend?* How gross.

Virgie Creed looked me up and down. Definitely making some sort of assessment. I should have just turned and walked away, followed Joe out of that church, or shop, or whatever it was, but something made me stay. She smiled again. Her teeth were a tobacco-stained jumble, dark yellow like the ends of her badly bleached hair. Looking at them, I felt sick.

"You have found them, my darling, haven't you?" she said in that sing-song voice. Deep cold settled over me. I fought the urge to turn and run. "They've turned your head, too. Or rather," she went on, "they have found you, pretty one. They must have been looking."

She knew about the boy. *Of course she does,* I thought, *he's carved on the font in the church, there for anyone to see.*

I opened my mouth to speak but couldn't. I was aware of Joe standing behind me, waiting. I sensed him watching, impatient, ready to leave.

Virgie Creed smiled, leaning across her table so that one of her heavy velvet scarves knocked over a bottle of shampoo. The dull plastic thud filled the church, a bubble of sound exploding. A dusty wave of incense and stale cigarette smoke drifted towards me.

"That's the trouble with Conway's land," she went on, still smiling, leaning closer. "The old magic is strong there. The Reach began as standing stones, before the monks came and went. Did you know that? It's an old, old place, Hopesay Reach." Her breath smelt of stale cigarettes. "Miles opened the Gateway, you see. Silly boy. He shouldn't have done that. He should've stuck with me, but she got to him and he was never the same. Never the same, do you hear me?"

"I don't—"

"No, no. It's no good pretending. They are here. They have come, and they'll be hunting for pretty young girls to breed with." She shook her head. "Now listen. Remember. They might grant your heart's desire, but be careful how you pay. Never dance with the Hidden, and if you shake their hands, you must count your fingers afterwards, do you hear? They can't be trusted."

I did remember. In my mind I was back in that wood, hand in hand with the red-headed boy, dancing among the trees. Wild and full of joy.

The warning came too late. I had danced already.

I felt a rush of hot, bitter nausea, reached out for the table to steady myself. I watched my reaching hand rest on nothing; my head whirled. A bright jolt of pain shot through my knees as I fell. The last thing I saw before darkness flooded everything was Virgie Creed's face, pale and ghost-like.

17

Joe

Lissy fell and lay dead still, right by the church door. The shopkeeper made a choking noise like she was about to hurl, fat pale hands pressed to her mouth.

Oh, great. Just great. This was all it needed.

I'd got the landline in my phone. Lissy's brother answered after two rings.

"Yes?" I couldn't stand the way he spoke: amazed anyone really had that accent any more. Sneering. Flat and glassy, like a villain in a black and white movie.

"It's Joe," I said. "Your sister's passed out in the village, in the shop. The church. We could do with a lift back if that's all right." I don't know why I was being so polite, maybe to disguise the gathering panic. All that creepy stuff about gateways and breeding. Lissy lay there on the church floor, head at an awkward angle, eyes shut, red hair in her face.

"For God's sake." Rafe put the phone down. No one had ever hung up on me before. Who did he think he was? I'd hated him on sight, posh southern private-school loser, and he wasn't growing on me, either.

I took a long steady breath, pocketing my mobile, trying

to get a grip. "*Lissy.*" It was the first time I'd spoken her name. Warily, I put my hand on her shoulder. "Lissy, wake up." She was still breathing: I could see the steady rise and fall of her chest. Her pale eyelids shuddered as if beneath the skin she was looking at something I couldn't see, staring wildly from side to side.

The Creed woman snatched my hand away from Lissy. "Don't," she hissed. "Don't touch her."

I stared, holding my hand close to my chest as if she'd burnt the skin.

"She's with the Hidden, dreaming their dreams. If you try and pull her away, she might not find her flesh again. Sometimes they wander, the Caught." Leaning close to me, she stank of cigarettes and something else, flowery and herby, that made me half want to sleep. "Sometimes they can't find the way back. Have you seen an empty body with no soul?"

An empty body with no soul*? The Hidden?* How was I going to get Lissy out of here and away from this freak?

I stared at my phone, not knowing whether to call Rafe again or my dad. I didn't do either. The last thing he needed was me ringing up in a state. I didn't want to chuck Lissy in the deep end, either. Judging by last night, she was in enough trouble already.

Lissy lay totally still except for her eyelids twitching, chest heaving as she breathed.

"She danced," the shopkeeper insisted. "Didn't she? You must be careful with the Hidden. They're very tricky, very sly. They don't think the same as us, you see. Don't see right and wrong in the same way."

I didn't know what she was on about so I just ignored her.

A car pulled up outside, a door slammed. Rafe came walking in, straight over to us. I hadn't expected that. He must've driven flat out.

"Lissy." He dropped into a crouch at her side. His voice was hard, like he was speaking to a total stranger, not his sister. *"Melisende."*

Lissy turned away from him so all I could see was the back of her head.

And then Rafe hit her across the face. So hard the crack of it echoed right up to the roof.

"Hey! Leave her alone." Hot anger flared in my belly. You just don't do that. He ignored me.

If there's anything you need, ask Rafe, Dad had said as they rushed out of the door. Obviously the golden boy in their eyes but he didn't fool me.

Lissy opened her eyes, looking confused, then started to cry, tears slipping down her face, quiet all the time.

The shopkeeper just watched us all, mouth hanging open like a ragged black hole.

"Get up," Rafe said. *"Now."*

What was he in such a panic about?

Lissy just held a hand to her cheek, looking away. Then she rolled over, pushed herself up and ran out of the church.

Rafe followed her and the shopkeeper put a white hand on my arm. "You need to watch out. They are coming. You will tell Mr Conway, won't you? That Virgie Creed says *watch out*." She hissed the last words through her teeth and fixed me with her pale boiled-pudding eyes and I went cold all through.

Get a grip.

"Conway knows what to do, what little there is," she said. "More than any one man alive, that's for sure. The dead know plenty. Poor Davy. He knew. Go up to Conway. The land is his; he keeps the Gateway. Don't let her rest, that's all I'm telling you. They will take her as she sleeps. And don't try to bargain with them, understand? They'll always manage to trick you somehow."

Pulling away from her, I turned and walked out after them. My skin prickled like someone was dotting me all over with a frozen pin. Davy? A gateway?

She watched every step I took. Mad as a sack of cats, daft old bag. All that crap about being dumped by Miles Conway. Must've been years ago and she was still on about it.

Rafe drove off without me in his crappy Renault, not that I cared. I didn't want to be in the car with them. At least he couldn't hit her again while he was driving. I sighed, hardly even moving as an expensive-looking black SUV shot past, spraying me with muddy water that splashed up the side of my face. The windows were darkened but as I glared after it, I saw one flat white human hand pressed up against the glass. There one second. Gone the next. As if someone were trying to get out but knew they couldn't.

Miriam had seemed OK at first, quite nice, not too weird or pig ugly like Dad's other girlfriends, but now *this*. Her kids were insane and Miles was just a liability.

What had Dad got us into with this family?

18

Rafe

I parked round the front. Lissy was silent in the seat beside me, a red mark on her face. Her skin was bone white and pale, streaked with tears, about Connie or because I'd hit her, I didn't know. I felt bad about the slap and I didn't need that irritating kid of Nick's preaching at me about it either. But Lissy couldn't faint; she couldn't sleep. Not now. They were waiting.

Mum had never told her a thing. Just tried to keep her locked up like a jewel in a box. How stupid can you get? Because now Lissy was not only useless and unable to defend herself, she was furious too. That train ride. I almost admired her for it. I couldn't blame her for that.

Just every other idiotic selfish thing she'd done. *Dad, who's Elena?* Holding up that birthday card. With an oh-so-innocent look on her face, but really she knew. Oh, yeah, she knew.

Lissy reached for the car door, her hand pale as china. Every other redhead I know is covered in freckles. Not Lissy.

I let her get out, leaving the door hanging open, raindrops patterning the passenger seat. She walked into the house alone, nearly having to duck so she didn't hit her head. Fourteen years old and almost six feet tall.

Your sister should be a model, Becks Dawlish said to me at her party before Easter. *My agent's looking for new girls. Lissy's got the looks and she's definitely got the height.*

Mum would never let that happen, never allow her to be seen by so many people.

I should have told Lissy then, in the car. I know that now. *You were stolen...* She would have believed me. Surely she'd guessed. But it was too late now.

I leaned back in the seat and swore to myself, flinching every time I heard a car pass in the lane. I lost the grey Alfa Romeo last night after four hours of twisting and turning down endless lanes till I nearly ran out of diesel, but it wouldn't take them long to find me. Would it?

Who were they? The police? Or something else?

And where was Miles? He hadn't shown his face once since we all arrived. Dad hated him, but I'd found photos of them together in the stuff Dad left when he moved out: two little kids Connie's age beside a chocolate birthday cake, a pair of lanky awkward twelve-year-olds in the rugby team. Later, standing beside the old pick-up truck Dad used to drive, smiling into the camera; sprawling on a chintzy sofa at a party surrounded by girls with big hair (one of them was Mum).

So what happened? I had asked Mum. *Why don't they see each other any more, Dad and Miles?*

Mum had paused. I knew she was choosing her words carefully. *It just happens, doesn't it? I think your father came to realize they didn't have that much in common any more, even though they'd been friends such a long time.* She laughed, looking tired. *Well, nothing in common except me. They started drifting apart when Miles was expelled in his final year of school.*

She was lying. It was part of the great unmentionable secret: Lissy disappeared. Then she came back. Anyone would think it had never happened.

Miles was Mum's stepbrother. Neither had any other living family. Both their parents were dead, killed in a car crash when they'd only been married a year. Miles and Mum were nineteen. Dad and Miles drifting apart as friends might mean awkward moments at Christmas or weddings if the conversation ever strayed towards the past. Drifting apart was not an explanation for Dad refusing to allow Miles into our house. Ever.

Which was what he'd done.

And why had I never seen Miles Conway, the closest thing I had to an uncle, since I was five years old?

The missing child in the journal, Philippa de Conway. She had to be an ancestor. Because it was *here*: she'd disappeared from Hopesay Reach three hundred years ago, a kid no older than Connie, and oh, God, Connie. It was bad. Anyone could tell that from the way the paramedics had rushed hard-faced through the house, up the stairs, but I couldn't think about that now because those people were hunting me. They were coming, and if I went then that wasn't going to help Connie.

Miles *knew* something about all this.

I had to find him.

19

Joe

Trudging back down the wet rainy lane, I tried to ring Dad but he didn't answer. There was a kid at school who'd died of meningitis, this guy in the sixth form. And now me and Dad were stuck in the middle of some other family's nightmare. I hoped Connie was going to be OK but what could I do?

It started to rain again, great gobbets of water from a boiling grey sky. Wet leaves torn from branches splattered on to the road. One stuck to my knackered waterproof, which was starting to leak. My shoulders were getting wet. I let myself in through the front gate. Rafe's car was quietly ticking on the drive as the engine cooled down. Rain hissed off the bonnet. Bastard, hitting her like that. I could see him still sitting in the driver's seat, leaning back, a dark shape. Waiting for something? The passenger seat was empty. What had happened to Lissy? Had they argued on the way back, had she forced him to stop the car and let her out? She didn't seem like the kind of girl who'd put up with being hit in the face.

The front door was open. Lissy must've left it like that. It creaked as I pushed past. The hall was quiet and dark. A cloud of dust motes hung in the air, lit up by a stream of rainy grey light coming in through a grimy window. Standing in the sitting room, all I could hear was rain drumming against the glass. The fire flickered lazily in the grate. I checked my phone again. Nothing from Dad, no messages. No reception now anyway. I had the weirdest feeling of being watched. I went into the kitchen and stopped dead. All the drawers were open: every single one.

Who would've done that? Miles?

I went upstairs, pausing when I heard the sound of a girl crying. Lissy in her room.

I would hate it if anyone saw me in a state like that. Unlike our parents, we didn't even know each other. At least she wasn't unconscious. Or dead.

I didn't go in.

The door next to Lissy's was open just a crack. Rafe's room. We were all on the same floor: me, Lissy and him. I waited outside a second. All I could hear was Lissy crying quietly. If I shut my eyes, I could still hear the sharp crack as Rafe's hand connected with her face in the church.

What was his problem?

I reached out and pushed the door wide open.

Rafe's room was bigger than mine but given the choice I'd not taken it. Gloomy wooden panelling covered the walls from floor to ceiling. It was like being inside a box. The door swung shut behind me. Grey rainy light filtered in through the two small windows. There was a bed pushed up against the far wall, white duvet piled up. A pillow on the floor. An empty rucksack, clothes chucked all over the room. It wasn't the normal kind of mess someone would make unpacking,

109

looking for a pair of socks or whatever. Rafe's stuff was everywhere. Books, clothes, the lot.

Like his room had been *searched*—

I was about to get out when I heard footsteps: someone moving about on the floor above. Cold fear washed through me. *Don't be stupid*, I told myself sternly. *It's probably just Miles.* I listened again. If Miles was up there, he had a friend with him. There were *two* sets of footsteps. Rafe? But I'd passed him, still sitting in his car. No way could he be up in the attics already.

Treading softly, I walked over to the window and looked down into the cobbled courtyard out the back of the kitchen where I'd found Connie and the white-haired girl the day before. An unfamiliar grey car was parked there now.

We had visitors. Visitors who obviously felt at home enough to let themselves in.

Probably just a friend of Miles. Up in the attics with him.

I was already going for the door. I listened for a second outside Lissy's room. All quiet now. Maybe she'd fallen asleep. I crept down the stairs and into the silent hallway. I waited outside the sitting room door but heard nothing. Even the fire had died down to a pile of glowing embers. I moved on into the kitchen, trying not to look at all the open drawers. There was something a bit mad about the way they'd all been tugged open and just *left*.

I heard the lean-to door shut, more footfalls, then a giant metallic *snap* and a ragged wild cry of pain.

The heavy thud of a human body hitting the floor.

"Jesus Christ. *Miles!*"

110

Rafe. I was sure of it.

Fear gripped my whole body, my gut clenched up like a fist; I was ready to run at any moment.

Someone had set one of Miles's traps. I knew it before I'd even run down the kitchen corridor and opened the lean-to door.

Rafe lay on the floor, the jaws of a gin trap biting hard into the leg of his jeans. He was just swearing to himself, very quietly. It had to be agony, surely. I couldn't see any blood, so the trap was one without serrated jaws. But still, they would have snapped shut with enough force to break his ankle.

Rafe had gone completely white. "Where's Lissy?" His voice sounded thick, croaky.

I knelt down at his side, trying not to look at the steel jaw of the trap biting into his jeans, forcing myself not to think about the ruined skin, muscle and bone beneath the fabric. I found the pin and pulled, hard. It was rusty. Stuck. Rafe hissed and swore. I pulled the pin again and the jaw jerked open, catching his jeans in the hinge. A patch of dark blood instantly soaked through.

Rafe lay back on the dirty concrete floor, swearing again. He shut his eyes, shaking like mad. "How did you know how to do that?" he said at last.

"My grandad used to be a gamekeeper. He's got a load of gin traps like that in his shed. He collects them. They're illegal now, I think."

"Jesus." Rafe sat up. He pulled up his trouser leg a bit and I nearly threw up. His leg was a mess. The trap had smashed through the skin, even without serrated jaws. Thick blood

111

seeped from the wound. "It's broken. My ankle's broken."
He swore again, in a furious whisper. "Is Lissy on her own?"

I wanted to ask if it was normal to hit girls where he
came from, but thought better of it. Instead I said, "There's
someone in the house. Upstairs in the attics. I heard them
moving about."

Rafe's eyes met mine for a second, searching and ruthless.

"I saw a new car in the yard out the back," I said.

I expected Rafe to tell me not to be an idiot, that Miles
had the right to visitors in his own house.

The right to leave a man-trap waiting by the back door?

Instead, he asked me what kind of car it was, what colour.

"A grey Alfa Romeo. Very smart," I added, sarcastically.

Rafe swore again, quietly. Again. "Look Joe," he said, "this
is going to sound – strange, but I need you to listen. I think
someone followed me here yesterday from London. From
what you say, it sounds like they're here. In the house. This is
nothing to do with you or Lissy. You and her need to get out
of here. Now. Do you have anywhere to go?"

"My Dad's at the hospital—"

Rafe shook his head. "No. Not there."

"My mam—"

"Good. You and Lissy need to get to your mother's house.
Walk into the village and catch the first train north. Get a
bus if you have to. Don't talk to anyone, don't let her argue
about it, just go." He tugged a narrow dark object from his
pocket. What was he involved in? Drugs? Crime? "Cut it.
I can't reach." Rafe gave me a knife with a leather handle
and a dark, nasty-looking blade. I sawed through his jeans;

112

the blade was surprisingly sharp. He didn't thank me, just got slowly to his feet. He tried to put weight on the bad one, swore again and had to lean on the wall.

Neither of us spoke but we'd come to a silent agreement: whoever might be upstairs was potentially more dangerous than either of us. We were on the same side. For now.

Rafe grabbed a plastic broom from the floor and leaned on it like a crutch. He was still dead white, but I was impressed at his stamina, not that I would've told him. He was arrogant enough already. Still. It must've hurt like something else.

"We need to find my sister and get both of you out of here. This place isn't safe." Rafe hesitated, leaning on the broom handle. His breathing sounded shallow, uneven.

Don't pass out, I thought. *Just don't pass out.* We had to get his leg dealt with. That basic first aid course in Year Seven hadn't covered medieval-looking wounds caused by rusting gin traps. People often think I'm older than fourteen, but Rafe was bigger than me and he looked heavy.

I remembered that black SUV splashing me on the lane earlier. Darkened windows, like the tour bus for a small-time band. A pale palm pressed just for a second against the back window. A human hand. My belly lurched.

Who did that hand belong to? We hadn't seen Miles all morning.

"Who did all this? Who's been following you?" I was trying not to sound scared.

"I don't know," said Rafe, leaning against the door frame again, drawing in another long ragged breath. "I thought I'd lost them, but obviously not. Jesus Christ, this hurts. We need

113

to be quiet. Don't make a sound till we've got Lissy and we're outside, OK?"

Don't let her sleep, the shopkeeper had said. *They will come for her as she sleeps.*

Rafe hauled himself up the stairs, mud from his boots hitting me in the face, rain shaking from his jacket.

Lissy's bedroom door was still closed. Rafe reached for the handle, twisted it.

Locked.

"Lissy!" he hissed, shoving the door, twisting the handle. His face was completely colourless now: he looked like a corpse. Droplets of sweat slid down his forehead, shining like bubbles. He took the knife from his pocket, unsheathed. Breathing heavily, he leaned on the wall, poking about in the door frame with the blade. I heard the snick of metal on metal. Rafe took the door handle and turned it.

He'd broken in. Was there nothing he couldn't do? He was like bloody James Bond. It felt like a hundred years till he pushed the door open.

There was nobody in the room. Just Lissy's bag, still unpacked: a purple girls' rucksack covered in stickers and black biro hearts. Her iPod lay on the bedside table. The bedclothes were rumpled.

"No," Rafe said. "No."

Where Lissy had lain, there was nothing but a drift of brown winter leaves.

She was gone.

Rafe sank to the floor. His shoulders slumped. He was beaten. I wished I'd not been there to see that.

It's fine, I told myself. *Maybe she's just gone out for a walk.* Leaving her room locked from the inside. All right. OK. What could I do? "I'll call the police."

Rafe looked up, facing me. "No. Don't do that. Oh, God, you're just a kid. You shouldn't be mixed up in this."

We both went for our phones at once, scrabbling in pockets. I still had no signal, no way of knowing if Dad and Miriam had tried to get in touch from the hospital.

Connie. Was she even still alive? She could be dead and we wouldn't know. But there was nothing: no text, no voicemail message. If the house phone had rung, we'd not heard it. We'd been out half the morning. I pictured Dad or Miriam trying again and again, it ringing out.

"I'm going to try the landline." Rafe struggled to his feet; I passed him the broom and followed him downstairs, both of us trying not to make a sound, not really knowing what else to do.

She was gone; Lissy had gone. I glanced at the kitchen clock. It was only quarter past eleven. I felt like ten years had passed since we'd walked into Hopesay Edge but it was only two hours.

Rafe leaned against the kitchen worktop, breathing harshly as he stared at the phone. "It's not working."

"Let me see."

He handed it over and I listened to the dead silence. Not even a dialling tone. The handset shook like mad as he passed it to me. "Look," I said, "we've got to get you to a doctor. You need a tetanus jab—"

That was when I noticed a severed cable sticking out

But really it was idiotic, swearing to save Connie's life. Because what could I do?

I stared, miserable, at the font. There were carvings in the stone but they'd nearly worn away. That's how old it was. I could just make out a snaking vine with leaves and flowers, tried to imagine a stonemason wearing the funny medieval clothes I'd seen in books: a baggy tunic, tight leggings. He must have crouched for hours with aching arms and legs, working slowly at the stone, perhaps almost a thousand years ago. There were people-carvings, too, mostly worn to nothing, but down near the base of the font I could clearly see a small group − saints maybe? − completely dwarfed by the tall slender angel standing in the middle of them all. An angel? I leaned closer. An angel with no wings.

Maybe it's Jesus or something, and they've made him bigger.

I couldn't stop looking at the tall figure: eyes, nose and mouth long worn away, the flowing robes. I knew it was looking back at me from somewhere within its blank face. This weird electric pulse shot through my body, and for a second I swear I was hit by that smell again. Mouldering leaves. Damp sheds. Hot sweetness.

The boy, I thought, reaching out to touch the tall, robed figure, pulling my finger back a millimetre before it brushed the stone. *It's the boy.* I shut my eyes and saw his eyes looking back at me, black as burnt wood, so old. Then, *Don't be an idiot. This isn't the time for stupid daydreaming.*

"Just the milk, cheers." Joe's voice jerked me back into the real world, where Connie lay in hospital. How could I daydream about some guy I'd met at a train station when the back of the phone. Someone had cut the line. Maybe whoever was in the house right at that moment.

"Oh, Christ," Rafe said.

We had no way of calling for help.

We both heard it at the same time: a floorboard creaking above our heads.

For a second, we just stared at each other. It was almost like in the panic over Lissy, we'd forgotten there were other people in the house. People looking for Rafe.

Rafe grabbed my arm. "Shut up and come with me. They might have people waiting outside by now. There's another way back upstairs." He was scared. I could hear it in his voice. Whoever was looking for him, they were here in the house right now. His little sister was in hospital, the other one had been snatched from her bed, he'd had his leg smashed up by a trap. He'd been cool as ice the whole time. Not any more.

I didn't argue. He limped out of the kitchen, down the corridor to the lean-to. He went to the door by the gun cabinet and pulled it open. A bare, uncarpeted staircase led away, and I remembered Dad telling me Rafe had lived here as a little kid. He instinctively knew the layout of this rambling house, and that was our only advantage. I followed Rafe, half shoving him from behind – every time he put weight on the bad leg he swore ferociously. We didn't stop at the first floor, either. The rank smell of his sweat filled my nose. His body was struggling to cope; he was probably going into shock.

Don't pass out, I remember thinking. *Just don't bloody well pass out. I can't do this on my own.* Still swearing and hobbling, he led me up the narrow twisting staircase. You could feel the age of the house here – worn stone steps, lathe and plaster walls like Grandad's cottage. I couldn't help remembering what that woman in the church had said: *the Reach began as standing stones.* It was so, so old. He was clutching at the handrail, breathing heavily, going as fast as he could. The bloodstain on his jeans was spreading. Far below us, I heard voices, the distant click of a closing door.

Whoever it was, they were still looking.

"In here." Rafe pulled me into a vaulted attic lit by a pair of dormer windows I'd never even noticed from outside. I stepped over the carcass of a dead bird – a knot of dusty feathers and blackish slime. Apart from that, the place was empty except for a huge old oil painting leaning against the wall: a portrait of some little kid in a white dress. She was holding a silver bell on a stick with a glossy pink ribbon tied around it. There was something freaky about the look in her pale grey eyes. *Help me,* she seemed to be saying. *Get me out of here.* It was like she was trapped in the painting. Her name and a date were embossed into a plaque in the heavy gold frame: Philippa de Conway, 1707.

"It's her." Rafe was staring at the picture like he'd seen a dead man walking.

"What do you mean?"

"Shut up, there's no time to explain now." Rafe staggered to the nearest window, standing slightly to one side so that anyone waiting outside wouldn't catch sight of him. I crouched by the attic door, thinking, *Oh, shit.*

117

We heard quiet voices. Two people walking up and down, nosing about. Floorboards creaking.

They'd been up here in the attics already. Now it sounded like they were coming back — obviously suspicious, wondering if they'd missed something. I really, really didn't want to be found. Rafe turned to me with this weird smile on his face, like he'd just reached the same conclusion.

"Rafe," I whispered. "We can't stay here. They're going to find us."

At the exact same moment, we both turned to look at the nearest window. We'd got to climb out of it. Up on to the roof. Hope they didn't follow us there.

I heard heavy footsteps on the landing below, in our bedrooms. I wondered what they'd make of the dried leaves on Lissy's bed.

"You go first." Rafe pushed the window open.

"If I go first, you'll never make it, not on that leg."

"For Christ's sake." Rafe heaved himself up onto the window ledge, gasping in pain. Blood dripped from his trouser leg and I scrubbed away as much as I could with the toe of my boot. The last thing we wanted to do was leave evidence. With a suppressed groan, Rafe stood on the ledge, swearing quietly as he pulled himself up onto the roof. I grabbed the good leg and shoved. He nearly kicked me in the face. I could hear footsteps on the stairs now and scrambled up. I made the mistake of looking down. The weed-choked front lawn spun below me. The lake by the yew tree looked dark and shadowy, evil almost. It was a long way down. Very. I turned and nearly fell, grabbed hold of the guttering, and

Rafe hauled me up onto the roof, cursing under his breath.

The window was still open. If they saw it—

I reached down, feeling blindly with one hand, and just managed to push the window shut.

Me and Rafe edged backwards and crouched behind a chimney stack. We'd have to time it right: get inside before whoever was in the house went back to their car. It was windy up on the roof and freezing cold. I looked down at the wet leaves stuck to the tiles, trying to forget how high up we were.

I heard the faint click of the attic door opening, more footsteps. Rafe crouched at my side, sweat running down his face. If he passed out up here that'd be it.

We heard the door go again, then no more footsteps. Time dragged and I stared out across the trees. Rafe followed my gaze but neither of us spoke. Now it was a waiting game. We sat there for what felt like hours and probably was. At last, the grey car pulled away down the drive, tyres crunching in the wet gravel.

"Bloody Christ," Rafe said, very, very quietly. "Who the hell are they?"

And I didn't answer, because I'd been hoping he'd tell me.

20

Miriam

It will be fourteen years tomorrow since Lissy was returned.

Tomorrow, they will come for Lissy. If I try to shut the Gateway, Rafe and Connie will both die.

All this time I've been expecting to find a way out of the covenant, hoping to cheat the curse. I even sent Lissy away to school. The truth is I hoped the Hidden would simply forget about all this if she wasn't with me all the time. They can be so capricious. I was wrong.

Time's up. Nothing worked. The Hidden didn't forget. *He* didn't forget.

So now I'm here with Connie in hospital, and Lissy's at Hopesay without me. The Hidden are close. So close. I hear them whispering, faint traces of their music. I shouldn't be here – I should be with Lissy doing something to protect her though God knows what – but Connie is so so helpless. It was an impossible choice. There was no way I couldn't come to hospital with her, but Lissy is at their mercy now. I'm outmanoeuvred at every turn: I can't be in two places at once. Connie looks very small under the hospital-issue blankets. I've been holding her hand but I don't think she even knows

I'm here. There's a purple bruise already spreading beneath the plaster on the back of her hand where they've inserted the drip. I can't fix this; I can't make it all better for her. I've only ever felt helplessness like this once before and that was fourteen years ago when the Hidden took Lissy.

The Hidden are showing me what they're capable of: Connie is a warning, in case I try to close the Gateway before the time's up. Larkspur told me what would happen. I know all my children are cursed to die tomorrow unless I give Lissy back. But I thought I had one day left.

Why didn't I shake Lissy awake this morning? Why didn't I force her into the car with Nick? There was no time to think about anyone except Connie. I thought she was going to die in the ambulance, my little girl. I was in a blind panic, not thinking straight. They say her condition has stabilized but she's not improving. What does that really mean?

I know what it means. Connie is cursed to die at midnight tonight unless the Hidden have Lissy. They have made her sick now to warn me, to make sure I don't forget. The poison in her blood, this septicaemia – it's no ordinary disease, I'm sure of it.

This is part of the curse.

I'm growing more and more afraid that they've done something to Lissy too. I know we're not in Oxford now and mobile phone reception can be terrible in the countryside, but I don't believe that explains why she's not answering. I can't get through to Rafe, either, and Nick can't contact Joe. We tried the landline earlier. It rang and rang. Now it's not even working. Where are they? I don't like this. I really don't.

Have they taken her already? Have they cheated?

Nick knows I'm worried; he's driven back to Hopesay to make sure they're all OK, promised to bring Lissy to the hospital for visiting hours. I'm not looking forward to that argument with the hospital staff: there's no way I'm letting her go back to the Reach without me. I'm not making that mistake again.

I can't just give Lissy to the Hidden without a fight. Miles will help. He's got to. He's the one who started all this, and he knows what we're up against.

Adam blames him for everything but it's my fault too. Of course it is. I had choices. After the car crash, Miles and I had no one to tell us to stop. I don't mean just the endless parties we had at the Reach once both our parents were dead. Nineteen felt very old at the time, but it's not really. I should have made sure Miles spent less time with Virgie Creed. She was completely unsuitable for him, and they were obsessed with her stupid old books about folklore: they talked about nothing but standing stones and portals. Instead, what did I do? I fell in love with Miles's best friend. I fell in love with Adam, and I left Miles and Virgie to their meddling.

What bloody fools we all were.

It was Miles's twenty-first birthday at the Reach that really changed everything, not even having Rafe so young or getting married to Adam while we were still at uni, like everyone said. My tutors had even agreed I could come back to college and do my final year again. Adam and Rafe weren't the reason I never did. It's easy enough to see all this with hindsight. I like to think my life would be so different now if we'd just never turned up to that party.

He would have found me anyway.

The party didn't take long to get completely out of control. I remember someone kicked a football through one of the bedroom windows – there was broken glass everywhere. Miles laughed, but I could tell he was upset. Adam and I were furious and terrified because Rafe was asleep upstairs – we nearly left there and then, but Miles persuaded us to stay. I remember how desperate he looked, so strangely lonely. In the garden, a girl no one knew fell down a flight of stone steps wearing a pair of glittery angel wings, and twisted her ankle. I went to the kitchen to get candles and jam jars, hoping we could at least light up the more perilous hazards outside: the lake, the steps, the ha-ha that dropped straight down into the paddock.

"You forgot the matches." I knew the voice, faint and girlish. Virgie. She offered me a box of Swan Vestas. I was careful to thank her – she already thought I was a snob because she was from the village, and I didn't want her to think I was being even more unfriendly than usual because Miles had finished things between them. Or that I'd heard those horrible stories about her family. Something about Miles's great-grandfather paying for one of the Creeds to go to Eton, but all he did afterwards was get shot for desertion in the First World War. Poor boy. He probably had shell-shock.

All the same. She shouldn't have been there. Miles had broken things off with her, so why was she still hanging around? Virgie Creed was a creep, and seeing her only made me feel more flat about the party. By then, I was really starting to wish we hadn't come to the Reach at all. I had the oddest feeling of foreboding and gloom. I should have run and found Adam. He would have come with me. We could have got in the car with Rafe and driven back to Oxford. But we didn't.

Instead of leaving the kitchen, Virgie just stood and stared at me. Miles must have invited her to the party out of kindness, or maybe she was just gatecrashing.

"Tell him," Virgie said. "Tell Miles he wants to be careful. He doesn't know what he's fooling with." Her forehead glistened, and I wondered how on earth anyone could be sweating. It was freezing in the kitchen, even with the range lit.

Virgie was sweating with fear.

I didn't know what to say, just stood holding the matches. Was that a *threat?* I could hear more voices now, footsteps out in the old stone-flagged corridor, and Virgie scurried off to escape into the garden through the lean-to. I was alone again.

I dropped the box of matches into my basket, unable to stop myself wiping my fingers on my jeans.

I turned as the kitchen door opened, heard Miles call my name. He sounded like he'd had too much to drink already. "I've brought someone to meet you, Mirry," he said.

And I *smelled* her before she even came in. Musty woodsmoke, something sweet and intoxicating beneath it all. I turned and there she was, so horribly tall and pale, white-blonde hair like a cloud around her head, smiling. And those terrible clothes, layers of mud-coloured wool and weird greenish silk.

God, she was beautiful. I could tell immediately that she wasn't human. You could see it in her eyes – something cat-like and merciless. Utterly without pity. I stood in total shock. Of course I'd heard Miles and Virgie's stories about the Reach, about the Hidden "folk" as they called them. But I'd never actually thought for a moment any of it was true.

It's all true. All of it.

She smiled, and I saw her glance around the kitchen, her eyes finally resting on a bowl of pink roses I'd cut earlier and left on the table. "I'm Rose," she said. I had the strangest feeling she'd made it up there and then, that Rose wasn't her real name at all. "And you're Miriam. Aren't you lovely? So perfect."

I stared at Miles, hardly able to speak. I couldn't believe what he'd done, the sheer recklessness of it. I couldn't believe what I was seeing. A girl who looked human, but wasn't. Another species.

"How did this happen?" I stammered, stumbling over my words, unable to take my eyes away from Rose. There was something both intoxicating and repellent about her.

All I remember is Miles laughing, walking over to the sideboard by the door, tipping out the contents of a plastic carrier bag. *Iron crosses*. The iron crucifixes which had hung for centuries over every window and door at Hopesay Reach, even the iron knocker unscrewed from the front door, all sitting there in a useless pile.

Miles had taken them all down. He'd removed our protection. I'd listened to enough of Miles and Virgie's tedious stories about the history of Hopesay Reach, that poor little girl who went missing hundreds of years ago. I knew the Reach was protected by the prayers of a terrified village priest, whispered over each iron cross. I knew why, too.

I'd always thought they were just silly stories. Till now.

The Reach was protected because of the Gateway. Because of the power in those old standing stones that now form the very fabric of Hopesay Reach, some left in their original position when the priory was built, others knocked down, cut, shaped and built into the very walls around us. A vortex of power which, left unsealed, allowed the Hidden to leave their halls and roam free.

"Miles, what have you done?" My voice sounded like it belonged to someone else, whispery and terrified.

He grinned. "I've opened the Gateway," he said. "Isn't it extraordinary? A whole other world, Mirry. Come with me – we'll be young for ever. We'll never die."

"Don't!" I hissed, thinking of every stupid fairy tale I'd ever heard. "Miles! You won't be able to get back. You'll be trapped!"

Rose was looking at the pile of iron crucifixes with the most extraordinary expression – fear and triumph all mixed into one. Yes, the Gateway was open now, but right there on the table was the only thing on earth that could kill her, were it heated, beaten, forged into a weapon with a deadly edge.

She laughed at me, as if I were the boring sensible one telling everyone to stop, which I suppose I was. She turned to Miles and kissed him full on the lips till my cheeks flamed red. They parted, his eyes still lingering on hers, his fingers tracing a line down her exquisite face. Rose turned to me, smiling. "Oh, Miriam, you darling silly thing, don't worry. I've brought someone just for you."

The way she spoke was so pretentious. Just one of the many things that annoyed me about her.

But as Miles and Rose stepped further into the kitchen, hand in hand, a boy walked in after them, taller than Rose, stooping through the door frame, standing, smiling too, just like her. Black eyes like smears of coal-dust, shiny black hair hanging loose past his shoulders, a gold band around his white throat.

"He's my brother," Rose said, so very proud.

And the boy smiled at me. "Hello, Miriam. I've been longing to meet you."

PART THREE
THE HIDDEN

21

Lissy

I'm dreaming again.

It starts, as usual, with the clear limitless light of a blue sky on a hot day. And the sky is all around me, air rushes past my face, between my outstretched fingers, into my wide-open screaming mouth, because I'm falling. I look down and watch the ground coming closer every second, the patchwork of green fields and darker smears of woodland, the glittering trail of a river, cars inching along a motorway, the grey sprawl of a town staining the beauty of it all—

I'm falling and I'm going to die.

Then that physical sensation across my back: muscles stretching, lengthening, something unfurling. I squeeze my eyes tight shut. And the lift, that incredible lift, warm air beneath, pushing me up, higher and higher. I want to open my eyes again, to look down and see those fields and forests, that ugly town, but I know what will happen if I do. I soar, wind rushing past my face, and when I can stand it no longer, I open my eyes and—

I woke with a jolt. Everything was dark, soft warmth. I spread my fingers and touched fur, the hard leathery edge of some animal's skin. One side of my face burned with a faint sting, as if I'd scalded myself.

Fear jolted through my body. Where was I? Not in my bedroom at Hopesay Reach. Not any more. Then where?

Chilly sweat broke out on my back and on my hands, sticking to my skin. My hair hung down, brushing against my neck. What was this place? I'd dreamed of freedom, of flying, but woken up in a dark prison. All I remembered was that woman in the church reaching out as I fell, and Rafe, Rafe *hitting* me. That was why my face hurt.

Why had he *done* that to me?

It wasn't quite dark. Not really.

"Rafe?" I called. "Rafe?" No reply. Deep down, I hadn't expected one. I knew even then that my brother was a long, long way away. I felt his absence, deep in my flesh and bones. More tentatively, I whispered, "Joe? *Joe*. Is anyone there?"

I had a sudden, absurd desire to hear Joe telling me not to be a daft cow, like he'd done outside the house earlier that morning. *Not boring after all. Just* safe. I would have given anything to hear Rafe's voice then, sarcastic and cold, even though he'd just hit me. Even being with Rafe would be better than this – alone, in the dark.

"Let me out!" I shouted, again and again, until I was only sobbing, not even able to form the words.

No one answered. No one came.

I sat back on my heels, trying to calm my breathing, knowing if I went into a blind panic I would lose my grip on reality and never get out. I wouldn't escape this place without at least trying to think straight.

My eyes were adjusting, and the dark seemed to lift. I crawled towards a circle of silver light like a rising moon, bare earth beneath my hands and bare earth just inches above my back. A tunnel. I *was* underground, soil and sharp stones beneath my hands, digging into my knees even through jeans.

Buried.

Had *he* done this? Rafe?

No. Not even he would leave me in a place like this.

Don't panic, don't panic.

I crawled to the end of the tunnel, broke out into a cave where at last I could stand, but the walls weren't rock, they were just earth. There were no windows, only a few openings leading off, dark like gaping mouths. But I could still see. At one end of the cave, flames leaped in a stone bowl on the ground. The smoke drifted off, fading into nothing. Lines of ragged silky flags hung from above like bunting left outside all summer, floating in a breeze that came from nowhere. There was a grease-smeared bronze plate on a table and a silver bell looped onto a white stick, trailing a few ragged scraps of what might once have been ribbon. A child's toy? Animal bones lay scattered on the earth beneath my bare feet. Or at least I hoped they were animal bones.

And now I remembered kicking my boots off before throwing myself on the bed. I'd gone to sleep there.

Woken up here.

Don't panic—

"They can't hear. It's no use trying. I cried till my voice died and no one came."

I looked up, swallowing my horror, but there was just a little girl standing in one of the dark doorways, maybe seven

132

or eight years old – about the same age as Connie. A little girl, underground. I had to push the thought away, concentrate on the detail, or I was going to panic, start screaming. Her brown hair hung in a tangle all the way down to her waist, bare legs streaked with mud.

"I've tried calling so many times." The little girl *curtseyed* then, before coming towards me, an odd little bowing bob, like it was something she did automatically. There was something strange about her voice, too: a weird, rolling accent I'd never heard before. "Once, I thought I heard my papa, calling back. But I was only dreaming. He never came, so don't wear out your voice. No one will hear. It's not worth your tears, boy."

I smiled at her, even though I felt sick with horror and fear. "I'm not a boy. I'm a girl."

"Oh. But you're so tall. And wearing hose." The little girl was staring at my jeans. "I'm looking for my bell."

"I'm definitely a girl." I reached across to the table, not really wanting to touch the greasy surface, handed her the silver bell. The white handle felt smooth, like polished bone. Ivory. She clutched it to her chest as if I'd been trying to steal it.

"What's your name?" I asked gently, like speaking to Connie when she was upset – *oh, Connie* – "Mine's Lissy." I didn't want to frighten her away. I didn't want to be left alone in this dark filthy place.

She smiled. One of her front teeth was missing. "I'm Philippa, but Mammy and Papa and Roger always call me Tippy." Her mouth twisted like she was going to cry.

133

I wanted to reach out and hug her, as I would if she were Connie. Her eyes stayed dry. I could still see the horror and misery in them, though, this terrible desperate *longing* for Mammy and Papa and Roger, but there were no tears. It was as if she had none left.

She turned and ran.

"No!" I called out after her. "Wait!"

But Tippy didn't stop, just disappeared through the farthest doorway, her skinny legs pale against the darkness. I stood, helpless. Now I couldn't even hear the silvery ring of her bell on its ivory stick. She'd gone.

What would Mum do when she got back to the Reach and found I wasn't there? I couldn't stand not knowing what had happened to my sister. Standing in the gloom, I dug into my jeans pocket for my mobile. There was no reception at all. I re-read Mum's text from that morning. I didn't have much battery left. Why hadn't she tried to ring or leave another message? Was Connie still in intensive care or— Or something else?

Tears burned my eyes but I rubbed them away.

Crying wasn't going to help. I'd been wrapped in cotton wool for years; I was the one who'd wanted to prove I could look after myself, catching that train alone. It felt like years ago but was only yesterday.

But how did I even get here? How—

I *had* to get back to the Reach. *No one will hear.* Such terrifying words. I pushed them out of my head. *She's just a little girl.* I was older. I was convinced I could think things through more clearly.

I'm going to get out of here. I am. I will.

I tried not to think about Tippy's strange accent, those old-fashioned clothes.

As if she'd been down here for hundreds of years.

22

Rafe

I sat on the front doorstep, leaning back against the old wood, gasping for breath. I couldn't believe I'd made it without falling and breaking my neck. Climbing down from the roof of a house isn't easy at the best of times, and especially not with one ankle smashed to hell. I patted my jacket pocket, and felt the reassuring presence of the manuscript, safely folded away.

They'd found nothing. Whoever they were. They'd be back soon. I knew I didn't have much time, and I could have very easily done without Joe to baby-sit.

My hands were shaking so much I gripped my leg, looking down at the mess. Blood everywhere. The level of pain was astonishing: a crazy pulsing agony. I was dimly aware of Joe opening the door behind me, sitting down at my side. He said something I couldn't concentrate on, pushing a pack of codeine tablets into my hand, then a half empty bottle of red wine.

"You want brandy but I couldn't find any." His flat, northern voice was oddly calming and businesslike. Maybe he was going to be useful after all; he'd definitely kept his nerve up on that roof.

I forced myself to focus. I choked back three of the tablets and swallowed a mouthful of wine, eyes watering.

"Listen," Joe said, "are you going to tell me what's going on? Who were those people in the house? What makes you think you're being followed—"

And Joe stopped mid sentence. Just stopped. I followed his gaze.

The creature stepped out between the trees on the front lawn with the silent grace of a deer in the woods. There he was, just standing and watching us, the hood of his black cloak thrown back, red hair everywhere, dark eyes shining like mackerel skin.

"What is that?" Joe kept saying, over and over again, repeating himself like a scratched DVD. "What is that thing, what is it?"

Not human, a voice screamed inside my head. *Run!*

He hadn't changed at all in fourteen years. I hadn't forgotten, not even in all that time. He looked the same. Ageless. A deep, unrelenting fury welled up inside me and burst. I struggled up, staggering towards him, speared with pain every time my bad foot touched the ground.

"Give her back!" I hardly recognized my own voice: a ragged, bloody roar. I hated Lissy for telling Mum about Elena, getting Dad kicked out, but she was still my sister.

"Where's my sister?"

The Hidden creature just raised one hand, gave us both a slight, mocking smile as if he couldn't decide which was more amusing: my rage or Joe's shocked confusion. Then he just turned and walked off to the lake, black cloak flowing behind like a crow dragging its wing. He stepped straight in without looking back at us, and first of all his cloak seemed to float on the surface, then he was gone, head and shoulders disappearing beneath the flat glassy water.

A freezing cold chill slid right down my neck as I stood on the lawn, wet grass soaking my bloodied jeans, gasping for breath, fighting the urge to sink to my knees, anything to ease the hideous pain in my ankle. They were back. The Hidden. For years they'd lived only in my worst dreams. Not any more. Now they were here in the real world, and they'd taken Lissy.

Joe stood beside me, staring fixedly at an ever-expanding circle of ripples left on the water. "What?" He sounded breathless, like he'd just sprinted a hundred metres, but it was just the shock. Understandable. "How did that happen?" He turned to me. "What was that – thing? It looked like a person but—"

My hands were shaking wildly, and I was starting to feel sick, unable to cope with the pain or the pressure. I had to get a grip. I looked straight at him. "They're not people. Laugh if you want but let's just say that now. I don't know what they are but they're not people."

Joe sat down on the grass, staring at the lake. I couldn't blame him. There are creatures here on earth who look human, pass for human, but are not human. I'd grown up with this possibility, now I knew it was true. To Joe, it was extraordinary. Devastating.

We didn't have time for it.

"Look," I said, trying not to let my impatience show.

"We've got to get away from the Reach. Those people with the grey Alfa. They could come back." I glanced at the lake. "For Christ's sake, Joe, *he* could come back, and you definitely don't want to mess with them."

Joe got up, slowly, watching me all the time. He obviously thought I was a complete nutter, to be treated with extreme caution. Quite justified, really. "OK," he said. "OK. I saw it. Him. That thing— But if they're *here*, more of the same, wouldn't someone else have seen them too? Isn't there some kind of record? Like an investigation? I mean, this is mad. It's a world-changing thing, it's crazy – a different *species*, you only have to look at them—"

"Why," I said quietly, "do you think we've just spent the last half hour hiding on the roof like a pair of idiots? Those guys with the flashy grey car. They *are* the investigation." With supreme effort, I clambered to my feet, doing my best to ignore the intense pain in my leg. It was so bad I now felt like throwing up.

Not only did I have a gang of crazed house-breakers on my trail, one sister in hospital and another who could best be described as missing, I now had a cocky teenage northerner to look after, ripe for collateral damage.

Great. Just great.

23

Lissy

I walked in darkness, earth and dry roots beneath my bare feet, mouth dry, fear fluttering in my belly. At last the dark lifted; another bowl of fire lit my way, lying on the bare soil. Again there was hardly any smoke, just bluish flames glowing like burning brandy on a Christmas pudding. A few metres on, more fire in a stone cup lit up a sheet of silvery-gold metal flattened against the wall. It was carved with birds and clambering roses, each petal perfect: so real. The birds looked as if they might fly away: bright-eyed, feathered wings full of life. But then the sheet of silver just curled away from the earthen wall, an abandoned project. Further on, a white stool lay discarded, one broken leg. It looked like marble. One leg had been just snapped in half.

Who were these people?

I thought of Tippy's dirty clothes and tangled hair. Living underground, all this grime and darkness and beauty jumbled up together. And then I heard music I recognized. Folky, wild: drums, a harp, and I was back in those dark woods, dancing with him. With the boy. I'd known all along, really and truly, that *he* was here somewhere. Cold fingers.

Eyes that shone like dark wet steel.

What do you want? Sudden fury overtook me. Connie was desperately sick, blood-poisoned. She might be dead by now and I wouldn't even know. Mum could have arrived back from the hospital with the worst news possible and found me gone because of his stupid games. Prancing about in the woods, mysteriously appearing in my bedroom like some kind of murderous creep. And now this.

I ran down the tunnel, following the music.

You'll just have to take me home.

The light grew brighter and brighter; soon there were bowls of fire every few paces, the music growing louder with every step. I passed a heap of sparkling fabric just left on the soil. It was draped with drifts of cobweb that made my toes curl – I didn't even want to think about how big the spiders were, and—

Someone was watching.

I turned to face a girl even more monstrously tall than me. Bright white hair hung wild and uncombed around her shoulders, all the way down to her waist, as if she were some old lady. But her eyes didn't look old, just all glittery and shadowy silver like the boy's. Neither did her face; she couldn't have been more than sixteen or seventeen. Her skin was pale and creamy smooth. She smiled, fast, like she was making a sudden tactical move, and I saw bright sharp teeth.

The words rose up from the back of my mind. *Not human. She's not human. Something else.*

"So, little sky-in-her-eyes. You came back."

Came back?

141

She leaned closer; I breathed in the throat-raking scent of stale woodsmoke, unwashed clothes and a wood full of bluebells on a hot day. "I've been called Rose."

She offered the information as if a name could easily flow into something else and change, like water into ice or steam.

"Where am I?" My voice sounded more trembling and tearful than I'd meant.

Rose shrugged: an odd fluid movement, as if the joints in her shoulders moved in a different way to mine. "Only where you have always been. What else is there but the world?"

"Listen." I tried to sound firm and confident, like I really didn't have time for this. Which I didn't. "I must go home. Please can you help me? I don't know how to get out of this place."

I was starting to panic, feeling in every bone and muscle the weight of all that earth above me and on all sides, *buried* underground with this Rose-thing. Not-human. I pushed the thought from my mind, telling myself, *Not possible, not really. She's just—*

"Oh," said Rose. "You want to *leave*?" She spoke as if I'd expressed the need to fly. And laughed. "Well, now you're here, that might be a little difficult."

My entire body froze with fear.

"I don't even know why I'm here. Look, my—" Instinct warned me against telling Rose about Connie. As if even from here in this horrible underground lair she might be able to harm her. "Listen, I need to get home. I don't belong here, OK?"

"Oh?" Rose sighed at my confusion. "Well, I'd better take you to find him."

And she just started walking off, muddy silk skirts swishing like wind through the trees, hair hanging in a great tangle all down her back way past her waist, dirty and freakishly white for someone who looked so young. It shone like polished silver.

The music got louder. I felt the drum beating through me, pulsing in my blood and bones, making me want to dance again, even though every nerve in my body sang with terror. Now everywhere I looked there were gold symbols hammered into the earthen walls; they reminded me of the Egyptian hieroglyphs I'd seen in books. An enormous horn about six feet long hung from glittering chains. What huge animal had *that* been taken from? An elephant?

"They're all dead now," Rose said, not turning to look at me. "The Horned Ones. In case you were wondering and most of you do. It's been such a long time since any of you *saw* one."

I didn't like the way she'd guessed what I'd been thinking. Or what she'd said. *Just keep your mind on the music.* I could hear someone singing now: holding a high clear note, bright and distant as a star. Rose picked up her pace and was now walking so fast I ran to keep up, nearly tripping on a carved wooden chest left open, spewing more bright silky stuff and a tangle of ribbons out onto the dirt floor.

Then, with no warning, Rose grabbed my arm and drew me off into a side passage so thick with cobwebs it was like walking through clinging mist. Her fingers were freezing;

a deep chill spread up my arm, and just out of sight jerky long-legged shapes scuttled away. I opened my mouth to scream, but nothing came out – just a dry little gasp. Cobwebs brushed my face, caught in my hair, unseen things crunched beneath my bare feet; I was dizzy now, head spinning with fright, burning nausea surging up my throat.

In the deep gloom I could just make out a sheer rock face ahead of us; Rose had led me to a dead-end tunnel, deep underground.

What was she going to do to me here?

I was so horrified my head swirled with dizziness; any second now I would faint, but just at the last second before I did Rose stopped and said *Open*. I had a sense that the ground beneath my feet was not to be trusted, of everything shifting, and before I had time to scream the darkness lifted. I was blinking in the brightness of it all, coughing as smoke raked the back of my throat.

The spidery tunnel had opened out into a cavern so high and wide I couldn't see where it began or ended, just earthen walls reaching up higher, higher, and finally lost in a swirling clot of green-tinged smoke.

The music stopped.

Fires burnt nearly everywhere I looked, flames in black charred bowls hanging from above or shoved up against walls, one enormous pool of greenish fire burning in the middle of the cavern. Tippy was sitting beside it like a pet cat, putting a little wooden doll to bed in a pile of rags. She stared at me, unblinking, still that terrible longing in her eyes as if I were someone – or something – that she recognized.

144

They were *all* looking at me, and all the time I was thinking, *How did she do that? A wall of solid rock, and now this—*

"Welcome," Rose whispered in my ear, mocking, "to the secret halls of the Hidden, where men could never find us." She smiled. Her breath smelled like crushed herbs on a hot day, spicy and weirdly enticing. "Until my dear beloved opened the Gateway."

Hadn't Virgie Creed mentioned Uncle Miles opening some kind of portal at the Reach? What had he *done*?

I stared around me, breathless with horror, with sheer disbelief. *This shouldn't be happening*, I kept telling myself. *It can't be real*. But it was. I could see perhaps fifty of the Hidden lounging in the shadows, stretched out in the fires' warmth like strange and beautiful cats. Were there *more*? They were too tall, their limbs too long. So cold and pale with long shining hair hanging in tangled plaits and coils around their shoulders, men and women alike. Male and female. It was clear straight away they were totally different from Tippy. Not only was Tippy the only child, but she glowed with heat, her cheeks flushed pink from the fire. Each and every one of the Hidden was whiter than the belly of a fish, weirdly gorgeous with dark eyes that glittered in the firelight as they watched, some holding flat drums, one sat by a harp. Watching me in silence. Just like in the woods, a half forgotten instinct shrieked at me that if they chose, I would be prey. Hunted. Down here, with nowhere to run.

"Child of my brother," Rose said, voice as sweet as honey, eyes harder than solid shining steel, "O child of my brother, claim your prey. Brought to ground at last."

Prey. I turned, about to run anywhere, even back into those webs and that awful darkness, but she grabbed me tight around one wrist. Cold shot up my arm and I knew there was no pulling away. Rose was straw-thin and delicate but stronger than a granite cliff. Her body obeyed different laws to my own.

Rose is not a person. She's something else. Hidden. They're all something else—

And I'm prey.

My head spun; everything was black. I dropped to my knees and heard Rose laughing, high and wild like a little girl Connie's age. She let go of my arm and I fell forwards, breathing in cold damp earth. I couldn't get away. I couldn't get out. How could I escape, when Rose could make a wall of rock just melt away into nothing?

"Leave her alone." I knew that voice.

I opened my eyes and looked up. There he was. The boy. Crouching right in front of me, like we were playing a game – smiling but sad and haunted at the same time.

"Hello, Lissy."

I said what I'd been longing to since I first saw him. "What are you?"

Elf? Fairy? Alien? Not human, though. Definitely not. His answer was completely way off what I expected.

"Did no one ever say?" The boy shrugged his shoulders with that same odd fluidity as Rose. "I'm your brother."

"No." The word came out, hard and choking like dry leaves.

Rafe's my brother. Not this creature.

I could feel them all watching me but none of them moved, not even Tippy, who was the only child in sight. A human child, down here among these *things*—

"Really?" said the boy. He reached out and without even thinking I took his offered hand, chilly to the touch but not the deep cold of Rose's. "Ah," he whispered, never taking his eyes from mine. "So warm with that mortal blood. But look, Lissy, at your hands."

I did. White and pale just like his. Never brown, but never sunburned either, not even a single freckle. And in that second I knew he was telling the truth.

Mum—

I was the only one. Not Rafe or Connie, blonde and tanned all year just like Dad. He wasn't my father, was he? It made sense now. If Rafe or Connie had spoilt Dad's secret about Elena, he would have forgiven them. I'd always known that. You could forgive your own child anything. But not the cuckoo hiding in your nest.

My eyes burned and tears poured down my face. The boy was telling the truth. My whole life was a puppet show. Nothing was real.

I stood, allowing him to raise me up, tears sliding down my neck as his cold hand gripped mine. "You might call me Larkspur," my brother whispered.

Everything was fake. Every Christmas, each family holiday. Even the way everyone blamed Dad when he left Mum. It hadn't been his fault. It was hers. They'd both cheated but she'd done it first. Such a long time ago.

"Why?" The word creaked out of my mouth. "It's not

your real name." He knew mine. They all did.

He smiled. "Call me Larkspur," he said, "because when I close my eyes, I do not see the walls of my father's kingdom. I see a knotted grey sky pouring fresh rain on my face, I see the seven hundred colours of a hedgerow: hawthorn, dead nettle, dandelion, cowslip, meadowsweet and larkspur. As blue as your eyes, my sister."

I drew my hands away, folded my arms across my chest. Even with bowls of fire everywhere, I still felt cold.

"Why am I here?" My voice sounded as if it belonged to someone else, cracked with fear.

And Larkspur smiled. "I will let our father tell you. Come with me. Kneel before the King."

Larkspur reached out for my hand again but I snatched it away. I wasn't going anywhere with him.

All I could hear was Rose laughing.

24

Miriam

I stepped out onto the lawn, alone, drawing the heavy oak door shut against the hubbub from inside: laughing, shouting, the clink of broken china. Miles's parties always got out of control, but now we'd entered a whole new league. The stars looked brittle and cold. The whole of the night sky was like a black glass bowl rising up above me.

I sensed he was there before he even spoke, caught that scent of woodsmoke and last year's leaves. He rested his hands upon my shoulders as if we'd known each other a hundred years. I held my breath. His fingers were so cold.

"The sky," he whispered, and I closed my eyes at the sound of his voice. "Doesn't it look as if it would break if you threw a stone high enough?"

I turned to face him, knowing what would happen even before it did. He was so beautiful, with that black hair, those shining eyes. I was married; I had a child.

I still didn't stop.

When he kissed me, his lips weren't cold; they were warm and so were his arms around my waist.

"Don't let me go," I whispered.

He laughed, a silvery, airy sound. "Have no fear. I will not."

And I felt the first cold touch of fear—

25

Joe

I sat in the driver's seat with the key in the ignition.

That thing. That creature. He was just like the girl I'd found in the yard with Connie. I could see it all now, what had frightened me so much about her.

She'd not been human.

You could tell straight away they were different. Not like us. Not the same species. OK, so they'd both been very tall, but so were lots of people. Basketball players. The Dutch. Those guys in Africa who live on blood and milk. No, it was the eyes that gave it away: those glittering and somehow metallic eyes. In a way, it was a relief to finally admit it to myself. I'd seen two creatures who looked human, might even pass for human – just. But they weren't human: they were something else.

I couldn't get my head round it.

I felt like the whole world around me had undergone this subtle change and taken on a new character, like I'd just noticed for the first time that the sky was actually green. We weren't at the top, us humans. There was *something else*.

It shouldn't be true. It was. I'd seen them. Two. With my

own eyes. Him and that white-haired girl. The first time, I'd talked myself out of it. Now there was no way of escaping the reality.

"Joe. Are you going to do this or not?" Rafe said. "We've got to get out of here. It's not safe."

I didn't need telling.

That *thing*. He was the one who had taken Lissy, leaving nothing but a pile of dead leaves on her bed, not the faceless people who'd driven off in their fancy grey car.

There were these wild inhuman creatures. And the others, those men searching the house. They were different. *They are the investigation*, Rafe had said. I couldn't take it all in; I was starting to panic.

One step at a time, I told myself.

I turned the ignition and the car leapt forwards, a huge, shuddering jolt across the yard. I slammed my foot on what I hoped was the brake; Rafe grabbed the handbrake.

"It's in gear," he said through gritted teeth. "Always start a car with your foot on the clutch. The pedal on the left."

Right, thanks for telling me.

I jammed my foot on the clutch and turned the key in the ignition a second time. The car started, engine humming. I tried to forget where I was and what had just happened.

He wasn't human—

I tried to pretend that Dad was sitting in the passenger seat, letting me drive his old Ford around the field at Grandad's.

Release the clutch as you press down on the accelerator, easy now—

I was driving the car, in charge of this huge lump of metal.

It was like someone had just handed me a detonated bomb.

"Left out of here," barked Rafe, gasping as he leaned forwards, clutching his leg just below the knee.

Just don't pass out, Rafe.

The hawthorn hedge scraped the window on my side with a shriek against the glass.

"For Christ's sake!" Rafe hissed.

"Just shut up and tell me where to go!"

"OK, OK, OK." Rafe craned his neck, looking back along the lane. "We've got to find out more about those people who were inside the house, all right? There's nothing in Hopesay Edge. We need to get into town, find an Internet café or a library or something. You're good this side. Pull out and stay close to the left. It's pretty narrow."

I inched out into the road. *Find out more about those people who were inside the house?* He had his priorities all wrong but I wasn't about to argue. What about that other thing? The creature.

"Get on with it – you've got to be decisive!" Rafe snapped.

I turned the steering wheel and the car went left. I was driving. Driving a car along a country road. A Landrover shot past, flashing its headlights.

"Speed up. You're going to draw attention to yourself driving at twenty. You should be doing fifty here at least."

I settled on thirty miles an hour, glancing down at the speedometer. What would happen if I got caught? Was it possible to lose your driving licence before you were even old enough to have one? Or would I just be sent to some young offenders' institution to learn about drugs and burglary?

We slunk along soaking wet country roads, hedgerows flashing past the windows. The sky overhead was filthy grey and hurling down rain.

"You're really not doing too badly."

He didn't have to sound so surprised.

"Look. Are you going to tell me what's going on, or not? What was that thing in the garden? Why are you being followed?"

"He was one of the Hidden. Any more than that, I only know that this isn't the first time they've taken Lissy."

"What do you mean?" I stared at the road ahead, concentrating hard on not veering into the hedge again. "What are the Hidden?"

"Our parents didn't ever want Lissy to know," Rafe said, slowly, "but she was taken away. For three weeks. It's one of the first things I can properly remember. I was the first to see – her empty bed. She'd just gone. It was in all the newspapers. Mum and Dad were suspects."

Was he making this up? All I had to do was go online and type in Lissy's name. If there'd ever been a big newspaper story about her I'd find it.

"I was there," Rafe went on, "when *he* brought her home. That creature we just saw walk into the lake. I was in the kitchen with Mum, really early one morning. We saw him out of the window. He was coming through the garden holding this bundle. Mum just ran outside with no shoes on. It was Lissy. He brought her home, then *went*. He just kind of melted away into the garden."

"So Lissy disappeared – and came back?" I could hear the

disbelief in my own voice, slowing down to take a corner.

"Believe me or not," Rafe said, like he'd read my mind. "It's your choice. I can't exactly blame you if you don't."

But if Lissy had gone missing as a baby, that explained a lot, didn't it? Miriam was so paranoid.

"Why hasn't Lissy ever found out about it? All she'd have to do—"

"She's vain enough to look herself up online if that's what you're wondering. But there's nothing there. Not a single newspaper story or mention of her name. It's all gone." Rafe shook his head. "Don't think I haven't tried to—" He paused. "I've got older and he hasn't." A blank, furious look crossed his face. "It doesn't make any sense."

I hadn't told Dad and Miriam about the girl-creature I'd seen with Connie. And now Lissy was gone.

I saw Rafe check all the mirrors. Again. Like he was expecting to see someone behind us, even though the road was clear the whole way. We followed signs for the town centre, passing an old-fashioned petrol station with pumps that looked as if they'd been there since World War II. A couple of fat old men sat on plastic chairs outside under a battered awning, one eating a sandwich, another reading the paper.

"OK, listen," Rafe said as I stopped at the traffic lights. "There's only one place I've *ever* read anything about – about all this, which even comes close to the truth. I spent years looking for stuff on the Internet and in stupid new-age books, trying to find out what had really happened to Lissy, why she was taken and who did it, and eventually I went on the British Library website. I found a record about this weird old journal." He paused, glancing at me. Maybe to see if I was laughing. I mean, it all sounded so ridiculous and unreal. "It was called *Investigations into a Hidden Race* or something. I stole it."

A Hidden Race. OK. He'd said what we both now knew: *there are things living here on earth who can steal a girl from a locked room, leaving nothing but dead leaves on her bed.* Race wasn't even the right word. No human can turn a girl into leaves.

I glanced at the traffic light. Still red.

"You *stole* it? From the British Library? No wonder these people are following us. That's a crime, Rafe. They're probably the police." I spoke slowly and carefully, as if to a very stupid person or a child. "All this is your fault."

"It might be my fault but I didn't exactly have much choice." I thought he was going to hit me like he'd clouted Lissy in the church. "Listen – I've spent fourteen years trying to find out what happened to my family, why Lissy was taken, and no one will ever tell me the truth. Mum's the worst. *Listen, darling, all that was so long ago. Let's not dwell on the past. Lissy was abducted by someone with a terrible mental disturbance. All that matters is she came home.*" It was a nasty but accurate imitation of Miriam.

He lowered his voice. "That journal. I'm sure it's some kind of trap – like there's an alert whenever someone asks to read it. Those people who followed me from London and then searched the Reach for us this morning are the response. They were literally on my back in less than an hour after I left the British Library, and I don't think they're the police." He shook his head, looking confused. "I was sure I'd lost them last night."

"Why'd they wait till this morning to break in, then, if they followed you all the way here last night?"

"How the hell should I know?" Rafe snapped. "None of it's exactly making much sense to me either."

"Another species," I said, gabbling really, thinking of that tall creature, just walking into the lake, disappearing beneath the water, leaving nothing but ripples. *He never gets any older*, Rafe had said. *He's always the same.* Was "he" or "she" even the right word? Did that distinction apply? "An immortal species. There can't be many of them. There's no way they could stay hidden. You can see they're not human."

"There's a café," Rafe said suddenly. "Pull in at the lay-by."

I waited for an old woman to lurch across the road with a tartan shopping trolley, heading for a shop with a load of rakes and plastic dustbins outside, then drew the car up close to the pavement outside an arty looking little place, tucked between a charity shop and an old-fashioned grocery with boxes of carrots and stuff on display right in the street, where anyone could nick them. There was a blackboard leaning up against the wall. Someone had scrawled "Free wi-fi" in pink chalk next to a price list.

"What are you going to do? Google 'fairies'?" I couldn't keep the sarcasm out of my voice. What was he, really? That boy? Not human. Something else.

Rafe opened the passenger door, hauling himself out. "Just shut up and pass me the broom."

I'd seen enough of Rafe to know he was half mad, unscrupulous, and potentially violent. I wasn't about to argue with him. I just obeyed, like he was some kind of army general.

I helped Rafe hobble into the café and found seats near the back. I still had change from my last motorway stop with Dad the night before. It felt like a thousand years had passed since then. I got us each a coffee from a bored girl behind a bar that was completely papered with comic book pages. The clear plastic laminate was pockmarked with old yellow cigarette burns. Either this place had been here since the days when people could still smoke indoors, or no one cared about the law. I got the feeling that this far out in the sticks anything might happen and the normal authorities would never know.

Not very reassuring.

Rafe had already found an ancient computer in a gloomy corner at the back of the café, just beneath a spiral staircase.

"Not even a password," he said, taking a swig from his coffee as I sat down beside him. "Not bad. Surprisingly OK."

The coffee *was* good. Bitter and strong. Dad thinks I'm funny for liking black coffee at my age but I needed it then. My whole body felt drained and empty. I'd hardly slept the night before, after Rafe had smashed the window. I'd just lain there on edge, watching the hours slide by.

Like I was waiting for something.

And then Dad had come in at six in the morning. *It's Connie. She's really not well, Joe. There's an ambulance coming—*

I glanced at my phone again. Still out of reception.

158

I'd had no signal for hours now. At the Reach, I'd managed to send texts to my mates the night before, moaning about how shit this holiday was going to be, and now we were in town. You'd think the reception would be better, not worse.

"Are you going to try speaking to your mam?" I tried to sound casual.

Rafe shook his head, not looking at me. "What's the point? Neither of us can do anything to help Connie." He sounded rough, aggressive. "I really don't think either of us should be using our phones. Just turn it off."

"I've no reception anyway." I hesitated, almost not wanting to know the answer. "Have you?"

Rafe shook his head. "Not since this morning."

"I know the house is out in the countryside and everything," I said, "And Hopesay Edge is tiny, but we're in town now. Why would the signal just disappear?" For a second, me and Rafe just stared at each other. "The police can jam mobile signal, can't they?"

He shrugged. "If you think this has got anything to do with the police, you're more stupid than you look."

I swallowed the urge to hit him and went to the bar. I was starting to feel light-headed, slightly sick. We had to eat. By the time I returned with some bags of crisps and a couple of flapjacks, Rafe had started his search. Not that I really knew what we were even googling *for*. There was a long silence as we both mechanically worked our way through the food, and I tried to read the latest website over his shoulder. It was badly designed – lots of cramped white writing on a black background. My eyes ached.

"What's the Fontevrault Group?" I asked. "It sounds sort of familiar."

Rafe drank the last of his coffee, still looking a bit green. "Just a load of businessmen and politicians from places like Germany and the US. Holland, France. Us, too. They meet in secret, so every conspiracy-mad lunatic has a theory. I just searched for 'the Hidden' and this page about the Fontevrault Group came up way, way down the list after all the usual crap about fairies and crystals – I can't find where the Hidden are even mentioned. I must have done a million Internet searches about them, but I've never come across this association before. It's really weird."

He scrolled through an article making out that this Fontevrault Group thing had control over the International Monetary Fund, and went right down to the comments.

There it was. One rambling badly spelled sentence, right there in front of us:

You can talk about money and politicians all you want but what they dont want you to know is that if the Gateway got opened the Hidden could take control any time they like and theres nothing anyone can do, no matter what the Fontevrault Group want us all to believe

"Jesus," Rafe whispered.

The Gateway's open, I couldn't help thinking. *They're already here.* Whoever had left that comment was behind the times.

I let my eyes travel down to the responses below it.

Save your pathetic vampire theories for
the fangirl websites, loser. This forum is
for serious political discussion about an
organization with Nazi origins who—

I didn't bother reading on.

And below that:

This person is clearly trolling, don't give
them the satisfaction.

The whole conversation was dated two days earlier.

"This website's based in the US," Rafe said, quietly, "they
must—"

I moved without even thinking, took hold of the
mouse and shut down the computer, heart racing. "We
shouldn't be looking at this. They could be monitoring it,
these Fontevrault people, if they're some massive powerful
organization. Checking the IP address of computers that
access websites which mention the Hidden."

Rafe reached into his bag and took out the manuscript.
"Look," he said, quietly.

I looked where he was pointing, reading the scrawled
old-fashioned handwriting at the bottom of the page.

They will kill you—

Both of us glanced towards the bar at the same second. The
girl had her back to us, emptying glasses from a dishwasher,

stacking them on a shelf by the till.

"I thought that meant the Hidden," Rafe said, so quietly she'd never be able to hear. "But now—"

"It's this Fontevrault Group thing? So they're the ones who've been following us? Why would a load of politicians and bankers care what we do?"

Rafe shrugged. "Maybe they don't care what we do. No one really knows what the Fontevrault Group is actually for, or if it even really exists. That's why there are so many conspiracy theories. What if it's the Hidden they're interested in?"

"Or people who try to find out more about the Hidden."

Rafe stared at me. "Even if you're right, they can't possibly know where we are. There's no way. We were on that site for less than five minutes."

"Come on – don't you feel like we've walked straight into one trap after another? First you with that journal, now this. And what about CCTV? They must know your number plate. Neither of us have had any phone signal for hours." Was it really crazy to suspect that someone had jammed all signal from the local mobile mast?

Why would anyone do that?

"CCTV? Out here? They've barely got fire and the wheel."

Rafe might have been right about the CCTV, but we were both already on our feet and walking to the door, out to the car, Rafe leaning heavily on the plastic broom and my shoulder. The girl behind the counter watched us leave, her eyes fixed on Rafe's knackered and bloodied leg. He looked a mess, white as a sheet and sweating like mad. We weren't exactly inconspicuous. I should've come in on my own.

Another mistake. The keys felt heavy in my pocket. All this was too much responsibility.

I'm supposed to be on holiday.

I was starting to feel a bit crazed.

Rafe leaned back in the passenger seat, breathing heavily. Sweat was now pouring freely down his face; I could see it trickling along his neck. Those painkillers he'd necked at the Reach weren't even touching the sides, by the look of it.

I started the car, following the signs on the one-way system out of town. "Look. We've got to get your leg sorted out. Is there a – a doctor or something?"

I didn't want to say the word "hospital". Connie was in hospital.

I looked up. And I saw that dark grey car coming straight for us, right in the middle of the tiny lane. There was no room to pass. I waited for it to pull over. Slow down.

It didn't.

Seconds flowed like hours.

Closer. Closer.

"Brake!" Rafe was yelling. "For Christ's sake, stop, Joe! Stop!"

The other car wasn't going to.

I pounded the brakes, yanking the steering wheel hard over, pulling in as close to the hedge as I could. Crabbed hawthorn branches screeched against my window, against the side of the car. The grey car filled our windscreen. I gripped the steering wheel, digging my fingers into the fake leather. Waiting for it.

We stopped just in time. I leaned back, gasping for breath,

but Rafe was already leaning over me, wrenching my door open, shouting into my face, "Run, *run*, don't you see it's got to be them? These Fontevrault people, whoever they are."

Surely these people were just coming to see if we were OK? They'd nearly crashed into us, after all.

"Don't be stupid!" I said. "It can't be—"

"Go!" Rafe yelled. He tore open the buckle of my seatbelt, shoved me out of the door.

I half fell out into the road and shoved past the hedge to Rafe's side of the car, hardly feeling the scratches; my legs weak with fear or exhaustion — I don't know what. He was right. He was right. Two men climbed out of the car, one on each side, quite young, each wearing a suit.

I tore open the passenger door, grabbing Rafe by the sleeve. "Come on! You can't just sit there!"

"*I can't move!*" He spoke very quietly. "Run, Joe, this isn't a joke. *Go.*" He shoved me into the hedge. "Here. Take this. It's the only thing that will kill them. The Hidden."

I looked down: he was holding out the iron knife. "Take it." Rafe looked away, staring straight ahead at the men running towards us.

I had to leave him there. I took the knife. It was heavy, the wooden handle a smooth weight in my palm.

"Go!" Rafe said again. "It's OK, Joe. Just go."

"But—"

I looked up — the men were only a few feet away now, faces set hard, smart-looking shoes pounding against the tarmac. They were coming for Rafe. They were coming for me.

My legs woke up and I started to sprint. My whole body

knew I was being chased because I've never run that fast in my life: the need to survive took over and I ran like a mouse from a cat, zigzagging down the lane back the way we'd come. There was a gap in the hedge a hundred feet away; beyond it a church spire. A village. No one could abduct me in the middle of a village.

I could hear them chasing me. They didn't speak; they never spoke. Just the drumming of their smart office shoes on the road. Ragged breathing. Rafe was alone in the car. Waiting.

I forced my way through the gap in the hedge, keeping to the edge of the field because it was thick mud, raining hard, clutching Rafe's knife all the time.

Rafe was gone. I'd just left him, like a bloody coward.

I was on my own.

26

Lissy

Larkspur held out one hand, his fingers swan-feather white in the gloom, still smiling, teeth shining, always on the edge of laughter despite the sadness in his eyes. As if I were some kind of giant joke that made him want to laugh one minute and cry the next.

"I don't care about your stupid king," I snapped. "I'm not going anywhere with you."

I whirled around to run, but Rose was waiting, thin arms folded across her chest. I noticed for the first time that her pale wrists were scarred, each marked with a livid purple band, as if she'd been horribly burned.

She smiled viciously. "Now *that*, my dear, would hardly be fair on the boy, with so much effort spent, and such a lonely punishment endured, all for your sake. Fourteen years of living alone with nothing to think about but how he betrayed his own father."

"I have not missed conversing with you, Rose," Larkspur said. "Every word a drop of poison. You'd kill me if you could – would you not?"

For a second they just stared at each other, her all silent

and calculating, Larkspur defiant, like he was daring her to say something.

At last, Rose shrugged. "It seems I could not, though, much though I'd like to have you out of my way. The path you long for is no longer forbidden, child of my brother. Take it."

Child of my brother. Rose was Larkspur's aunt but they both looked exactly the same age. I couldn't process this information. Any of it.

Larkspur just stood waiting with his hand held out for mine, his face now blank as a mask. It was impossible to guess what he might be thinking.

Everyone was watching, even Tippy. Drums and pipes still silent and waiting for this drama to end. Tension bounced through the stale smoky air like a sonic boom.

I ended it myself by taking Larkspur's hand, my brother's hand, thinking: *And what does this really mean, if he's my brother?*

I'm not—

I'm not – human—

But the grateful way he pressed his fingers against my palm felt so totally normal that for a second I almost forgot he wasn't either.

Hand in hand, we walked through the chamber, all of the gathered Hidden watching our every step. There were more of them than I'd first realized, perhaps two hundred: the shadowy cavern stretched on into the firelit darkness like the great hall in a stately home. At last, Larkspur held aside a tattered tapestry and led me out into a tunnel that reeked of damp sheds. Behind us, the music started up again. Drums, pipes. Someone sang in a wild voice; I half remembered the tune. Laughter, too.

I couldn't shake the idea they were laughing at me. And Larkspur.

He turned, looking down at me. For once no trace of a smile. "Come."

Before I could answer he held aside another heavy curtain, alive with grey mould. As Larkspur touched the fabric, thousands of tiny spores drifted from its folds, hanging in the silver light. I heard him whisper something beside me but didn't catch the words. And Larkspur led me forwards into sheer white brightness. I had to cover my burning eyes, squirming and unprotected like a blind worm.

I squinted into the light.

We were facing guards. Two Hidden cloaked in black. Each held a long spear, dark against the brightness. Moving quicker than falling stones, the guards crossed their weapons before our path.

The clash of metal echoed, bouncing around the bright white vastness. There was no way past.

One spoke, face shadowed by the hood of his cloak: "What can you want, traitor?"

"I'll speak with the King and no one else." Larkspur sounded so calm, but when I looked down at his hands they were shaking.

Traitor? A word from another time: when queens and kings ruled the world. What kind of mess had I walked into? I was part of a game, but no one had explained the rules.

I wasn't human. *I'm a monster.*

The other guard turned to me, reaching out to touch my face with the tip of one finger. His skin was so cold I gasped; the chill spread through my entire body. It was like falling into a well. A faint musty smell rose from the guard's black cloak as he moved, the wide hood completely shadowing his face. "Let the traitor by." Slowly, slowly, the guard's finger moved down my face, tracing a line of burning cold. How could anything be so deeply frozen and still alive? The guard laughed. "Yes, let him by. It is part of the covenant."

Cold air rushed past my face as the guards stepped away, bowing low.

My eyes adjusted to the brightness. There was no daylight; I couldn't bear to ask myself how I was even able to see. We were in another cave, but here the walls were not hard-packed earth but white, glittering quartz. Flowers glowed like bright coals in shining bowls: dandelions, clambering roses tangled among ivy, daisies with middles like bright yellow buttons. Trees grew up through solid rock – silver birches with pale trunks and tiny bright leaves. It was an impossible place.

In the middle of the cave, a dark pool of water glittered. Lily-pads floated on the surface.

"The White Hall of the Hidden, Lissy," Larkspur said.

I turned to stare at him. "Look, what did those guards mean by a covenant? Isn't that some kind of bargain? I shouldn't be here. My sister's in hospital, and if my mum comes back to find me gone—"

But there was such desperate sadness on Larkspur's face I was glad when he walked away from me, moving fast as if I'd stung him.

And the air was thick with white feathers, feathers everywhere I looked, tumbling down from the soaring heights of the cave above.

By the dark water, Larkspur dropped to his knees and I was left standing alone in a raging swirl of soft whiteness. When I reached out, pearl-white petals fell into my hands and the feathers were gone.

It was beyond nature. "Magic," I said.

And Larkspur turned to face me. "No, sky-in-her-eyes, just the way of the world, if you live long enough to really know it."

He turned away, kneeling again, bowing his head so low it touched the chilly quartz beneath our feet. Petals settled on his back, bright against the darkness of his cloak, tangled in his red hair. They touched the floor and melted into nothing like snowflakes. When the still, flower-scented air was clear again at last, I saw a white swan waiting on the water, watching us.

Larkspur stayed utterly still.

Who comes to the Hall of the Swan King? A voice filled the cave, so furious and terrible my stomach lurched and I had to shut my eyes because I couldn't bear it, knowing that burning voice came from the swan on the water, which hadn't moved or made a sound.

The voice was inside my head.

Still Larkspur knelt, a hunched figure on the cold white floor.

The swan lifted its wings as if to fly, raising them higher and higher. A giant crack of thunder tore the air; once again the cave was full of twisting falling feathers and my face was wet with rain; hammering rain *here* below ground. Feathers kissed my skin, tangled in my hair.

When I looked up, the swan had gone. A young man stood with the pool at his back, wrapped in a cloak of white feathers. Black hair tangled around his shoulders, shining like the dark waters of the pool – but it was clear straight away he was closely related to Larkspur; one face echoed the other. A gold band glowed against his white throat. He was impossibly tall and, even I could see, in a fierce rage.

He spoke: "I ask again. *Who comes to the Hall of the Swan King?*"

"You *know* who I am." I was terrified but so angry at being in this horrible place when I should have been waiting for Mum, waiting to hear if Connie was alive or dead. I forced out the words: "Why am I here? I want to go home."

The Swan King raised one hand and I flew backwards, hurled through the air till I hit the wall, cracking my head against the quartz. A sharp ache jolted through my skull, down the back of my neck, shooting up my elbow as I landed. Instinctively, I curled up into a ball, arms clinging around my knees, watching in horror as the King waited, so pale and cold, for Larkspur to speak. My whole body sang a bright note of shock and pain; all I could do was watch as Larkspur sprang up, a cloud of petals bursting away from his cloak.

He ran forwards, stopping just inches from the King himself. "I did not bring her back to be thrown aside like Tippy's discarded hoop."

"You forget yourself." The Swan King spoke so softly I could hardly hear. "You disobeyed me. You took my daughter back to her human mother. You acted against my word, and I see that fourteen years of punishment have not been enough to correct your faults, child. Seven years and seven again, walking alone through these halls, shunned by all. So much silence. So alone. How many more will it take?"

Larkspur flinched, as if he had just been pinched or hit. "For ever," he said. "It will take for ever. It was right to return her. How can I help it if age has not yet made me cruel? You were just angry Miriam wouldn't leave her mortal lover, her mortal son."

Oh, my *God*. He was talking about my mother. He was talking about Dad, about Rafe. I sat watching them, unable to move or speak. My hands shook with the shock of it. *Mum*—

"Miriam wouldn't come here to be with you!" Larkspur's voice was rising. "That's the true reason you were so angry. She wanted her child back but she didn't want *you* – Oh, Father, her sorrow was everywhere, in my dreams; I heard her voice on the rain—"

"How dare you call me that name after such a betrayal?" The Swan King's voice was cold and furious.

A look of anguish passed across Larkspur's face. "Forgive me. Please. I did what I thought was good."

"When you came into the world," the Swan King said to him, "I held you red and bloody in my arms, and I burned with joy I had never known, not in all the ages I have lived. The only one born to our kind for more than two thousand years. That delight is now ash in my mouth. What use to me is a disobedient child?"

"Then what use to me is a heartless parent?" Larkspur looked straight at his father, and I thought the King would hurl him through the air, smash him against the cold hard wall, but instead he just said, "She would be ashamed of you."

Larkspur looked away, then back up at the King with such misery and rage I knew his mother must be dead. "I have brought my sister to you now," he said. "Don't you remember what it was like to be young and feel compassion?"

"I may well remember," said the King, "but you must learn what it is to see across the ages, and only then will you have the wisdom to make these choices you presume to understand. You had orders; it was not for you to act against them."

"No," said Larkspur. "It is *you* who does not understand. Miriam wept so much when Lissy had gone I couldn't bear it; her sorrow leaked into my dreams. It was everywhere, bigger than the earth itself. You ignored it; I could not. Tippy cries out for her mother as she sleeps and not one of us has the courage to admit that everyone she knew is long since dust, that her father came looking and starved to death, lost in our halls, never to find her. Mortals feel so deeply, their hearts burn. We can't just *play* with them like this, but I cannot bear to be alone any longer, either. So I have brought her back, as I promised I would, and now I beg you to forgive me."

Everyone she knew is long since dust? Tippy's father had come looking for her and *died* down here without ever finding her?

How long had Tippy been in this place? I thought of

173

her strange accent, that odd little curtsey. A hundred years? Two hundred? A prisoner for all time, kept alive among these immortal creatures. *How?*

"Let me go!" I cried out, still too afraid to move. "Please let me go." I turned to Larkspur. "How could you do this to me? What have I ever done to you?"

I would be like Tippy, ragged and forgotten, aching to see daylight and the faces of my long-dead family. Tears burned my face. I couldn't stand it. *I'll have to escape or kill myself.*

But both Larkspur and the Swan King completely ignored me. I was just a weapon in some battle between them that I had no way of understanding.

"So you do not repent, but only ask me to forgive?"

Larkspur shook his head. "I don't repent. I gave Miriam fourteen years with her daughter. She and I agreed it, and it was right."

"Fourteen years?" said the Swan King. "You foolish child! It would have been kinder if the girl remembered nothing. Now you have condemned her to the same fate as Tippy, always remembering, yet never able to go back."

"She can go back!" Larkspur shouted. "She has our blood. She *can* move between our world and theirs, even once she has lived many years more than a mortal lifespan. She won't crumble to dust beneath the sun after three hundred years, even a thousand years down here in our halls. She is one of us. Wasn't that the whole point of Miriam? Do you know nothing?"

Even I could see Larkspur had gone too far, even though it was my life they were arguing about and my head was ringing with terrified questions. Was I immortal? Never to die, but never to see my family again?

The Swan King took one single, sharp step forwards.

Quickly, Larkspur looked down, then up into his father's face. "I should not have said such a thing. Of course, your wisdom is beyond anyone else's."

"No," said the Swan King, "it was foolish. You have learned nothing, so you will not sit by me, always away. Should I come near, you will go into the shadows. No one will speak with you beyond what is essential. No one will share your cup or dance with you. I condemn you to be alone among the Hidden. Always."

"Please no," Larkspur said, quietly. "It has gone on so long already. My desolation knows no end. I know you must punish me but do it another way." His voice cracked. "Don't send me away from you again."

"You made the choice with those words," the Swan King said. "It is as it is, and shall not change."

Larkspur got up and walked out without speaking another word. All I could hear was the heavy swish of the hangings as he went, but I actually felt his despair, a cold and relentless anguish that swept up in me as he passed, overwhelming, fading a little when he had gone, replaced by my own fear.

I crouched against the wall, hugging my knees against my chest.

And slowly, slowly, the Swan King turned and he held out his hand to me.

I shook my head, still hardly able to believe what I'd seen. "I don't want anything to do with you. That was so – so cruel. He's so unhappy, and he's your son. How could you do that?"

He smiled. *So young*. But thousands and thousands of years old.

My father.

Even though I didn't want to, I found myself taking his hand, gasping as the coldness of his touch shot through me.

He shrugged, raising me to my feet as if I were lighter than air. "My blood is in your body." The Swan King smiled again. "And, my darling, we are so very, very few." He leaned closer, so close his breath chilled my face. "But now you are here, my lovely one, the world is mine again."

What was that supposed to mean?

The words he spoke were gentle and caressing, but his inhuman eyes blazed with hatred and fury. What had I ever done to him?

I got up and ran, but as I shoved past the guards and tumbled out into the darkness beyond the White Hall, all I could hear was the Swan King laughing.

27

Miriam

The consultant has just left. I'm trying not to think about what she said. I'm writing this to escape from it, watching Connie all the time. Her fringe still hasn't quite grown out, and it hangs in her eyes no matter how many packets of hair clips we buy. I've still got one in my pocket, pink and glittery with a plastic cherry. Her favourite. Her skin feels warm when I touch her. She's still alive, for now. She's in there somewhere.

I can't help it: the consultant's words are going round and round in my head. When I close my eyes I can still see her kindly eyes, with those red-rimmed spectacles, her curly greying hair. Does this kind of thing ever get easier for people like her?

"Well, I'm afraid there's good news and bad news," she had said. "Connie still isn't responding to the antibiotics, but her condition doesn't seem to be deteriorating, either."

I tried to ask what this meant, but could no longer seem to speak. I couldn't force out the words.

The consultant carried on talking, but nothing she said made sense to me. I felt as if the room was spinning, with me and Connie in the centre of it. Waiting.

I watched her walk out of the room, moving on to the rest of the ward. *Come back,* I wanted to shout. *Help me, help her – you can't just leave us here like this. There must be something you can do.*

But there wasn't. She'd just told me.

Miles left the Gateway open. I'm cursed. By midnight, the Hidden will have Lissy – or Rafe and Connie will both be dead.

Virgie Creed used to say the Reach was built on tainted ground. It was certainly foolish and arrogant to have built a Christian priory actually over a stone circle – the church trying to steal the power of the old religion. The Reach is completely deconsecrated now. It's totally unsafe, like a hole dug in the pavement for anyone to fall into. Going back to Hopesay will be dangerous for ever: the temptation is always going to be too great. It's hard to resist immortality. It's hard to pretend it isn't an option, when it is. At a price.

I remember the last time Adam and I went back to the Reach together, a year after Larkspur brought Lissy home. Adam knew everything by then, of course. He knew that I'd been unfaithful since before Lissy was born, that he wasn't really her father. It would have been impossible to hide that from him. I didn't want to go, and Adam would rather have jumped off a bridge – he was so terrified I'd leave him for ever if I saw the Swan King again. We owed it to Miles, though – despite everything, he was still the closest thing I had to a brother, and Adam's oldest friend. Lissy was protected by the covenant then, but taking her there still felt like such a risk.

Even so, of course I couldn't resist. The archetypal bad mother.

I'd left Adam and Miles inside, Adam trying to persuade Miles he was wasting his life pining after Rose, drawing far too much attention to himself and, by association, to us.

Never mind the Hidden – if the Fontevrault ever found out about Lissy, I knew I'd never see her again.

I stood alone on the lawn, watching the round disc of the moon shivering on the surface of the lake. The breeze died, and I turned to glance back at the house. There were only two windows lit, the hall upstairs for Rafe and the kitchen where I'd left Adam arguing with Miles.

I counted three windows along from the hall to Maman's old room where Rafe and Lissy were sleeping: Rafe in the canopied four-poster bed, Lissy curled up in a travel cot she was already too long for. Rafe still had night terrors, a year after all the horror. I was worried Adam wouldn't hear Rafe from the kitchen if he screamed.

Lissy's gone! Lissy's gone!

Rafe didn't have to worry. Thanks to Larkspur, she was safe. For now. Another thirteen years. I came to dread every birthday.

Miriam.

I heard the trees call my name. Shivering with horror, and anticipation too, I turned to face the water, standing alone on what had once been the lawn. Brambles trailed through overgrown tangles of thistles and bindweed. The Reach had fallen into decay, neglected and unloved. Miles thought about nothing but Rose, even though she'd already

179

started to lose interest in him. His beauty was already fading, the years and his desperate obsession with her taking their toll. He wouldn't go to the Hidden. Either too conscious of that ridiculous inherited duty he harps on about when he's drunk, or too cowardly to risk stepping out into the sunshine again only to find three thousand years had passed, his mortal body crumbling into dust, no longer protected by Hidden magic.

Oh, yes, they can make you immortal, the Hidden, but only if you never leave their halls. Only if you stay for ever.

I didn't want that. I was determined not to be like Miles, so desperate and hopeless. The Hidden are addictive, worse than heroin. Once tasted, their kiss – you have to get more. And more.

I was luckier than Miles. Stronger. I had Adam. My children.

I could no longer see the moon in the water, even though the pale silver disc still glowed in a cloudless sky.

I knew he would find me here. He was coming.

Shaking, I watched a mound of water rise out of the lake like a blister.

His head broke the surface, black hair shining wet, then his bare shoulders, pearl-white. His smooth chest. His arms. He looked up, smiling, and stepped out of the lake and onto the grass before me, water running down his chest, pale skin shining, wet fabric clinging to his legs, droplets shaking from the dull silver straps on his boots.

"Miriam." And the Swan King stepped closer, still smiling even though I knew him well enough now to spot the raw hatred at the backs of his eyes. He reached out and ran one cold finger down the side of my face. He loved me, I knew that, but he always hated mortals. He loved me, yes, but despised me for what I was. For what we did to Larkspur's mother. "You grow older."

I shrugged, no longer half afraid of him as I had been once. "Two children," I replied, and was about to say, *You try it*. But I had to choose my words so carefully. Making sure there was nothing he could interpret as an offer — another covenant — which might strike out the one I'd made with Larkspur. "Even you would look older," I told him instead. "There's no use asking for her. I won't give her back to you. So don't bother."

A look of torment crossed his face. He was genuinely lonely, I'll always believe that. "Then why are you here, Miriam? Why did you come back?"

"Miles. We're trying to get him to leave Hopesay. He needs to forget about Rose."

"He never will." The Swan King smiled, bitter and cruel. "But Rose grows weary of him."

"It's not just her," I said. "Adam thinks the Fontevrault suspect Miles. Not me, not yet — I've stayed away from you, and I've always made sure that Lissy isn't seen by many people, just in case. But Miles can't keep away from Rose. They don't know the Gateway is open, but Adam thinks the Fontevrault are watching him."

He smiled when I mentioned the Fontevrault. "They're all fools," he whispered. "They made me a promise and broke it. But they will learn." I felt uneasy when he said that. "Oh,

181

will you not come with me, Miriam? You could be young for ever. At my side always."

"And never see the sky again? No thank you." I shook my head. "It's not just that—" There was no point making him angry by telling him that despite what had happened between us, I loved Adam, and wanted to love Adam more than him. "You must understand: I have a little boy as well. I couldn't watch him grow old and die."

"Bring the child," the Swan King whispered. "Miriam, bring all you want to, bring your mortal lover if you must. In the Halls of the Hidden your hours will be as days, your years as centuries. Just come. Be with me for thousands of years, my love. My loneliness knows no boundary."

"What about Larkspur?" I hardly dared ask.

He turned away. "His punishment will see no end till my daughter is at my side."

That's never going to happen.

"What have you done to him?" I had to know. It was my misery that had condemned Larkspur to whatever fate his father had chosen, my misery and the spark of mercy that shuddered and flickered within the Swan King's only son.

"He is an outcast among his own kind. He suffers, alone and despised. That is all. Another thirteen years you have with her, Miriam. Don't forget."

I didn't dare say anything else. All I knew was that Larkspur had brought Lissy home, and if he would be an outcast for it till I gave her back, then he would have to be an outcast for ever.

I'm sorry, Larkspur.

★

Connie's eyelids shift and twitch. I wonder what she is looking at, there in the darkness of her dreams.

It's my fault she's in this hospital bed. I know why the antibiotics aren't flushing the poison from Connie's blood, why those steroid drugs are seeping into her body through a thin plastic tube but haven't kick-started the healing process. I know more than the kind consultant and all the medical staff put together, but they would never believe me.

Connie is dying because I was cursed. I've spent fourteen years wondering how on earth I could fool the Hidden into not giving Lissy back. I thought I had till midnight to think of a way.

In the end, they just cheated me. They're going to take Lissy, and they will have Connie's life, too.

What about Rafe?

28

Joe

I tore across the field, wet mud caking around my soaked trainers, breath rasping in my chest. When I glanced over my shoulder no one was following.

Rafe must have been giving them some trouble.

For a second, I slowed, half stopping. Should I go back? Try to help? Had I made a terrible, gutless mistake? I should have ignored Rafe's order to run and stayed to help him. There must have been something I could've done—

It was too late now. *Nice one, Joe.*

I was a coward.

Behind me, I heard the distant roar of one engine and then another. The grey car and then Rafe's— Had he got away?

Or were the Fontevrault Group just removing the evidence? Impounding Rafe's knackered looking Renault behind barbed wire in some innocuous suburb, like the police had done that time Dad parked in a loading bay.

High above me, a lone blackbird hung in the sky like a ragged shadow. Across the field, a church tower reared up above the trees, huge and grey.

Maybe I wasn't being chased because they knew I had nowhere to go.

So I ran.

The straggle of houses looked familiar; when I passed the butcher's shop I knew why. I was in Hopesay Edge, the village itself. I was so disorientated as we drove out of town I'd not realized we were so close.

There were at least four dust-caked cars parked outside the butcher's; a load of old women and a fat bloke in overalls and workboots queued outside, eyeballing me. My trousers were soaked up to the knees, heavy with wet mud. My senses must've been sharpened by fear because I could smell blood: the heavy stink of wet rust. This was all wrong. I shouldn't be standing out, so screaming obvious—

For the second time in one day I headed into the church. That freakish hippy woman had clearly known something. What if it *wasn't* the Hidden she'd been so afraid of?

It was dark in the church even after the feeble overcast daylight outside. At first all I could really see was a huge stained-glass window I hadn't paid much attention to earlier. It floated in the gloom: a tall figure surrounded by kneeling men with haloes and flowing robes.

I saw it differently now, that story told in the glass.

The tall figure in the middle had no halo. It wasn't Jesus or some kind of saint but one of *them*: the Hidden. An immortal creature frozen in bright blues, greens, yellows and reds, arms lifted to the sky without appearing to notice the kneeling men clustered at his feet.

"What are you doing here? What do you want?" Virgie

185

Creed's voice rang out, high and breathless. "Stop meddling with what you know nothing about."

My eyes were used to the dim light now; she stood up behind her table of random groceries, closing one boneless white hand over a black metal cash box.

I took a chance. "You know, don't you? You know about everything. The Hidden. The——"

"I don't know what you're talking about," she snapped. I could hear cars on the road outside. Were the Fontevrault among them? Coming closer. Finishing the job.

"You've got to help, please. I'm being followed." Where could I go? Who else could I ask? I was on my own. My whole body tingled with horror and fear.

Virgie shook her head. "I tried to warn you, didn't I? Go through the lychgate. You'll come out in the orchard – it's a private way into the Reach. If that's the Fontevrault coming you must go *now*." She reached into a leather handbag and pulled out a folded wad of yellow paper, shoving it at me. I took it without even thinking. "Now go," she hissed, fixing me with a wild gaze. "Shut the Gateway. You must shut the Gateway. Miles should never have opened it. I told him. Don't fail. You can't."

"But I can't shut it if I don't know where it is."

"You need to walk into the lake. That's the way down."

I stared at her. *What?*

"Go! There's no time to explain."

I didn't need telling again, just forced the wad of paper into my back pocket and went for it.

As I was about to run out the way I'd come in, Virgie

shook her head, beckoning at me to follow.

Outside, I heard doors slamming. Driver's side. Passenger side. Two of them after me.

Without a word, she rushed me into a chilly stone room where a set of long white robes hung from the wall. A place for the vicar to get changed before his services.

"Go," she hissed, shoving me hard out of a narrow doorway; I was blinded by daylight. I'd come out by a high thick hedge. Right or left? She hadn't said. I ran to the left, banging hard into a gravestone on the way. Pain shot through my hip, down my leg. It was only luck that took me to a faded oak gate, silvery grey wood against the greenery. I grabbed the rusting latch, shoved the gate open and found myself in an overgrown orchard, four times the length of a football pitch. Through some apple trees, I could just make out the Reach: black and white timbers, rain-wet stone, windows glittering like the eyes of a reptile.

I broke into a run, tearing as hard and as fast as I could across the grass till my chest was on fire and my lungs were burning. The house wasn't getting any closer. A nightmare. I was going to be caught. Taken, like Rafe.

They will kill you.

Was Rafe dead?

I scrambled over a half-rotting fence into the back garden, past a long-neglected veg patch, the shell of a greenhouse and flowerbeds choked with weeds.

I could hear voices now – people shouting behind me, yelling at me to stop, but ridiculously polite. "*Excuse me! Excuse me! Can you stop, please?*"

187

Not a chance was I going to stop for anyone.

By the time I reached the lean-to my chest was burning, sweat pouring down my face. I threw open the door and more broken glass smashed out of the panel Rafe had knocked through to break in. The kitchen drawers were all still yanked open where the Fontevrault had searched for Rafe's manuscript. I ran down the dark corridor and out of the front door. On the overgrown lawn, I had to stop for a few minutes, gasping for breath. I could see the lake now, glittering and all innocent-looking, there by that big old yew tree.

All I could do was hope Virgie Creed hadn't been lying, because I couldn't see how this murky lake, with a couple of lily-pads floating there in the rain, could possibly be of any help to me now. The Hidden creature had gone in there. Just disappeared into another world.

I did the only thing I could.

I stepped forwards, into the lake, just my right foot. One step at a time. Cold water flooded my trainer. There was nothing to stand on, my foot just swished around in the blackness. It was deep, very deep.

That creature. The Hidden. He'd walked straight in, hadn't he? I'd watched the waters close over his head.

"Excuse me! Can you please stop immediately?"

I had nowhere to go. There was no other way out. Because I knew that if I was caught now, I would be killed. Rafe had history with the Hidden. The Fontevrault Group must have been observing his family for years, suspecting they'd had contact but not doing anything about it. Which didn't make any sense, now I thought about it. Whatever the reason, I was different.

I was expendable. If the Hidden had Lissy, I had to help her. Had to try and protect her in any way I could.

I fell forwards into the water, and I went down.

Down.

29

Rafe

I woke in a blazing fluorescent glow, curled in a ball on a metal bed jutting out of the wall like a shelf. I had to blink: half because of the unbearable light and half in pain, the quality of which had now changed from shooting agony through my ankle to a dull relentless throb.

What had they done to me?

I sat up, looking down at my ankle, what was left of it. The wound had been bandaged and set in one of those flexible plasters – how long had I been unconscious? – but it still felt as if my leg was on fire.

Why take the trouble to tidy up the god-awful mess I'd made of my ankle but keep me locked in here?

I leaned back and the cold steel wall chilled my skin, even through my t-shirt. It was like being inside a meat locker. A windowless room, walls, floor and bed all stainless steel. Bed was too generous a term for the bare metal slab. There was no blanket, no pillow. Even the bog in the corner was steel. A cell. I was in prison. A prison without windows. Weren't there rules about that? Regulations?

The whole place reeked of stale air and the faint,

sickening-sweet odour of other people's terrified sweat, not quite masked by disinfectant.

The door was just as shining and impenetrable as the steel walls. Not even a millimetre of space around it. Perfectly fitted. There was no handle on the inside. No keyhole. There had to be a lock. Unable to stop myself I got up, pain shooting through every shred of bone and muscle; I had to breathe through my teeth. I pushed at the door; you never know till you try. Of course it didn't budge. That was when I saw what they'd done to my hand. A purple bruise spread from behind a dab of cotton wool taped to the skin. I had been sedated.

Another wave of freezing cold fear washed through me.

How long had I been down here? Long enough to be glad of the metal bog. I peed in it and sat down on the bed again without flushing, not wanting to alert anyone to the fact I'd woken up.

I had no way of knowing what time it was, or even which day. If I'd been taken by the police, Mum would surely have been involved by now, tracked down at the hospital. I fought an acid surge of nausea. Connie. What if—

I couldn't think about that. Not now. I was always the strong one, the oldest. Never in trouble. Too clever for that. Till now.

I stared up at the ceiling. A metal grille no larger than my palm had been screwed into the wall near the ceiling. Air conditioning of some kind. The closest I got to a window. Even if I could reach up there and undo the screws, remove the grille, I wouldn't fit more than one arm through the hole. So far that and the drain were the only way out.

The door slid open without a sound.

I hadn't heard anyone coming. The realization hit me like a train. *This whole cell was soundproofed.*

What did they *do* to people in here?

I watched the door open.

"Mr Harker." Two women stood in the corridor outside. One looked slightly older than Mum, the other was maybe about thirty: old but not that old. They seemed so completely normal – one wearing suit trousers, the other a dark, narrow skirt. Both wore wrinkled shirts and shoes that probably came from a catalogue. Ordinary on the surface of things but they were *here*, which made them serious.

And very, very scary.

"Unless one of you is my solicitor I don't want to know." It took a lot to sound so unconcerned, but I was proud that my voice didn't shake. God, I was hurting.

The older one was holding a crutch. She held it out to me with a disturbing motherly smile. "You might be needing this. Quite a nasty injury to your leg there, Mr Harker. Come with us, please."

I took the crutch and hobbled to the door. Every time so much as a toe touched the floor, burning pain shot up my injured leg, snatching the breath from my lungs. I was already calculating how easy it would be to get rid of them. I could probably move quite fast with the crutch, even though I'd probably regret it later.

Who was behind these other steel doors? More prisoners – and if so what had they done?

The younger woman closed the cell door behind me.

It locked with a quiet, heavy click. She then pulled a gun from inside her jacket and let it nestle in her palm, dark and heavy. Away it went, hidden again. A chilly flutter settled in my belly. Unlike the rifles we use at school in the shooting range above the gym, I guessed that this was fully loaded with live ammunition. The woman smiled. Her teeth were slightly too bright, as if they'd been artificially whitened. "Obviously, Mr Harker, you're a resourceful young man. Please do be aware that my colleague and I are authorized to carry firearms, and to use them if necessary. Obviously we're trained to fire only warning shots but sometimes accidents do happen in the course of an incident."

"Obviously." I didn't bother to hide my contempt. They were just a couple of idiotic patronizing jobsworth – *what*? Policewomen? Government endorsed psychopaths? But doing what? None of this made any sense. I hadn't even been accused of anything. Yet.

All I'd done was steal an old manuscript from the British Library, which I admit was not exactly ethically pure, and I was being held under the Terrorist Act.

I was kidding myself. The Fontevrault Group. The grey car. I was here because of the Hidden. Because I'd stolen that manuscript.

I staggered between them to another steel door, but this one led to an elevator. Even so, I was still trapped in a room without windows. With *them*. No one spoke. I didn't want to give them the satisfaction of asking questions, only to be refused a single answer. It was clear enough who had the advantage. I looked down at my boots, my torn and bloodstained jeans, trying not to panic. My legs were still caked with mud. What had happened to Joe in that lane? He was just a kid no older than Lissy. Even if those men had called for back-up and managed to catch him, surely *he* couldn't be held in a place like this? But then again, I'd read newspaper reports of immigrant children being chucked into prison, and they hadn't even stumbled into an enormous scary cover-up operation that was trying to disguise the existence of—

Of what? I still didn't even know what to call them. The Hidden, but what did that really mean?

All I could do was hope I'd bought Joe enough time to get away. He was cocky and annoying and northern but he didn't deserve to be caught up in this mess. What would he *do* by himself? Try to reach the hospital? He'd talked about going back to the church to find that woman who ran the shop at Hopesay Edge, he'd seemed convinced she knew something and might be able to help.

I didn't really see how *anyone* could help.

I tried to imagine what Dad would say if he knew I was here. He'd kill me, then kill me again. He's got a contacts book the size of a brick, website designer to the rich and famous. He's the kind of guy who always knows someone in the right place. But I knew that even Dad would be helpless in the face of this place, these people. Because who were they even authorized by? Rooms with no windows. Middle-aged women with guns. It was just ridiculous. I'd heard about the police using mobile signal jamming to break lines of communication during major criminal activities. Could that really be why our phones hadn't worked for God only knew how long? Were Joe and me now considered such major deviants that the authorities wanted us all out of contact?

Normal authorities or the Fontevrault?

The lift stopped with a jerk. The doors slid open and we stepped out into another corridor. This one had windows – high, pointed Gothic arches. A hellhole hidden inside a beautiful old building. Where? The walls were painted bare white, the floor dark polished wood. My whole body sagged with relief just to see daylight: weak rainy daylight, but real. I was still a prisoner but didn't feel like one any more. I stepped across and glanced down, trying to get my bearings, and just caught sight of a grey city street far below, glimpsed the London Eye rearing up from the skyline, a flash of sunlight glancing off water.

London. Not far from the Thames.

For God's sake. I'd driven for hours to escape this place, these people. Here I was again. More or less back where I'd started.

"Come with us, please, Mr Harker." The older woman reached out, steering me away from the window. "I hope I'm not going to have to use force."

So did I.

As we went on down the corridor, the atmosphere changed. The bare dark boards were covered in worn-out carpet now. Old but clearly once extremely expensive: you can tell by the way they fade. Dad told me. Oh, God. What the hell *was* he going to say about this? I'd been in trouble before but this time was different. This time I'd been caught.

The same questions whirled around in my head without end. *Someone* had searched the Reach. Had they found the manuscript in my pocket? Who were these people, really?

We stopped before a door – another Gothic arch, heavy wood, but the younger woman reached out and spoke quietly into an intercom panel screwed to the wall.

What were they going to do to me?

The door swung open with a soft metallic hiss.

And instead of walking into another cell, I stepped forwards into an office. More tastefully faded old rugs covered the floor from wall to wall. Light shone in through another arched window overlooking the street far below. All those people down in the street below, none of them knowing what was hidden in an ordinary London street: windowless rooms with soundproofed walls—

The door shut behind me, a gentle click. I sensed that the women were no longer behind me; I'd been left alone, or not quite.

"Rafe?"

A man was sitting by the desk, watching me. I hardly recognized his face. It had been years since I'd last seen him. He was skeleton-thin now, grey-skinned, smudges of purple beneath his eyes like a pair of bruises.

"Miles." I tried not to sound too horrified.

"I warned your mother not to try keeping it all secret." He even sounded different to how I remembered, so tired. "Clearly, she didn't listen. You found out, didn't you? Or did you just remember?" He laughed, but nothing was funny. "It started with these Internet searches, didn't it? They've been watching you for years, Rafe. That trip to the British Library was your biggest mistake. You led the Fontevrault straight to me."

For once, I had nothing to say.

30

Lissy

I ran through twisting gloomy corridors, tears streaming down my face. At last, I found an empty chamber lit by a faint silvery light that shone from above. A heap of wizened apples sat in a corner. I reached up and felt a sticky bump on the back of my head where I'd hit the wall. Been *thrown* against the wall. I couldn't stop shivering even though it wasn't cold. When had I sat at the kitchen table with Mum, Nick and Joe, pushing that spaghetti Bolognese around my plate? Last night? The night before? I was already losing track of time, just like Tippy. I thought of Mum, of Connie, and I couldn't stop sobbing.

Till the moment Rafe told me Connie had gone to hospital, death was something that only touched other people, like a virus I'd been immune to up till now. I still didn't know what had happened to Connie, trapped down here, but the Swan King's words echoed in my mind again and again. I had immortal blood, genetic material from an inhuman creature who had lived for thousands if not millions of years. Even if Connie fought the poison in her body and survived this illness, one day I would still watch her die. And not just her but everyone I knew – an endless cycle of knowing people, loving them and losing them while I lived on, grieving. For ever.

And then I heard footsteps. Someone coming. Fear gripped me again; I was frozen with it, totally unable to move. If the Swan King had sent someone to bring me back to his hall, I wouldn't go. He had thrown me against a wall without even touching a single hair of my body: powerful, cruel and heartless. Not even Mum and me at our nastiest could beat what the King had done to Larkspur, torturing him with every word.

He was my father, too.

I clutched my knees and stared at my hands, long-fingered and paler than the belly of a fish. No matter how hard I gripped my legs, I couldn't stop my fingers shaking. There was alien blood in those veins knitted together with inhuman DNA. I was a freak, a monster.

"Mum, what did you do?" I whispered, *"Mum."*

"Those tales about never eating the food, they're not true. You can have an apple."

I looked up, wiping my eyes. Tippy stood watching me, tugging at her nightie: it might have fitted a five-year-old, but it was obviously tight under her arms and too short, dangling above her knees. They hadn't even bothered to find her any proper clothes. Sudden anger burst inside me. How dare they treat a child like this, neglecting her like an unwanted pet?

"What tales?" My voice was shaking just like my fingers. I tried to breathe steadily; I had to calm myself and think clearly or I'd never find a way out. I reached out and took an

199

apple, though – I had no idea how long it was since I'd last eaten, and I was hungry. It tasted sweet and dusty. The juice ran down my chin.

"Oh, you know. Nurse was always telling me I must never eat fairy food, or I'd have to live in the fairy hill for ever. Well, it's not true. I never ate fairy food. Nurse wouldn't have let me. And I was still caught. I remember her kissing me good night, then Mammy. And I woke up here."

"Come over here." I tried to stop my voice shaking, not wanting to frighten her. "Your hair's a state." I could at least try to make her more comfortable.

Tippy stared at me. "A state?"

She didn't understand; she was hundreds of years old. I tried again, choosing my words more carefully. "Your hair's all tangled. Where can we find a brush?"

Tippy smiled, and for the first time she looked happy and excited, like an ordinary child. "Oh, please let's get one. You're the King's daughter. You only need to ask anyone at all and they must bring whatever you desire. Only not Rose: she would have to do it, but she'd find a way to make you pay."

"I can see that," I said. "Come with me, then."

When we reached the main hall, the great bowl of fire was still flickering, but everywhere I looked, harps and drums lay discarded on the cold earth and the Hidden had gone, as if they'd just melted away into the darkness.

"They've all gone to dance somewhere. They do that now the Gateway's open, places they can be sure they won't be seen." Tippy rummaged in a wooden chest with a broken lid that someone had shoved against a wall, tugging out handfuls of glittery cloth and a ragged cape of mouldy-looking feathers, which made us both shudder. I couldn't look at feathers without thinking of the Swan King, sick with anger and terror.

My father.

Tippy tossed the cape into the fire where it exploded with a burst of foul-smelling smoke, and emerged from the box with an old-fashioned silver hairbrush. "I knew there was one somewhere." She sounded so excited, just about having her hair brushed. I tried and failed to imagine what it was like to have bed-head for centuries.

We sat alone by the fire, Tippy now dressed in a blue gown I'd torn the bottom off. She smiled every time she ran her fingers over the silk. "It's so beautiful. Thank you, Lissy." It had taken me two minutes to rip away a metre of fabric, making the dress short enough to fit her. Not exactly difficult. And not one of the Hidden had bothered in hundreds of years to find her some proper clothes.

What had happened to Tippy down here? If she was stolen in a nightie that would have fitted a five-year-old, why had her body aged so slowly? She didn't look more than eight – it was as if her physical age had slowed down to a rate of one year for every hundred. I couldn't help shuddering, and she looked away, as if ashamed.

"I know I'm enchanted," she whispered. "I'll go to hell. I've been here such a long time, but I'm still so little. It's the Hidden – they know such powerful songs. Rose gets cross with me. She says I'm useless."

"You're not going to hell. Why did they bring you here, Tippy?"

She shrugged. "They're dwindling. They can't have their own babies." Tippy's face twisted with misery. "I want my mammy so, so much. I've wanted her every day since I was taken. It's a long time, Lissy."

I didn't know what to say. Tears sprang to my eyes, and I didn't want her to see, so I just hugged her, a rigid little body till she relaxed in my arms.

"Do you want a bath?" Her neck was filthy. If all I had to do was ask, and be obeyed, I should be able to get some hot water. I could at least make her feel washed and clean.

Tippy pulled away to look at me, smiling. "A what?"

"Don't worry," I said, quickly, and concentrated on her hair instead, working through the knots.

"It's nice." Tippy arched her back like a stroked cat and I couldn't help smiling. "I think they grew tired of me. I've been little for so long, you know. Mammy would be very surprised." Then her shoulders started to shake, jerking up and down. She was crying. I put down the brush and hugged her again; we clung to each other, and I whispered to her all those things I'd say to Connie if she were upset: *It's OK, it's going to be all right.*

A lie, because I didn't have a clue.

At last, Tippy pulled away, rubbing her eyes. "Rose is always saying I'm less use than a bent spoon. They wanted me to have Hidden babies of my own one day, but I'm taking too long to grow."

I suppressed a shiver, not wanting Tippy to see how

disgusted I was. She was being kept here like an animal reared for breeding. What had the Hidden done to her? A new fear clung to me like wet cloth, chilly and unsettling, impossible to shake off.

With the force of a blow, I remembered what Virgie Creed had said to me in the church: *They want pretty girls to breed with.*

Why was I here?

If the Hidden wanted to use human girls like cattle on a farm, why weren't people always going missing? Even if there was something special about the Reach, I wasn't the only girl in Hopesay Edge. What did the Hidden want from Tippy? From *me*?

"I don't understand." I finished brushing one section of hair and moved on to the next. "Why did they take you in the first place? Why do they want us?"

Tippy stared at me. "They've stolen hundreds of children, men and women too, and I'm the only one still alive. Larkspur told me they all just withered away down here; he thinks they died of grief. I don't remember any others except the baby, so I must have been one of the last before the Gateway was closed and they were stopped." She turned and stared at me. "*You're* the baby, aren't you? You came through after they opened the Gateway again. You did nothing but cry; I had to show them how to feed you milk from a rag like the village women do."

I still couldn't get my head round having been down here as a baby. Tippy must have saved my life, and all I could do in return was give her a stolen dress.

"What *is* the Gateway?"

"It's in the house where I was born," Tippy told me. "A door between God's earth and this place. Larkspur told me my kinsmen guard the Gateway to this day, and must swear to keep it secret from other men. He said my brother Roger's son had the Gateway shut when Roger and Pappy were both dead. Roger always refused to try, in case I ever got out of these halls only to find the way home closed. Now it's open again, and the Hidden have been dancing in the woods again."

I put down the hairbrush. "Where were you born?" I wasn't sure she'd be able to remember, but Tippy turned around and looked straight at me.

"In the manor house of course," she said. "It's called Hopesay Reach."

I remembered those patches of bare paint where crosses had once hung at the Reach — by the windows, above the doors — and a cold chill passed through my body. The Gateway.

Someone had opened it.

It was clear what I had to do, even though I was already dreading it. I didn't know if I could face Larkspur after seeing his naked despair: it was like reading someone's diary, knowing too much about them. Or snooping in your dad's laptop bag and finding a birthday card from his girlfriend.

As if she'd read my mind, Tippy turned to look at me, her grimy face cast into shadow by the fire. "You want to find him, don't you?"

I put down the brush. "I've got to, Tippy. I need to know how to get home." I squeezed my eyes shut a second, desperately trying not to cry.

I needed to find out what had happened to Connie.

"They won't let you go," whispered Tippy. "I know."

I had to go home; I had to find Larkspur. I had to get us both out of here: me *and* Tippy.

Whatever it might take.

31

Rafe

So it was my fault we were both here. I'd led the Fontevrault to Miles.

"I'm sorry. I thought I'd lost them before I got to the Reach." I stared at him. "What did the Fontevrault want *you* for, anyway?"

He just gave me a small, odd smile, looking down at my ruined ankle. "It looks like you walked straight into the trap I left the Fontevrault," he said. "Miriam will be furious." I felt all cold when he said that. Miles was *scared* and ruthless – a pretty lethal cocktail. I kept my mouth shut. He might've been responsible for crippling me, but I wasn't about to antagonize him.

It was weird how the Fontevrault waited till the next day before making their move, though. Taking Miles first thing in the morning. Then me. Why not the night before? It was like they'd had to retreat for a few hours to consider their options. *Analytical* and ruthless: a rather scary combination.

"So I take it you've guessed." Miles leaned back in his chair a little, watching, blatantly not answering my question. Despite his skeletal and dishevelled appearance, there was still something weirdly glamorous about him. His eyes were the pale grey of a rainy morning. Mum always said Miles had buckets of charisma. She was right. Had he been held in one of those airless steel cells, too? Or was that just me?

"Guessed that Lissy isn't human?" I stared him out. "Oh, yeah, a while ago actually."

Dad would have gone ballistic if I'd spoken to him like that. But Miles just sat there; he wasn't even looking at me but out of the window. The branches of a huge old ash tree tapped at the glass. How long was it since I'd seen him? Well over ten years.

I had to know. "So who's her father then?" I asked. "Who's Lissy's real dad?"

"The Swan King," Miles said, and I laughed.

"Lissy's dad is a king? That beats it all."

Miles just sat back and watched me. He looked so old and raddled compared to Mum and Dad it was hard to believe they were the same age. "The Swan King is nothing to laugh about. He's lord over all the Hidden, for one thing. He hates mortals, and he's extremely dangerous. Lissy has spent her life in danger of the Fontevrault Group finding out what she is. You must understand that now she's with the Swan King anything the Group might have had in store for her pales into insignificance. I've always thought he had some kind of plan regarding your mother, some sort of ulterior motive. It's remarkable," he continued quietly. "Very few hybrid children survive. Usually, the mother dies in labour—"

"Wait. This has happened before?"

Miles turned back to me, face deadly serious. "Well, clearly it's not something that could ever be proven, but the Group

207

has always suspected there were others, before we agreed there should be no more contact between humans and the Hidden. No more than a handful over the entire course of human history, of course. The human mothers had to be exceptionally strong to survive the birth, in physical terms and psychologically. It's hardly ever successful. For a hybrid to survive in the womb and grow, the Hidden always had to choose a human girl with the right genetic characteristics, and even then, both she and the baby usually wouldn't survive childbirth. Of course, human blood contains iron. Any hint of human blood physically contaminating the Hidden bloodstream would be fatal to the Hidden parent, too. It's said that the hybrids are immortal, but immune to the effects of iron. Lissy can't be killed by anyone or anything."

I gazed down at the swirling floral pattern on the rug, trying to squeeze the vast enormous truth of all this into a shape I could understand. "It's strange," I said, "but my granny once said that Mum nearly died when Lissy was born, and it was all very dramatic, but that Connie and me were just kind of really easy."

Gross. I didn't want to think about Mum in childbirth. Lissy was never, ever going to die. I couldn't get my head around it.

Miles nodded. "It's true."

"But listen," I said. "The Group? You're involved with these Fontevrault people? Don't you have to be some kind of government leader or own about seven companies? What have they got to do with the Hidden?"

"That's nothing but Internet gossip," Miles said, looking bored. "Membership has always been inherited. The group got its name from a council held at the court of Eleanor of Aquitaine at Fontevrault Abbey in 1153 – the Fontevrault Convenant. We each agreed not to harm the other, and not to make contact unless it was absolutely necessary. It's a long story, but humans and the Hidden have lived alongside one another a long time, and it was becoming clear that too much contact was dangerous."

"Why? Why don't these Fontevrault people want anyone to know about the Hidden? For Christ's sake, Miles – who would even believe it? I mean, who *are* these people?" I gazed around the palatial office. "Is it something to do with the government? And if they've been killing anyone who makes the mistake of becoming seriously interested in this—"

"David Creed," Miles interrupted. "His parents worked for my family at the Reach, but he was clever, and my great-grandfather paid for him to go to school. He found out about the Hidden – about the Gateway too – and got his hands on the journal. David knew too much, and he lived dangerously close to the Reach itself. His mother was the housekeeper – it would have been easy for him to get access. The Fontevrault Group was afraid he would find out how to lift the protection and open the Gateway." Miles smiled. "I don't think they ever suspected that one of their own would eventually do that, and particularly not the Gateward."

"You did it," I hissed. "*You* opened the Gateway, didn't you? All this is your fault. Lissy – everything."

Miles shrugged. "Look at it this way: Lissy wouldn't even exist if I hadn't done it. Doesn't she deserve to live, Rafe? Look, I'll admit I was naïve to believe that humans and the

Hidden could live alongside each other after what we did to the Swan King's queen. She was murdered just after the Fontevrault Covenant, hunted down by a gang. The Hidden don't age or die like mortals, but iron will kill them if the skin is broken, if it gets in their blood, and they cut her throat. The Hidden don't *think* the same way as us, you see. They don't even view time in the same way – a murder committed nine hundred years ago is still a recent injustice in their eyes."

"What happened to David Creed?" I had to know.

"The Fontevrault had him falsely accused of desertion, and he was executed in 1917. Particularly nasty because it got out locally that he'd deserted. The family suffered for it. He was only eighteen years old."

Eighteen. Just like me, but born over a hundred years ago. And if the Fontevrault Group had killed a teenage boy in 1917, what was to stop them doing the same now?

I could imagine the terror David Creed had felt, scrawling that warning on the journal. *They will kill you.* Had he done it just before they took him away to be shot?

"I always thought Miriam should have told you both the truth, you and Lissy. You would have been better able to protect yourselves. Particularly her."

"Truth's not exactly Mum's speciality." I managed – barely – to keep the bitterness out of my voice. He'd managed to not really answer any of my questions, like some kind of politician. I tried again, attacking from another angle. "Listen, Miles. If David Creed was shot just for *reading* about these – these immortal things – how come I'm still here? Mum? Lissy, even?"

Not that I knew where Lissy was or what had happened

to her. I'd let them take her, again. Failed to protect my sister. Was it because of what she'd done? Showing Mum that birthday card from Elena? Had I subconsciously just let it happen, to punish her for destroying our family?

"Ah," Miles said. "Well, there is a decent explanation for that, at least. You'd better come with me."

"What's the deal with you and the Fontevrault Group, anyway?" I asked again, out in the corridor. Miles had opened the door with a flat grey plastic card unclipped from the waistband of his trousers, like the office ID I was always given if I visited Dad at work. Obviously not a prisoner, then – so what was Miles's connection? "They searched the Reach—" I nearly told him about Connie, but couldn't make myself form the words. Not without knowing. Maybe he'd still have his phone and I could try calling Mum. But if Connie hadn't made it—

Miles moved surprisingly fast for someone who looked so skinny and weak. "I didn't come here by choice, but it hasn't turned out quite how I'd expected. I'm part of the Fontevrault, of course, just as my father was and his before him – there have been Gatewards at the Reach a long time." Miles turned and smiled at me. "But unlike the rest of them I committed a serious breach of the rules. I didn't just open the Gateway – I fell in love with one of the Hidden. Difficult times lie ahead, Rafe. For everyone." The look in his eyes was kind of desperate, as if he was seeing something he wanted but could never have. "I've never had the courage to pass through. I couldn't do it, knowing there's no way back if you lose track of time. Never seeing the sun again. Sometimes

I think it would all be worthwhile, just to be with Rose."

God, how embarrassing. I really didn't want to know about Miles's love life, even if he was talking about some beautiful immortal creature who wasn't even meant to exist.

"Elves? It's not exactly a fairy tale."

Miles whirled around to face me, his face thin and pale. "Why not, Rafe? Let's call them what they are, after all. Elven, the Sidhe, the Hidden, they've had many names."

"But that stuff's just— They live for years – I've seen them, Miles. They never get old. They never change. They must be some kind of alien—"

"Did you ever stop to think that they might have been here first? All young people are so stupendously arrogant. Consider this, Rafe: *we're* the invading species that got out of control, like some kind of virus."

"But I don't understand why the Fontevrault didn't just close the Gateway again. It's been open for nearly fifteen years. Why?"

Miles laughed, and I started to think he'd gone a bit crazy. "They don't even know it's open, Rafe, that's why. The Fontevrault are useless – outmoded, concerned with nothing but tradition. And the Hidden are biding their time, just waiting for your sister to return. Believe me, it's been in their interest to keep a very low profile as Lissy grew nearer her fourteenth birthday. The last thing the Hidden wanted was to risk the Fontevrault finding out about the Gateway. They needed it open for Lissy to return."

Before I had time to even attempt an answer, Miles reached out with the grey key card just as we approached another arched wooden doorway, and touched it against a metal sensor panel. A small green light flashed, and the doors swung open. Inside, light flooded in through huge leaded windows. A polished wooden table ran down the centre of the room, seating four men and the two women who'd collected me from my cell. They were all so bland – wearing plain suits and smart shirts, like I'd interrupted some kind of board meeting. They all looked just like faceless office drones. Except one. I scanned the table again, trying to conceal my shock.

I just stared, unable to register what I was hearing or seeing.

How could *he* possibly be here?

A tanned, fair-haired man sat at the far end of the table, deep in conversation with the woman beside him. As usual, he looked as if he'd just stepped off a yacht, not quite at home in a suit.

"That's your answer," Miles said, a thin smile creasing his face. "Going to the British Library? You've gone to a lot of trouble to bring yourself to our attention, Rafe. All you had to do was wait till your twenty-first birthday, and you would have received an invitation, just like I did. Membership is yours by birthright, the Fontevrault inheritance."

My dad looked like I'd just walked into an elegant dinner party completely naked, and then thrown up on the table. "Rafe." He sounded very reasonable but I knew him well enough to wish I could turn and walk straight out. "Would you mind telling me what you've done to your leg?"

I didn't even know where to start.

32

Joe

Water flooded my mouth and nose; I coughed, choking, sending up bubbles of wasted oxygen. Pain shrieked inside my chest. I tried to swim, arms and legs flailing and useless, but it did no good because I wasn't sinking, I was *falling*. The pain shot to unbearable heights. Everything went black and then I felt solid rock beneath my feet. I stood up streaming water, choking again and spewing, but breathing. Actually breathing. I crouched down, getting wet all over again but not caring, gasping in as much air as I could. I stood up, staring down at my clothes.

They were already dry: my thick heavy jeans dry as a bone after a massive soaking.

And I was *somewhere else*. This wasn't the overgrown front garden at Hopesay Reach, but a huge glittering white chamber, bright even without a window or any kind of obvious light. And trees were growing up through solid rock. Actual trees with green leaves, silvery trunks. Unsteady, slipping, I stepped out of the water, dropped to my knees, pressing my hands to the ground. Yes, rock. Solid quartz, it felt like, bone-white and glittering.

This wasn't real. It wasn't right. I knew straight away this couldn't be a place that had ever been touched by human hands. It was like being in a giant ants' nest. Somewhere imagined by inhuman minds. A place built by them, the Hidden, whatever they were really called. Hot nausea shot up my throat and I was sick right there on the shining floor. I sat back on my heels, cold with horror. No one came. No one saw. I was alone. I reached round to move whatever was jammed into the side pocket of my jeans, digging into my hip.

The knife. Rafe's iron knife. *Kill them with iron.* The wooden handle was smooth and plain, the blade protected by a simple leather case, clumsily stitched with yellowish thread. If I had to use it, I didn't like my chances. I tried to imagine plunging the blade into the flesh of something that looked human, a shrieking wide-open mouth—

I wouldn't be able to do it.

I shoved the knife back into my pocket, a cold heavy weight against my leg, and pulled out the bundle of yellowed paper Virgie Creed had given me in the church. The edge that had been poking out of my pocket was slightly damp, unprotected by whatever strange forces had kept my clothes dry.

Why had the Hidden taken Lissy again? She had to be down here somewhere, too. I could find her. Together we could escape.

Yeah, right. What a hero, choking and spluttering then chundering on the floor.

And escape how? There was nowhere to run, no visible way out.

I couldn't sit there staring at my own regurgitated crisps

and coffee, so instead I rinsed out my mouth with water from the lake, tasting only the tangy edge of hard water, nothing else. I got up and staggered – I felt like the bones in my legs had just dissolved, and my head was still spinning. I sat down, leaning against one of the trees, resting my head against my knees. What was I going to do? I couldn't walk without puking. Trying to take deep steady breaths, I opened the letter, rolling away the elastic band that held it to a thin leatherbound notebook I hadn't noticed before.

The letter was dated August 1930, typewritten in faded black ink.

Dear Mrs Creed

I am sorry to write quite "out of the blue" in such a way, and to rake over an upsetting matter that perhaps you and your late husband would rather be left well alone. I hope that the news I have may offer some small consolation.

You were told that your son David had been convicted of deserting his post a short while after the Somme, an offence which led to the capture of several men by German ground troops. It was the loss of these other men and the valuable intelligence thus obtained by the enemy that led the military court to deliver the harshest possible sentence. I was deeply sorry to learn that this story got into the local paper, and that your family had no means of shielding yourselves from unpleasant consequences within the village of Hopesay Edge itself and even beyond, with malicious letters and so on.

Now that I am shortly to die of a malignant tumour, I feel an urgent need to offer what solace you might gain from knowing that your son did not desert his post. No fellow Allied soldier, to my knowledge, was ever lost as a result of his action. In actual fact, David had been recommended for honours after risking his own life by picking up an unexploded grenade and throwing it back across enemy lines. As you may always have suspected, knowing David as you did, the charge against him was an outright lie.

What I am about to write will never be believed by anyone you might tell, so I advise you not to tax yourself with this matter. Indeed, any attempt to take this matter further will almost certainly result in serious danger to you and your family. This risk is one of the chief reasons I have never written before now, and my main misgiving about finally doing so. I hope I can trust you to burn this letter: unfortunately there is no hope of using it to obtain an official posthumous pardon for your son.

David had stumbled on certain information, and this placed him in grave danger. It was extremely unlikely that anyone would ever have believed his story – he would be more likely considered mad, but we had no way of ensuring that David would use his new-found knowledge wisely. It was a risk to the saftey of not just our country, but the wider world. He knew too much, and the authorities at the time believed the only solution was to put an end to his life. I am ashamed to say I was one of those men. I can assure you, Mrs Creed, that this was one of the hardest choices I have ever made, and that David's life was not lost for nothing. Had your son acted on his discovery or, much less likely, had anyone believed his story, the consequences would have been nothing less than disastrous. It was extremely unfortunate that David learned what he did, and I regret immensely the pain his family and friends must have endured as a result of his false conviction and unjust execution.

It may also help to know that David faced the firing squad with utmost courage, never flinching, and those who witnessed the event remarked on his unusual bravery.

I hope that this letter restores some peace of mind, Mrs Creed, which I am sure you must have lost for ever when news of David's death, and the manner of it, arrived in 1917.

I will not insult you by asking for forgiveness.

The letter was unsigned. Not a huge surprise. I sat there wondering who had written it. Someone in the Fontevrault Group, about to die themselves, wanting to offload their guilt. *They* were the killers. They must have been terrified David might go to the Reach and try opening the Gateway.

Virgie Creed knew; she had to be some relation of this David guy; he'd stumbled on the truth about the Hidden long before us and this letter to his mother had been passed on down the family.

She'd saved my life. In a weird way, David Creed had, too. Now the Fontevrault Group had Rafe and their major fear was a reality: *someone* had opened the Gateway at Hopesay Reach. Rafe had been abducted by an organization that killed people for knowing too much: that was the truth of it. I had no idea where he was or who I could ask for help.

I stared down at the blank screen of my phone. I should have been calling the police. Doing *something*.

I folded the letter and slid the elastic band away from the leatherbound notebook. Opening it, I recognized the handwriting from the margin of the diary straight away, I knew who had owned this: David Creed. His possessions must have been handed down too, kept safe alongside the letter. I felt cold inside, holding something that had once been owned by a dead boy, wondering what it must be like to face a firing squad, tied up somewhere just waiting for the bullets, unable to do anything about it.

I turned the first page. There were doodles covering every blank space, little sketches of leaves and birds. The leaves weren't anything special but the birds looked like they might fly off the page: chaffinches, a ragged crow and some kind of falcon, the head of a swan. David had been a good artist before the Fontevrault Group blew his brains out. I swallowed a surge of rage. They'd squashed him like a fly just because he knew about the Hidden.

So what were they going to do with Rafe? OK, Rafe could look after himself, but David Creed had picked up a live grenade and thrown it back at German troops, and the Fontevrault Group had killed him without even trying.

This wasn't good.

It was weirdly comforting, though, holding something human down in that chamber, with those impossible trees growing out of cold rock – like me and the long-dead David Creed were in this together. The same panicky thought rolled round inside my head like a pebble in a bath: *how did I get here, how did it happen, how?*

I was losing it again. I breathed out, trying to concentrate on that for a moment. I had to get a grip.

David's handwriting started mid-sentence on the first page, as if he'd just filled up an old diary and started a new one.

and I believe Philippa de Conway is still alive, lost in the realm of the Hidden. How she must have suffered, missing her home. It's my duty to find her: I know that. It's the least I can do after all the Conways have done for me, Eton and everything. But even if I were to learn how to open the Gateway, would I ever be able to come home? Every child knows those fairy tales. The knight who dances for one night with his fairy lover, and leaves her domain only to find thousands of years have passed. And now there's no time. I've been called up. It'll all have to wait till I get back from France. I hope I don't die out there, not just because I don't _want_ to die yet, but because I'm that little girl's last hope of escaping. Still, a few months won't make *a difference to her, and everyone says the war will be over by Christmas.*

There is more to the world than most men and women ever dream of.

That was it. Underneath, David had just scribbled "2.19 for Birmingham", which must have been a train time. There was no more – the rest of the diary was empty, except for a tissue-thin dried flower that fell from between the pages, leaving a tea-coloured stain on the paper. I sat staring at the white walls, at the still black water I'd climbed out of, impossibly, just a few minutes before.

There was no way out.

33

Lissy

"We'll have to run." Tippy smoothed the blue dress out around her legs. "No one cares what I do but they'll all be watching you. If the King finds out we've gone to find Larkspur—"

I reached out and grabbed her hand: her warm, human hand – still so smooth and young after hundreds of years. "Listen. I don't want to put you in danger. Just tell me where Larkspur is and I'll find him."

Tippy shook her head. "You'll get lost. I wandered for years."

I pushed away a nightmarish image of drifting alone down those tunnels for centuries, desperate for water. I wondered if she knew. I hoped not. "No," I said, "I'll be all right if you tell me where he is. It's too dangerous for you."

"You don't understand how much I hate them," Tippy whispered, fiercely. "All except Larkspur. Rose stole me from my mother and they all just *left* me to rot down here as soon as they realized how long it would take me to grow big enough to bear a Hidden child. I want to help you. If you must see Larkspur then come now, while the others are gone."

We both stood up, Tippy's new plaits shining in the

firelight. She looked almost like a normal little girl now, wearing someone's old evening gown from a dressing-up box. I was starting to panic, heart pounding, burning nausea forcing up my throat. What if somebody caught us? *Rose?* She was the King's sister. My aunt. I took a long, steady breath. Tippy might have been hundreds of years old, but really she was just a child. I had to show her I wasn't scared.

"Take my hand," Tippy whispered, and we ran.

I followed her down endless twisting corridors. The light changed as we got further away from the White Hall and that huge central cavern: the silvery glow was replaced by smokey flaming torches; the air grew thick and I couldn't stop coughing.

Tippy didn't seem to notice; when a fit of coughing had me leaning against the dank earthen wall, trying to drag some air into my lungs, she grabbed at my hand, hissing, "Come on, they could be back any moment. No one is meant to talk to Larkspur – he's an outcast because he took you home. If the Swan King finds out I'm taking you to him there's no knowing what he'll do."

The only thing he couldn't do was kill me. I pushed the thought away. *I'm not human.*

At last, Tippy stopped. "Come." And I followed her into a side tunnel that wasn't lit at all. I felt the weight of the earth above pressing down on the tunnel. I'd never known such complete darkness; I had to swallow my panic.

Tippy's voice sounded louder away from the smokey torchlight. "Count your steps," she said. "Don't think about the shadows."

"I'm all right," I said. Her bravery made me want to cry. "Don't worry."

And at last, at long last, I sensed the tunnel opening out into a wider space. The air grew warmer, thick with the warm harsh scent of wet dog.

"The King's hounds. They steal them from above to please him," Tippy said, just a voice ahead of me now; she had melted completely into the black and so had I. "The finest hunters from a royal pack, a lord's prize gazehound. They never seem to die unless they get hurt in the chase."

Like me, I thought, and remembered that night in the woods, running terrified from Larkspur, listening to the wild call of the dogs. Fairy hounds. I half wanted to laugh, because how could it be true? I still felt the chill of Larkspur's touch, his cold fingers entwined with mine, and knew I'd feel it till the day I died, like a tattoo that never healed. I'd danced with the Hidden. How could I not have seen that I was *like* them?

The day you die? You're not going to die.

I pushed the thought from my mind. Tippy reached back to take my hand again and there was no time; I had to follow her.

"Why is he down here with his father's hounds?" I asked. The smell and the heat grew thicker, more intense, and I could hear them now, too, the occasional high-pitched whimper of a dreaming dog.

"The King's hounds aren't bound by his rules. If Larkspur hunts in the world above, they share his kill. No one else will."

Her voice grew faint as we turned a corner, and then I could feel the dogs: warm slinky bodies pressing against my legs, I heard the soft rhythm of their breath.

"*Larkspur,*" whispered Tippy in the darkness.

And then, bright like a winter snowdrop breaking from its bud, pure silver light began to glow. Larkspur sat slumped against a dark earthen wall, knotted hair hanging in his face. Cupped in his hands was a globe of light, a miniature moon.

Magic. *No, sky-in-her-eyes, just the way of the world, should you live long enough to really know it.*

If the Swan King could make trees grow in a cave, and I heard Larkspur's voice inside my mind, and he plucked silver bubbles of light from nothing, what else could the Hidden do?

What could I do?

Tippy had lived down here for hundreds of years, frozen in time as a child, never to grow up. Even the dogs never died. The Hidden could work miracles.

Maybe they had the power to save Connie. If she was still alive.

"You came." Larkspur's voice was so quiet, as if he could hardly summon the strength to speak. He blew, and the glowing silver moon rose up, floating like a bubble. He sat alone among the dogs, face and hands smeared with something dark. *Blood.* "You should not have. If my father knew—"

"You know I don't care," Tippy said. "He can do no worse to me. Anyhow, what fault is it of mine if I come to the hounds and she follows?" I felt her fingers brush mine, reaching out in the shadowy silver gloom.

"Thank you, Tippy," I whispered.

"It's too dangerous for you here, Lissy. Go. Don't become an outcast for my sake." Larkspur blew gently on the ball of light. It spun, hovering just above his blood-stained fingers, sending wobbly shadows around the cave. "Mine is not the life you want."

He was here because Mum had wanted me back so much, because he'd shown mercy. It wasn't fair.

I crouched down in front of him, trying not to retch at the thought of hot raw meat, crunching bone, fur or feathers in his teeth. "Listen. Please. Why does the King want me?"

Larkspur looked up; his black eyebrows were like flicks of ink. "To save the Hidden, before we are all gone for ever."

"What do you mean?"

"Mortals can never have enough, Lissy. They poison the earth; they breed into every crack and corner. They learned how to render metal, even questioned the existence of their own gods, and they killed one another in tens of thousands and discovered how to crack the very fabric of the universe itself. Mortals grew in learning but not in wisdom. Everything they touch, they destroy. We grew afraid that the Hidden would finally be flushed out like rats, and killed like rats, too."

They. Not you. *They.*

"It's not just that though, is it?" I whispered, watching the silver light flicker in Larkspur's hands. "The Swan King can't stand humans. He really hates mortals, doesn't he? He's not just afraid you'll be outnumbered like, like – red squirrels being killed off by all the grey ones." I'd seen it in the Swan King's eyes – a terrifying, slow-burning rage. "There's something else, isn't there? Some other reason."

Larkspur looked away; when he spoke again his voice was hard. "They hunted us through the woods, my mother and I, nine hundred years ago when I was a child and could do nothing to help – a pack of men and women with filthy faces and ragged clothes, crazed by fear and longing for blood. They cut her throat with an iron knife. I couldn't save her. She bled to death in my arms."

"I'm sorry." My voice shook. "That's terrible. But nine hundred years is such a long time. Why has your father waited so long to get revenge? And I still don't understand what it's got to do with me. Why did he want a half-mortal child if he hates them so much?"

"Nine hundred years is nothing to my father." Larkspur gave me a beautiful, tormented smile. "I'm just a little older than that, and he still considers me young and foolish." He shrugged. "The mortals closed the Gateway, Lissy. They *trapped* us."

"Because the Swan King kept stealing girls and letting them just wither away and die down here. Using them to *breed*, or trying to. It's cruel and disgusting. You deserved to be trapped."

"You don't know the truth of it," Larkspur said, and I flinched at the anger in his voice. "At Fontevrault, mortals and the Hidden swore an oath to live in peace, side by side, but always apart. The mortals cheated. They killed my mother. After that they spread too far, too fast, laying waste to all they found, driving us into our secret halls. There was a bargain, Lissy, but the mortals broke it first. We had to fight back or dwindle to nothing, driven underground like hunted rats."

"That still doesn't justify stealing girls away from their homes, using them like animals. That's not fighting back. It's just evil."

Larkspur stared at me. "Maybe so. But it was necessary. Either way, it did not work. They all died except Tippy, and her body is still too young. My father always plays a long game, Lissy, and the mortals had their chance. He's going to kill them all – every last one."

"What?" I said, disbelieving. "*How?* There aren't enough of you to kill us, you don't understand the weapons we've got, and you can't touch iron—"

Larkspur shook his head. "We do understand; we have seen how you murder thousands of your own kind. No, my sister, our father has made his own weapon. For centuries, he searched for a mortal girl strong enough, with enough spirit. He took living girls the right age, but down here they all died before they could be of any use. He even took young children, hoping they might more easily forget what they'd left behind. They died, too – all except Tippy. We sang our immortality into her blood, into her bones, but she's still just a human child with Hidden powers. She can't breed, not yet. It might be another five hundred years before she is ready, and the mortals will have poisoned every ocean and burned every forest to dead ash by then."

"She's just a little girl," I said, fiercely. "You had no right to steal her."

Larkspur frowned. "Taking Tippy was Rose's greatest mistake. Tippy was the Gateward's daughter, and when he died down here in search of her the Gateway was shut by his grandson, prayer-bound in iron by the village priest so no one could pass through it, human or Hidden, for centuries." Larkspur passed his silver light from one hand to the other, just watching me. "And then," he said, "the Gateway was opened again. We hunted in the night air as we had not done for three hundred years. The right girl came to Hopesay Reach, almost as if she had heard us calling. Her name was Miriam. Lissy, you are the weapon."

I could only stare at him.

Larkspur blew on the silver ball once more; it spun in his hands, lighting up the dark stains. I could smell the blood smeared on his fingers, across his face: a faint metallic tang.

"Your *blood*, Lissy," he said. "With just one drop, my father will make a plague that will spread through the waters of the earth before the moon has risen even twice. He has that power – you must see it. He will spread a plague born out of human blood from a girl who will never die. A sickness with no end till every last man, woman and child is dead, and the earth can breathe again." He shrugged. "They should have known better, those mortal leaders, than to break a bargain with my father. They should have known better than to kill my mother."

I stared at him, disbelieving. "Why now?" I demanded. "Why didn't he just take my blood when I was a baby if he wants it that much, if it's that special?"

"He did," Larkspur replied, simply. "He tried to brew the plague then, but it didn't work. You were too young. The quality of your blood wasn't rich enough until you began to bleed with each moon. Now you're ready."

I felt my face burn even though it was dark. "That's disgusting."

"It's the truth."

"No," I said, "I won't let him do this. There must be a way out. Show me. We could go, we could *all* go, Larkspur, please—"

And, as I watched, his black eyes stretched wide in horror and the whole cavern filled with piercing white light. The air split with the howling of dogs, I could see their swarming bodies: white, golden and black.

Beside me, Tippy screamed and grabbed onto my arm. "Oh, God save us!"

I turned and there was Rose standing in the cavern entrance, smiling, reaching out to stroke the nearest hound; it cowered away from her outstretched fingers.

"Oh, Larkspur, my dear child," she said. "Now you will learn what it is to suffer."

Larkspur just stared at her with such an intense look of hatred that even I was shocked by it. He didn't say a word.

Rose only laughed.

34

Rafe

"What are you doing here, Rafe?" Dad shot a cold glance up and down the conference table. "Would someone care to explain?" Everyone sat back a little in their seats but I stood my ground. He was the one with no right to be here.

He should have been with Connie.

"How is she?" I said. "How's Connie?"

Dad shook his head, very slightly – a silent signal that this was not the time or the place. I ignored it. I had to know. How could he even *be* here when she was lying in the intensive care unit of some hospital? Waves of pure hot anger washed through me watching him just sit there, too big and too important to bother with his own kid. She was only eight years old.

"She's alive." Dad's voice was clipped and furious. "We'll discuss it later."

Relief washed through me, and I felt so weak I had to grab onto the table.

The woman sitting closest to me gave me a smile that was half totally embarrassed, half seriously concerned, and pulled out the empty chair beside her. I sat down, leaning forwards onto the table, fighting a sinking black exhaustion I'd never known before. Miles sat down next to me.

Me included, there were eight of us.

"Thanks," I said. It was all just so completely *bizarre*, like I'd stumbled into an alternative reality, except Dad still looked like he wanted to rip out my soul. There were empty coffee cups all over the table, sheaves of paper spread everywhere, a water cooler by the door. It all looked so *normal*, just like the office I'd spent three brain-numbing weeks in on work experience at Easter.

A grey-haired man sitting next to Dad smiled at me down the table. "Rafe," he said, "thank you so much for joining us. We really must apologize for any inconvenience, but I'm sure you'll come to agree how important our work is here, how seriously we take it."

Dad looked as if he was fighting the urge to strangle me, but said nothing. I'd never seen him look so angry; actually, it was kind of impressive.

"When did you first become interested in the Hidden, Rafe?" asked the guy next to him. I stared wildly around the table. Except for Dad and Miles, they were all so indistinguishable, so bland. Plain suits, forgettable faces. "Could it be that your father—"

"He's never said anything," I snapped. "What's going on? Who are you people?"

Dad gave me another terrifying look but I just stared back, ready for a fight. I'd waited long enough for answers.

Miles turned to me. "Where's your sister, Rafe?" he asked. "Where's Lissy?"

I turned to Dad. "They took her," I said. "Again."

Dad closed his eyes for a second, as if he wanted to pretend that we had all just disappeared.

"I'm sorry," said the woman beside me, looking puzzled. "I'm afraid I really don't see how this is relevant."

Dad shot Miles a look of purest hatred. "It's relevant because Melisende Harker is not really my daughter."

"She's a hybrid," Miles said. "The Gateway is open."

Everyone just sat and stared at him.

"What do you mean, Miles?" the older man said, tapping the end of his biro against the table.

The woman beside me turned to Dad, looking disbelieving. "Your daughter is fourteen years old. If this isn't some kind of childish joke, and the Gateway really *is* open, why haven't there been other indications? And for God's sake, Adam, why didn't you just shut it again?"

Dad glanced at me sideways. "It's a long story. They placed Rafe and Connie under a curse. If we tried to shut the Gateway or not give Lissy back, they told us Rafe and Connie would both die. We couldn't take the risk. Also I presume they didn't wish to draw undue attention to the fact that we're now completely unprotected against them, in case *you* did something about it." Dad gave Miles another filthy look. "They don't think like us: they don't need to. The Hidden make long-term plans."

A few people actually gasped. Dad just stared steadily out of the window. What had it been like for him, all these years, knowing Lissy wasn't really his kid? That she was some kind of *monster*?

233

"What, you're saying interbreeding is genuinely possible?" asked the older man. "But this is extraordinary, if it's true—"

"What *I* find extraordinary, Professor," interrupted the woman next to me, "is the fact that Adam hasn't chosen to share this information with us before now." I could feel the hostility burning off her in waves. She was furious.

"I really must apologize." Dad's tone was pretty acid too, but I felt a fresh jolt of fear. He'd hidden the truth about Lissy for fourteen years. It must have been horrendous: an endless source of worry, stress and paranoia, always wondering if tomorrow would be the day his secret got found out. I surprised myself by feeling sorry for him.

What would they *do* to him? David Creed had been shot in 1917 just for knowing too much about the Hidden. Dad was one of the Fontevrault, and he'd been harbouring a hybrid child for years.

"Adam," the professor said, "so, are we to assume that your – daughter – is *not* sensitive to iron?"

"Of course not," Dad snapped. "How could a girl live for fourteen years in the modern world if the slightest contamination of her bloodstream would kill her? If even touching iron would burn her skin? Iron's in every car, every home, in various compounds and forms. It's everywhere. She's half human. Her blood contains an element of iron – Lissy is immune."

The younger woman who'd shown me her gun earlier gave Dad a tight, angry smile. "So, if Melisende Harker really is a hybrid, we're now faced with the very eventuality the Fontevrault Group was established to prevent: an immortal girl with no sensitivity to iron. Unbeatable and unstoppable. The Hidden's perfect killer. And now they have one hybrid, perhaps soon there'll be more. We all know the dangers, the possibilities. Within a few generations, the human race could be outnumbered by an immortal hybrid species of infinite capability. Those left would be ruled over by despotic leaders who know they will never die, and can't be destroyed. You failed in your duty, Adam. You've betrayed us all."

"Lissy might not be my real daughter," Dad said, "but she is my child. My first duty is as a father, to protect her. We have to bring her home – not just for her own safety but for everyone else's."

The silence fell again, and I began to see what they were all so afraid of.

Lissy was capable of anything.

Anything at all.

35

Joe

I woke to the sound of drumming: a slow steady beat that grew louder every second. I had no way of knowing how long I'd been asleep for, but someone – or some*thing* – was coming closer every second, by the sound of those drums.

If I stepped back into the pond what would happen? Would I find myself back in the garden, with the Fontevrault Group waiting for me? I couldn't risk it. I was caught between them and the Hidden.

And I couldn't exactly try to escape, leaving Lissy down here on her own. Bloody Dad and his stupid bloody girlfriend Miriam and her stupid bloody kids.

Behind me, a row of stalactites hung down like frozen spittle. Heaving myself up, aching in every bone, I scrambled behind them and crouched in the shadows. The drumming got louder still, a steady unstoppable beat. I reached into my pocket, closed my fingers around the smooth wooden handle of Rafe's knife; I tried to imagine using it.

And they came.

They walked in from the shadows: tall, wild-haired, with ragged clothes on their backs, trailing glittering swathes of fabric, leather boots with elaborate silver buckles that clinked as they walked, scrappy furs and skins wrapped around their thin shoulders. The breath froze in my lungs. OK, I was so scared I was terrified I might actually spew again, but it was pretty incredible to see them, these fairy tale creatures. One by one, the Hidden drifted in, melting in from the darkness: they were so human. But *not*.

There must have been a few hundred of them, at least, crowding in, standing so still. Waiting.

There had to be some kind of tunnel, then, an entrance to this place other than the pond – a way out.

The drumming stopped. Silence. They'd hear my heartbeat. Know I was here—

The Hidden gathered around the pond: all silent. Not a single word spoken.

I gripped the handle of Rafe's knife. *Kill them with iron*—

One walked in on his own, a white cloak of feathers hanging around his shoulders. Silence thickened as he sat in the carved chair, facing that black water, black as his hair. The atmosphere was electric; I could feel power in the air, I mean it. Excitement, fear. He was a leader.

He sang in a language I didn't understand and the silence afterwards seemed to last for years before Lissy walked in with one of the Hidden. His hood slipped back, showing his knotty red hair: I'd seen him before – the creature who had disappeared into the lake. A little kid stumbled in behind them, as if she'd been pushed. If David Creed had got it right, she was Philippa de Conway. I stared down at my knees pressing against the cold white quartz.

I couldn't look at her: it was just wrong. A three-hundred-year-old child who looked no older than seven or eight, like Connie.

Did this mean the Hidden had the power to make humans immortal? I started shivering and had to sit down, holding onto my knees. If people knew about this it would change the world completely.

Everyone would want to live for ever.

Not that it looked as if anyone would find out, because how could I escape this place? Maybe this was why no one knew about the Hidden. Nobody ever left their hideout alive, and if they did, the Fontrevault Group would be waiting to eliminate all the evidence.

The leader in the feather-cloak spoke again. Lissy and the red-headed boy kind of huddled closer together, and that was when I saw it: *she looked like him*. OK, she was very tall for a girl, and they both had red hair, which always stands out. But it wasn't just that.

Her face was the echo of his.

Lissy was one of them.

A wave of cold horror rolled through my body.

Now all I could see was how inhuman she was: that quick, snake-like way she moved. I'd no idea how I hadn't noticed it before. I'd known all along she was different.

Just not *this* different.

I couldn't understand what the feather-cloak freak was saying, but the boy flinched every time he spoke. Lissy looked terrified, wrapping her arms across her chest, shivering. The little girl crept across and Lissy took her hand.

The red-headed boy stepped forwards, shouting in a wild ragged voice.

And then Lissy spoke, too, almost whispering. In that same whispery sing-song language I'd never heard before.

How could she do that? It took years to learn a language. Had Rafe known all along his sister was one of them? This was why she'd been taken, why Miriam was so protective.

Miriam wasn't just afraid the Hidden might come after Lissy, but the Fontevrault Group as well.

The feather-cloaked guy just snapped out what had to have been an order, and a whole mass of Hidden moved in as one, hundreds of them stepping closer, ragged black cloaks swirling around their ankles. The sound of their footfalls echoed through the cave like a drumbeat, the glittering clink of inhuman jewellery as they moved, the swish of ragged cloth through the still air.

The boy shouted out again.

"No!" yelled the little girl, in English. "Leave her alone!"

Lissy. They were going to do something to her. I stood up, gripping onto the nearest stalactite. It felt slippery and cool, hard but brittle, like I could have ripped it right off the ceiling of the cavern.

Feather-cloak took hold of Lissy, grabbing her by the arm, and I caught a flash of glinting metal. He was holding a knife.

He was going to kill her.

The boy dropped to his knees, whispering something I couldn't hear. The little girl started to cry.

Lissy just stared straight ahead. Right at me. Her eyes widened. She'd seen me.

Moving fast, Feather-cloak reached out and pulled Lissy towards him; she pushed at his arm, speaking in that weird language again, but he was obviously far stronger than her. He turned her facing out towards the crowd, put his hand on her forehead, tilting back her head.

He held the blade to her throat.

"No!" I shouted before even thinking, lunging out from behind the crop of stalactites: all I knew was I couldn't stand by and watch a girl being killed.

I had the iron knife.

Everything froze. Lissy just stared at me, her eyes wide with fear. The Hidden all turned to stare, all with the blank, know-it-all expressions of cats.

I tried to step forwards again but I couldn't move my own legs, never mind lift my right arm, never mind the knife, my only weapon.

No one spoke. Not a word. All I could hear was the little girl, crying quietly.

Feather-cloak just smiled, and drew the knife across Lissy's throat.

36

Lissy

Joe—

There he was, so close, looking at me. Green eyes with grey flecks, the first time I'd noticed them—

A line of burning pain spread across my neck.

Tippy screamed.

I was dying. Down here in this hole. I would choke, drown in my own blood. So I *could* die, after all; well that was something worth knowing. I could die and this was it.

I heard Joe yell, "Let her go, let her go!"

But the Swan King only laughed. I was still breathing. My neck stung; I felt a line of something warm oozing down my skin, but that was it. I saw a flash of silver, and he let me fall to my knees. I leaned forwards, drawing in gasps of cold air. I was alive. The knife had barely scratched my skin, just enough to draw blood. I staggered to my feet, nearly knocked straight over by Tippy who rushed across and hugged me hard around the waist. We held hands, her fingers warm in mine.

"Joe!" I gasped. "What are you doing here?"

But he just shook his head, and I started crying, tears

streaming down my face. Joe had come for me when no one else did, and I thought there was no hope of escaping. Now he was a prisoner.

"Stop crying, you daft cow." Joe's voice was even and steady, as if we'd just met in the park. "I don't know what your mam's been up to, but I need to have serious words with my dad about his choice of girlfriend." And he smiled at me.

Brave and stupid. "You idiot," I said. There was no way he'd be allowed to live after this, after what he'd seen.

But Joe just reached out and pulled me to my feet. We hardly knew each other, and he'd followed me *here*. Of all places. With a friend like that at my back, I could have gone anywhere, done anything, knowing I was safe.

The Swan King held up a small silver bowl. Had he taken my *blood*? The Hidden watched, each one silent and still as a hunting cat ready to pounce.

He looked at Joe. "Well now. And what's this?"

"Leave him alone!" My voice rang out, echoing around the cave. "This has got nothing to do with him."

And the Swan King said to me, "Well, you do learn quickly."

I managed not to flinch. "What are you talking about?"

"Perhaps I'm not so cruel as my son would have you think. I will let mankind die quickly, and the poison I'll brew with your blood, child, will spread faster even than the fear of it. You brought me the means to test the poison."

"No," I said. "No! You have to let him go. You must. He's done nothing wrong. It's not his fault humans killed

Larkspur's mother. The ones who did it have been dead hundreds of years, please—"

The Swan King stepped closer, closer, till we were standing face to face, except he was taller and looked down on me, black eyes blazing with hatred. He reached out and lifted my chin with one ice-cold finger so I had no choice but to meet his gaze, and I swear I felt it then: centuries of grief, of anguish and hatred. I would have done anything to turn away, not to look, not to feel his misery, but I couldn't move.

By the time he let me look away, I knew why he hated humans so much. He had wanted Larkspur's mother every day for nine hundred years. He was condemned to spend eternity without her. She was gone for ever.

When he finally spoke, his voice was soft, almost gentle. "All mortals have done wrong. The oceans are empty of fish, and still they cast out nets. The great ice melts year by year, and still they burn the skies. They all must die." He looked across at Tippy. "I could poison the girl, but she's tainted with immortal power. I'm afraid the sickness would not take, and there is little enough to waste."

I stared at him, not looking away. Everyone was watching us. I could feel it. *They like tricks and riddles*, Tippy had said. I thought back to Virgie Creed in the church at Hopesay Edge: *They will offer you your heart's desire, but take care how you pay.*

"I've given you my blood," I said, quickly. "You owe me something in return."

The Swan King smiled, ferocious. "I gave you life; without me, you would be nothing."

"But I didn't choose that. Don't I have the right to choose the price of my own blood?"

He laughed. "You are hardly in a place to strike a bargain, although I do admire you for trying."

No. This had to work.

Larkspur looked up, still on his knees. "If it's taken by force and not given freely she might curse every drop of blood in her body."

Thank you, Larkspur, thank you—

"Be silent." The Swan King's voice stung the air like a slap. "She wouldn't know how. She hasn't lived among us long enough."

This time, I smiled. "No, but I could try."

"Very well. Name your price, daughter."

"A life," I said. "Just one life."

The Swan King looked at me hard. "Very well. The bargain is made, and it is done."

Joe didn't lift his gaze from the floor.

I'd made a mistake. The worst.

I should have asked for two lives. Now it was too late. I had nothing left to bargain with. Every drop of my blood was spoken for.

"Remember your sister," Joe mumbled, still not looking up. He was so brave. He didn't deserve to die. None of this was anything to do with him.

"Choose the life you will save," the Swan King said.

The silence stretched on for ever. I had to break it.

"Connie." I spoke so quietly, ashamed to look at Joe. "My little sister. She's sick in hospital. She might even be dead.

Please make her well again. You can have my blood if you make Connie better."

The Swan King reached out and pushed the hair away from my face, hooking one cold finger beneath my chin, tilting it so that once again neither of us could look away. My eyes filled with tears. "Daughter," he said, "if she is dead then there is nothing even I can do."

Joe just carried on staring down at the floor, which was fine because I couldn't look at him.

He'd come to help me and I'd as good as killed him.

37

Rafe

Dad, Miles and I sat in silence as the SUV shot down the motorway. Miles was in front of us, just behind the driver and another boring-looking suited-up guy doubtless carrying so many unpleasant weapons he would have caused an airport metal detector to explode. Dad and I shared the back seat. You could have cut the air. It was pretty tense. Silence – real silence – is unnerving. Nine times out of ten, someone cracks and mentions the weather, in even the most awkward situations. Not this time. Not one of us said a single word. The grey leather interior of the SUV smelled of vanilla air freshener. I was filthy, wearing the blood-soaked clothes I'd slept in: cold and itchy at the same time. I could have been unconscious in that steel prison a whole twenty-four hours and I wouldn't know. It was raining outside and the driver had the windscreen wipers working full speed, but still it was hard to see in the rain, in the dark. We had left London hours earlier, and this part of the motorway wasn't lit.

It felt like hardly any time at all since I'd driven this way with the journal on the passenger seat, dodging that grey Alfa Romeo. Now here I was again, a prisoner. They'd won.

I'd pretty much abandoned Joe to his fate with only that stupid knife. Joe wasn't the type to use it. I could tell. Stupid idiot, getting me out of the man-trap. He should have left me there, walked back into Hopesay Edge and caught the first train home.

Miles's head lolled against the immaculate upholstery. He'd fallen asleep.

"Dad," I said, speaking as quietly as I could. I didn't want the driver or his henchman to hear us. "The Hidden have got Lissy. Are we really going to close this Gateway and just leave her there?"

Dad sighed, leaning his head back against the seat. He looked suddenly a lot older. "We don't have much choice."

"What do you mean? We can't just let them take her. In the meeting you said that we have to protect her and bring her home. You've already screwed things up with the Fontevrault Group, massively – why should you do what they say? If we shut the Gateway, she'll be trapped for ever—"

"Rafe, listen." Dad sounded totally desperate, completely at the end of his rope. "The Hidden made a bargain with your mother. They promised to return Lissy – but only for fourteen years."

"But why? Why fourteen years? None of this makes sense."

"Listen. It does make sense when you know the full story. The Hidden knew we'd try to keep Lissy. There was a curse. It's lucky for you they've already got her." Dad glanced at his watch. "You and Connie would both be dead by midnight otherwise. Either Miriam took Lissy back to the Reach, or all her other children would die."

247

"A curse? Come on. You know how this sounds, don't you, Dad? Like a fairy tale. And fairy tales aren't true." Even so, I still felt an extra level of cold and uneasy fear: I was cursed to die. And the Hidden shouldn't be real, but I'd still seen them.

"It might sound like a fairy tale but Connie is in hospital. They don't know what's wrong with her." Dad shook his head. "I don't trust the Hidden not to let Connie die, even though they've got Lissy. Just to punish us. They're malicious, and they never forget a thing."

I just stared at him. I didn't even know where to start.

"I knew all along, in case you've been wondering," Dad said, breaking the silence. "Your mother had guessed when she was pregnant that the baby wasn't mine." He half smiled, looking away. "Miriam went to the clinic for the three-month scan and Lissy arrived two weeks later. I wanted to leave the Reach as soon as I knew, but Miriam was too ill: it was extraordinary, Rafe. When your mother was pregnant with Lissy, she grew by the hour, like watching bread rise. She could hardly move – she was totally drained. When Lissy was born, the doctors just said she'd got the dates wrong, but the dates weren't wrong. So she told me. Of course, I believed her. I'd been initiated into the Fontevrault Group a few years earlier. I knew all about the Hidden. I knew Miles had become too obsessed with them, too, wasting his time with that idiot Virgie Creed from Hopesay. What I couldn't believe was how stupid and selfish Miles had been, opening the Gateway."

What was I supposed to say?

"I thought I'd hate the baby when it was born," Dad went on. "But I didn't."

"You didn't tell the Fontevrault Group what Lissy is, even though you're one of them."

Dad shook his head, staring out of the window at the streaming rain. "How could I have done? Lissy wasn't my child, but I loved her just the same as you and Connie. For fourteen years, I've been trying to hide Lissy's true nature. Particularly from them. The Group was founded to keep humans and the Hidden apart, to protect them and us. I swore an oath to uphold that purpose. I tried my best to keep it, but unfortunately for the Fontevrault Group, I was in love with your mother. And the rest you know." He turned to look at me. "I still don't know if keeping all this from you was the right thing. It was easy enough installing protective software on your laptop and phone, but every time you did a web search about the Hidden on a school computer, I had to delete the evidence before anyone else saw it. Miles aways said we should tell you the truth."

"But why did you swear to keep humans apart from the Hidden? Why all the secrecy? It's not like anyone would believe they even existed now, anyway."

"It's a hereditary position, Rafe. I didn't choose to be part of the Fontevrault Group. Humans and the Hidden don't mix well; we envy their immortality, the undying power of their king, they envy our biological capability to reproduce. And the fact is, the Hidden do exist. If they were to move freely in our world, sooner or later people would come to believe in the evidence of their own eyes. Think of all the fairy stories that exist in almost every single culture around the world. The seed of the idea is already there. If powerful men could harness the Hidden trait of immortality, think about all the tyrannical rulers who would still be alive today."

"Hitler. Stalin. And if the Hidden could have as many children as they wanted—"

Dad nodded. "They don't die a natural death: the hybrids would overrun us, if we hadn't already been destroyed by some crazed human despot with the power of immortality. And Lissy was just a little girl like any other. The Fontevrault Group would have insisted on testing everything about her – she would have ended up in a laboratory. Somehow we managed to keep it all secret – your mother's affair with the Swan King, and Lissy's true nature. I knew if I tried to stop you finding out about the Hidden, you'd only look harder for the truth. You're not easily fooled, Rafe. A dangerous personality trait, sometimes."

"What's going to happen to Connie now then?"

Dad didn't answer.

Her name hung between us in the silence. I don't know about Dad but I was thinking about the last time I'd seen Connie, a small humped shape on a stretcher, Mum scrambling into the ambulance, Nick running to his car.

She couldn't die. I wouldn't let her. She was only eight years old.

"The Hidden have got Lissy now," I said. "So that means this curse isn't going to happen. Connie's going to be OK, isn't she?"

I'm not going to die either. Am I?

Dad just looked at me. "The Hidden can't be trusted. They cheat. They change the rules."

So Connie could still die. I could die too. *Not if I can Christing well help it.*

I had to say something or I was going to explode. "You don't hate Mum, after everything she's done? That's just pathetic, letting her make a fool out of you."

Dad just looked away again. "No one talks about mercy any more. It's an underrated quality."

We were still a long way from the Reach, but with every mile I was closer to the ultimate betrayal. I knew what was in Dad's briefcase. Iron crosses. One for every window, one for every door.

We were going to trap Lissy in another world. For ever. I don't even know if I would have sacrificed my own life to save her.

All I knew was that I couldn't sacrifice Connie.

38

Joe

I could hear Lissy and the Hidden creature breathing, but everything was black. The little kid was crying. It was a lonely sound in the darkness. I reached out and my fingertips brushed cold wet rock.

I was glad I couldn't see. How are you meant to look anyone in the face when you know you're going to die?

When I knew I was to blame for all of this.

I didn't want to be poisoned without ever seeing my mam and dad again. I didn't want to die in some hole without trying to make it right.

"Joe," Lissy whispered. "Joe, I'm really sorry—"

"It's my fault," I said. "About Connie."

No one spoke. It just went quiet. I heard water trickling somewhere.

Then Lissy said quietly, "Joe, what are you talking about?"

I squeezed my eyes shut, even though it was dark. "It happened before you got to Hopesay. They were looking for Connie upstairs; it was time for her tea. She was in the yard, though. In the rain. Talking to that *thing*— The girl with white hair."

For a moment, there was nothing but the trickling water and the disjointed jerky rhythm of our breath.

"She did something to Connie," I said. "I'm sure she did. I should have told your mam I'd seen her, but she looked so harmless—"

"You don't know that, Joe." Lissy's voice had an edge of kindness. "And even if it's true, you couldn't have guessed how dangerous Rose is. I mean, she hardly looks it."

"He's speaking the truth," Larkspur said, quietly. "It was part of the covenant I made with your mother, Lissy. If you weren't returned, she had to pay with the lives of her other children."

"Connie," Lissy whispered. "Rose poisoned Connie – like a warning to Mum that her time was running out?"

I felt dizzy. This was my fault. "So Rose used Connie as insurance. To make sure Miriam didn't try and get out of the deal?"

"Yes," Larkspur said, simply. "Your brother's life is forfeit, too, Lissy."

The silence went on and on.

So I had pretty much put Connie in hospital myself by not speaking up when I should have. If Miriam had known, if she'd seen Rose, maybe there would have been time to negotiate. But I'd said nothing, and instead Connie was taken away in an ambulance.

We didn't even know if she was still alive.

I wished I could die of that filthy sickness there and then. Just for it all to be over. I squeezed shut my eyes in the darkness and all I could see was Connie crouching by that puddle, turning to smile at me as Rose watched, her stripey t-shirt and red shorts, just a little kid. She'd trusted me.

"Larkspur," Lissy said, "apart from paying with Rafe and Connie's lives, is there any other way out of the bargain my mother made with you?"

"As I told your mother, the only other price I can accept is the life of a Hidden, willingly given."

Silence.

"You made the bargain," I said. "Why can't you break it? Why not just say you've changed your mind, that Lissy can go back to her mam for free, without anything bad happening to Connie or Rafe?"

"Because I spoke the words. I made the pact. There is power in a Hidden promise. Once made, the bargain exists for all time. One cannot just be unmade."

"That's just bloody stupid!" I hissed.

The Hidden sighed. "I cannot expect you to understand, but believe me."

"It's true," the little girl, Philippa de Conway, said. "Their bargains are unbreakable. They're so cunning, you see. Men make pacts with the Hidden and think the Hidden have cheated them. But it's only because they haven't thought carefully enough about the words. If Larkspur made the pact with your mother, she won't be able to break it. He will make it impossible for her to cheat."

"I'll have to stay, then," Lissy whispered. "I'll stay with the Swan King if he makes Connie better, if Rafe doesn't die too."

"Look," I said. "Can't you see that the Swan King tricked *you*, anyway, Lissy? What's the point in him saving Connie's life if everyone's going to be killed by this plague? She's going to die anyway."

And Rafe: Lissy had no idea he was gone. I didn't know where to start. I couldn't stop thinking about that letter: David Creed shot dead in 1917 just for knowing about this.

Rafe's probably already dead, I told myself. *Just get used to the idea. There's no way he could have escaped.*

"The boy is right," the little girl said. "It *was* a trick."

"No," Lissy said. "I'm not going to let him do it. We're going to get out. All of us. And we're going to *stop* him. We can steal back my blood, escape from here and then if the Swan King has the power to save Connie that must mean *you* could, Larkspur."

The Hidden just sighed. "I have the skill, but I've told you: a bargain woven tightly enough cannot be broken."

"What, we're just going to let Connie and her brother die, or Lissy has to stay down here in this dump for the rest of all time?" I couldn't keep the sarcasm out of my voice. "It doesn't seem very likely that one of you lot would give up the whole of eternity."

"We've got to try *something*. We can't let the Swan King do this!" Lissy hissed. "There must be a way around it."

"Right. And how are we meant to escape? A, we can't see. B, this place is heaving with freakish alien creatures who aren't exactly on our side." There didn't seem much point saying what I really thought, which was just *I may as well sit here and wait for it.*

"I really am sorry, Joe," Lissy whispered. "You should never have been involved in this."

"I'm the one who's sorry. I should have told your mam about Rose."

No one argued with me. And now Connie was going to die unless Lissy returned to the Swan King, or one of the Hidden gave up their life without a fight. Either way, whichever way you looked at the deal, either Lissy or Rafe and Connie were going to lose.

39

Miriam

I'm writing this in the last few hours of Connie's life. It's nearly midnight. Lissy will be gone by now, my Lissy. I never even said goodbye. I never explained. Even so, they're going to kill Connie. Is the Swan King punishing me for choosing Adam instead of him? Or even doing this just for fun? I wouldn't put that past him.

When I reach out and hold Connie's hand it still feels so warm and alive. I want more than anything to climb into the bed and lie beside her as I did those endless nights when she was a tiny baby, and we weren't quite two separate people yet. I'm afraid to disturb the drip line coming out of her hand; I don't want to hurt her, so all I can do is hold her hand. My little girl.

Her condition is deteriorating. She's still not responding. The consultants and nurses were so kind, so expert at dispensing the cold, bald truth, using my first name as if we were old friends. It won't be long now, Miriam.

The Hidden cheated me. Larkspur or his father, I'll never know which. They demanded Connie and Rafe if I didn't bring them Lissy. Well, they've got Lissy. They'll have her by now.

I never even got to tell her I'm sorry.

The Hidden have got what they wanted, but Connie's not going to live through the night. God knows what's going to happen to Rafe—

My little girl.

I don't want to say goodbye. Someone told me that hearing is the last sense to go before you die. I don't want her to be frightened, but I want her to know I'm here.

I'm going to put down my pen now, to hold Connie's hand, and hope she knows it's me.

They cheated me.

And where is Rafe?

All my children will soon be gone. The ultimate punishment for a bad mother.

I'm sorry, Lissy.

40

Lissy

I turned to Larkspur, a patch of deeper darkness at my side. My eyes were adjusting, getting used to the black; I was starting to make out shapes, outlines.

"Are you really going to let your father do this, Larkspur? He banished you for fourteen years. He's thrown you down here with us. He treats you worse than a slave. You don't owe him anything. Help us escape. We can stop him. There has to be a way."

"Stop it!" Joe said. "This is all just stupid. Shut up, Lissy – there's nothing we can do—"

"Larkspur!" I found his hand in the darkness, gripped it with mine. *"Please."*

He spoke so quietly I could hardly hear. "You don't understand. He's my father. I've betrayed him so many times already."

Larkspur pulled his hand away.

"What's he going to do to *you* anyway?" Joe shouted at him. "It's not like he can kill you, is it? You're the one who took Lissy – it's your fault we're all here in the first place."

"Shut up," I hissed. "No one's going to escape if you bring all the Hidden running back here, are they?"

"What difference does it make?" Joe snapped.

"There are things worse than death," Larkspur said, simply.

"Great," said Joe, sarcastically. "Sorry I won't be able to share them with you."

"In all these many years," Tippy said, "I never thought you were a coward, Larkspur. Help us leave this place. I want to see the sky again."

The cave lit up around us as Larkspur balanced a ball of light on the palm of one hand. There *was* a way out. A dark space in the glistening wet rock face. A tunnel. We'd work the rest out later. The Swan King was not going to hurt Connie any more.

I refuse to let it happen.

But deep down I was terrified that we'd fail to cheat the bargain. Connie and Rafe would both die. Because of me, no matter how much Joe blamed himself.

"Right," said Joe, "and how many of them are waiting to catch us?"

We couldn't just walk out.

"It's time, Larkspur," Tippy whispered. "I know it's time."

There was just silence. Larkspur reached out and rested a hand on Tippy's shoulder.

Tippy took his hand in hers. "It has been long enough. Please, Larkspur."

"I don't understand," I said. "What are you two talking about?"

"I'll do it," Larkspur said. "I will fight him." He stood up with all the loose, easy grace of a cat. "But you must come, Lissy. You alone."

"I can't," I whispered. "What do you mean? We can't just walk out of here. The Swan King must have this place guarded—"

"But he won't expect you to try escaping," Tippy said. "Your brother and sister are like hostages. They're cursed."

Larkspur knelt down to her height and they hugged, holding each other tight.

"I can't do this," he said, quietly. "I can't bear it."

"You must," she said. "It's the only way. Where shall we meet?"

"The Western Caverns. There's a way out." Larkspur sighed. "Tippy—"

"Go! There is scarcely time to waste!"

"No way," Joe said. "Lissy, come on — that lunatic's not just going to let you wander away. What are you going to do, just *ask* him for the blood? Come on. Let's think this through properly—"

"You don't have to walk," Larkspur told me. "You know the truth, Lissy. It's the royal gift of the Hidden, and you have it."

No, I thought. *You can't mean that. Not the dream. Not that—*

He held out his hand and I took it.

"Yes," Larkspur said. "Yes."

For the first time ever, his fingers felt warm in mine. Hot, even. And the heat spread across my skin, up my arms. A searing pain shot between my shoulders and I cried out.

"Hush!" Larkspur said, gripping my hand. "Look at me, Lissy."

"It hurts—" I gasped. "Larkspur, stop it – this really, really hurts, *please*—"

"You can do this, Lissy," he whispered. "You know it's true. You've dreamt of it so many times."

All I could hear was Joe, just *Oh, my God, oh, my God,* over and over again, and when I looked into Larkspur's eyes all I saw was tumbling feathers reflected. And there were feathers in the cave, feathers swirling everywhere.

Larkspur and I were no longer holding hands. I had no hand to hold.

My whole body shrieked in agony I'd never thought possible.

I was thrown through the air by a force I couldn't see; I was lifted, rising, rising, rising.

I flew. The Swan King's daughter.

In my mind, I heard Larkspur's voice, full of laughter, joy and red-hot rage against his father. *My sister, the hawk. Fly with me.*

And so I flew; and so the dream was true.

41

Lissy

We soared through the dark; cold dank air slid over my wings. My dream was real at last. I was flying. A hawk. I was filled with a deep tearing hunger, I couldn't stand this blackness: there was no prey to be had. I followed Larkspur, my hawk-brother, matching the shadow of his wing-beats with my own.

I had changed.

I was something else.

And even now, the thrill of it swept me forward faster and faster.

We were going to get out of this place, Tippy too – she could come and live with us. It would be hard knowing that all her family were dead, but she'd have the chance to grow up like a real girl, have friends to play with, maybe Connie—

Stop. Don't think about it. We can't get this wrong. We can't.

The White Hall. I heard Larkspur in my mind. *They will be feasting but it will still be guarded. Take care.*

The tunnels were lit now and I watched the rise and fall of his wings; my eyes were so sharp that I could make out every grain of soil in the earthen walls. A glossy black beetle inching along below made me thirsty for blood again but I fought it away, followed Larkspur as he banked off to the left and swept into a side-tunnel.

I saw the Hidden guards turn after us, their grimy beautiful faces shadowed by black hoods.

I heard one call out: "He has come, Lord – the traitor!"

The White Hall opened out before us, blinding and bright, full of Hidden. Hundreds of them. They lounged in groups like beautiful ragged cats; most sat around a fire flickering by the black pool, passing cups from one to the other; they played pipes, they played lyres. Someone was singing, and all fell silent when they saw us, tarnished rings glittering on long fingers, ragged silk, cloth-of-gold stained with aeons of woodsmoke and the darkened blood of their prey. The trees were green, the waters of the pool so flat and dark against the glittering quartz.

Stay high. I heard Larkspur in my mind again, and in a burst of tawny hawk feathers that turned to ivy leaves as they fell, he took his own form again, landing in a crouch right by the fire.

I banked and hovered, looking down, my wings knew what to do; once again I wanted to shout out with the thrill of it. The Swan King got to his feet, letting a glass cup fall from his hand. It shattered against the white rock.

"You will have to try better than that if you want to confine me." Larkspur's voice rang out, harsh and mocking now rather than anguished and afraid. "No guard by the cave but my fear of you, *Father?* You show me no respect."

The Swan King stepped forward, wiping dark liquid from

his mouth. "I will bind you in rock for a thousand years."

Every eye in the room was fixed on the two of them. The Hidden were silent, horror etched on their filthy faces.

"So try," Larkspur said.

And I saw it. The silver bowl resting in a crevice high above the water, a dark wrinkle in the rock face.

My blood.

I had one chance. I flew.

Whirling faster than a cracked whip, the Swan King turned from Larkspur to me.

He held out one hand and I felt the heat of his eyes on me till I burned from the inside out; screaming in agony I fell hard to the floor.

"You are only just learning your true strength, daughter. Know that I will always better it." And he laughed.

I couldn't escape the pain; it was everywhere. I tried to shut my eyes but I couldn't even do that. The Swan King had control of me. He had changed my shape. My fingertips shook with agony, scraping helpless at the cold hard ground.

My one chance to save Connie and it was gone, unreachable as the bowl of blood high above my head.

I heard Larkspur's voice in my mind. *You have mortal powers he can only dream of; mercy, compassion, Lissy—*

He might have control of my body but the Swan King couldn't stop me loving my little sister. I could see her in my mind's eye, asleep at Hopesay Reach in her pink and white striped pyjamas, already poisoned by Rose. I remembered Mum and Dad bringing her home from the hospital; I was six and I loved Connie so much the moment I saw her wrapped in a white blanket, her small red face, the thatch of black hair that fell out and grew back golden, her tiny soft fingernails. Dad smiling, looking strangely fragile, saying, *Do you want to hold her, Tinkerbell?*

I'll do anything to save you, Connie, anything—

The pain drew back like a wave on a beach.

I won't let them hurt you any more—

And the pain came rushing back with the force of a tsunami; but this time I was riding it, I was in control. The air thickened, swirling with green leaves and white feathers.

I flew.

I looked down, glimpsing frozen shocked faces looking up at me as the Hidden watched. For once they weren't calm. Now they cared. Now they were afraid.

Of me.

The Swan King's cry of rage filled the White Hall.

Higher. Higher. I could see the bowl, dull grey silver, standing out against the white quartz. The entire world, wiped out with my blood. I had to reach it. There was no choice.

I flew at the bowl, knocking it from the ledge with the outstretched tip of a wing, just had time to see a glossy red smear in the bottom before the silver bowl fell, and fell, and fell.

Time stopped.

The bowl spun.

The Swan King turned away from Larkspur as the bowl tumbled, his face bright with rage.

Closer to the water.

Closer. Milliseconds dripped past like centuries.

"Stop." The Swan King held out his hand and just before the bowl hit the water it hung in the air, suspended.

He was too late. One last drop of blood slid out and slipped into the pool, lost for ever.

We had done it.

The Swan King's voice filled my mind: *I will empty your body of every last drop—*

I heard Larkspur again – *NOW, LISSY, NOW* – and that burning agony tore through my body again; I hit the ground running in the body I'd grown up in. He reached back and grabbed my hand.

"Run!"

We tore through the tunnel, twisting, turning, ducking stalactites, slipping on the wet rock beneath our feet.

"This is it," Larkspur said, breathing hard. It was the first time I'd seen anything cost him physical effort. I couldn't seem to get enough air into my lungs; I buckled down on the floor, half choking. "Come on, I know it's hard but there's no time, we must go—"

He pulled me upright and I forced myself to run. I could smell fresh air. New rain. Wet earth. The darkness had lifted a little. Moonlight puddled in. Real moonlight.

"Lissy!" I heard Joe calling. "Lissy, *quick!*"

Larkspur and I ran towards the moonlight, a tunnel leading up and out. It was so quiet; all I could hear was our breathing and wind rustling through the branches of trees in the world above.

Joe and Tippy were waiting at the tunnel's end, crouching on the ground, breathing hard; they must have got here just seconds before us. Clean woodland air filled my lungs and tears of relief stung my face.

Joe stood up. "We thought we'd better wait."

"We did it!" I said. "I spilled my blood into the water. He can't use it any more."

"Then let's get out of here before he decides to come after you and take the rest."

Tippy was staring out at the moon, just visible between tangled branches.

Larkspur crouched down beside her and for a moment they held each other, her head buried in his shoulder, his hand in her hair.

"Come on!" Joe hissed at me. "What are they doing? We haven't got time—"

"Go no further."

I turned, my whole body alive with panic.

Rose.

She stepped closer, so ancient and beautiful. A killer.

She ignored Larkspur and Tippy, who still clung to one another. She ignored Joe.

She came to me.

"Don't you remember your bargain with my brother, Melisende? It is most unwise to break a pact with the Hidden, you know." Rose ran one finger down the side of my face. "You gave your blood for a life, Lissy."

I'd failed. Connie was going to die after all.

Rose smiled. "Now you have taken your blood away, and my brother cannot brew his plague. He can't take the revenge he deserves. The life is forfeit."

Larkspur stood up, holding Tippy's hand.

"You forget, Rose," Larkspur said, "there was a caveat to my agreement with Miriam. She agreed to pay for Lissy's life with another as dear. Or the life of a Hidden willingly given. As you well know."

Rose just shrugged and smiled. "Indeed. Well, it is a great shame about that pretty little girl, but we always knew Miriam would not hold to her word unless we forced her hand. She is a mortal, after all, and they do cheat. Miriam tried to cheat, and now you have cheated, Lissy. The child's life is forfeit, but you will stay with us for all time. My brother will teach you how to pay for your dishonesty. You shall be with us, Lissy, and watch them all die, every last man, woman and child." Rose laughed. "Oh, please don't tell me you were hoping one of the Hidden would give up eternity to save your sweet little sister?"

"Connie's life is not forfeit," Tippy said, "blood for blood, a life for a life. I have been with the Hidden more years than I know how to count and I am still a girl. Your magic is in my blood. I am like you, Rose. I was Hidden." She turned to Larkspur. "Come with me." She looked at me. "Hold my hand, Lissy."

And I knew. I knew what she was doing.

"No," hissed Rose. "You would not. My child. My little child."

"She was never yours!" I said. "You stole her. You never looked after her properly. She's lived in agony – you didn't even try to comfort her."

"You will crumble to dust, Philippa de Conway!" Rose

shouted. "Your flesh will melt from your bones the moment your feet touch the earth."

She started towards us, one hand raised, a flat white palm, and in a moment that stretched on and on, Joe snatched something out of his pocket and threw it at her.

A knife.

It spun in the air for ever.

The knife hit Rose in the face, right between her eyes, breaking the skin. A shriek rang out as she fell that I knew I would hear till my last day on earth, ringing in my dreams no matter if I lived a million years.

Her body slumped forwards.

"What have I done?" Joe looked down at his hands as if they belonged to someone else. "All I did was throw it, I didn't—"

I could hardly breathe. "You killed her. She's dead."

"You saved us," Larkspur said, grim. "But he will avenge her. He will make you pay. He will make us all pay."

"Come with me!" Tippy shouted, and started running. We couldn't let her do it alone.

I took Tippy's left hand, Larkspur grabbed her right, shoving Joe out of the tunnel before us and we ran out into the moonlight, out into the night, the echo of Rose's dying scream fading behind us.

And as we ran Tippy's face was wet with tears and she laughed. "Mammy!" she called.

She'd known all along she could never go home.

I squeezed her warm hand, unable to stop myself crying because she was so brave.

My fingers closed tight around nothing.

Tippy didn't crumble to dust. She didn't become some nightmarish rotten corpse.

It was only that where Tippy had been, she was there no longer, only a thousand white feathers tumbling in the darkness. When the feathers landed on the dead leaves at our feet, pearl-white flowers opened, unfurling from their buds as we watched, petals spreading as cold stars hung in the blackness above.

42

Lissy

Larkspur dropped to his knees in the flowers that sprang open where Tippy had been.

She had given herself to save Connie and Rafe. I was free. No longer the Swan King's weapon. For now.

I stood with tears pouring down my face, unable to move, to comprehend the enormity of what Tippy had done.

Joe turned to me. "We've come out in the woods above the Reach. I can see the lights from here – look, just through those trees."

"How can you say that?" I gasped, sobbing. "Tippy just, she just—"

"I know!" Joe shouted. His hands were shaking, he was stammering. "But if we don't get out of here she'll have done it for nothing. Do you really think that *thing* is just going to let us go? I killed one of them. I *killed* her. Come on, Lissy! He'll be after you, the Swan King. He'll want more of your blood. He's not just going to give up because we've managed to get out."

Further down the hill, half hidden by trees, the kitchen window glowed yellow, bright in the darkness.

"Look," Joe went on, "if Larkspur can help your sister then you've got to get to the hospital *now*. You can do it – how you did before, in the cave." He half laughed. "Fly, Lissy. You and him. I'll be all right here, don't worry about me."

I turned to Larkspur, but he was still kneeling. He turned, his face wet with tears. "I must go alone. You won't have the strength to fly again so soon, Lissy. Not after what you did in the cave."

"Alone?" I said. "But Connie— She's my little sister. I need to go. In case the Swan King gets there first."

If my father got there first, before Larkspur had the chance to heal Connie, what would I do? I was shaking with panic. If I went with the Swan King to save Connie's life, he'd have my blood. *Every last drop.*

And then everyone would die.

Joe just shoved his hand into his jeans pocket and pulled out a set of car keys.

Rafe's keys.

"Rafe's not at the hospital?" I asked. I didn't like the look on Joe's face. Guilty. As if there was something else he didn't want to tell me. "Joe, where's Rafe? Why have you got his car keys?"

Joe just stood there. "Lissy, he's gone. The Fontevrault have got him."

"Who? What are you talking about?"

But Larkspur just grabbed my arm. "Hurry, if you want to save her."

We had no time, but we had to try.

43

Lissy

Joe slammed on the brakes and swerved into a bus stop opposite the entry to the Accident and Emergency department.

I screamed.

"I'm sorry, all right?" Joe yelled at me. "It's not like I've had lessons, is it?"

I couldn't argue with that.

The Fontevrault. Rafe? I didn't understand. All I knew was that my brother had gone.

We tumbled out of the car, just leaving the doors hanging wide open, running towards the entrance.

"Why's it dark?" I asked, panicking. "There aren't any lights on inside—"

"He's here," Larkspur said, quietly.

"Where is she?" Joe demanded, turning the torch on his phone at a colour coded map of the hospital. "Which ward?"

I thought back to Mum's text. "C3 or D3, I can't remember—"

Rafe. My brother. *He's gone*—

"Lissy—" Larkspur hissed. *"The Swan King is here."*

Tears streamed down my face. "I know, I know!" I stood at Joe's side, trying to make sense of the map key, a block of bright colours. The letters jumbled before my eyes, making no sense.

"D3 is Geriatric," Joe said, quickly. "That's old people. It must be C3 – here it is, Intensive Care. We've got to go left after Reception."

We ran.

44

Joe

We ran past bodies: doctors and nurses just lying flat out on the floor, a patient in a tartan dressing gown crumpled by a drinks machine. They were still breathing, or looked like it anyway. It was as if everyone had just fallen completely asleep where they stood, like all the people in Sleeping Beauty's castle.

"He's done this," Larkspur said, looking back at us. He was the faster runner. "My father. So no one can help us or hinder him."

Great. Just great.

I was hard pushed to keep up with Lissy and Larkspur but I did, driven on by sheer panic, chest tearing, legs burning. Bodies lay everywhere, littering the hospital corridors: a nurse with a clipboard, a patient slumped in a wheelchair by the lift. Everyone was – what – asleep? Half dead? In some kind of coma?

We had no back-up. Nothing. It was just going to be us and the Swan King.

And Connie.

"It's here!" Lissy shouted. "She's in here!"

Connie had been put in a private room. Not a good sign even if your life wasn't in the hands of a freakish monster king.

We ran and stopped, all except for Larkspur, who just walked over to the bed where Connie lay, a small heap beneath the blankets.

My dad was lying on the floor, collapsed beside Miriam's chair. She'd slumped over Connie's bed, still holding her hand. Two shattered mugs lay on the floor beside Dad in a puddle of still-steaming tea.

I knelt down at his side. "Dad!" I hissed, shaking him. "Dad, what's wrong?"

He just lay there, in some deep dark sleep.

"What's going on?" Lissy said to Larkspur. "What's wrong with them?"

I watched Dad's chest rise and fall. His eyelids shivered, like he was dreaming. "They're still breathing," I said.

"My father did this to them," Larkspur said again. "A sleeping song."

"To make sure we've no help," I said, and Larkspur just nodded, like this was the most ordinary thing in the world, not a hospital full of people in an enchanted stupor like Sleeping bloody Beauty.

He turned back to Connie. "She looks so innocent. I didn't think of that when I cursed her."

You might have that on your conscience, I thought, *but I'm a murderer.* I'd killed Rose, put an end to a life that had lasted more than a thousand years. It was my fault Connie had come to hospital in the first place. I'd stood in the yard and *watched* her with Rose. I should have done something.

Larkspur gently lifted the oxygen mask from Connie's face.

"No!" Lissy shrieked.

I stood, completely frozen and shocked.

He wasn't going to heal her after all—

He was still loyal to the Swan King. Larkspur had betrayed us.

Lissy ran to his side, but Larkspur just held out his hands, letting a white flower fall onto the pillow.

"Larkspur, *don't*!" Lissy cried.

"Hush," he said.

And Connie stirred. Turned one way, then the other. She sat up, looking around the dark room, not at all afraid.

"Lissy?" she said, looking down at Miriam slumped next to her. "Lissy? Where are we? What's wrong with Mum? Why's Nick lying on the floor?" She stared at Larkspur, then at Lissy. "Who's *that*? Lissy, he looks just like *you*—"

And just as Lissy reached out to hug Connie, before I even had time to work out if Larkspur was really on our side or not, the air filled with whirling feathers.

45

Lissy

The feathers turned to dead leaves as I watched, torn away by a wind that roared wild and loud, then faded to nothing just as suddenly as it had come.

Holding onto me, Connie screamed.

My father stepped out of the darkness, white cloak trailing behind, leaves caught in his black hair. My real father.

The room filled with silver light.

He knelt down at Mum's side. He reached out and touched her hair, her face.

"What's he doing?" Connie gasped. "Lissy, why is Mummy just lying here like this?"

It was as if the Swan King hadn't even noticed us.

He just crouched at Mum's side, watching her. "How they fade," he whispered. "She was so beautiful, and the years have gone in a heartbeat."

He stood up, and Larkspur faced him. Joe and I stood in silence, watching.

"You betrayed me," the Swan King said. "Time and again, Larkspur, time and again. Can't you see they must all go?"

"The mortals betrayed you, too – and what they did to

my mother was unforgivable. But give them another chance," Larkspur said. "Please."

The King smiled and nodded at Connie. "A pretty child," he said. "What a shame."

"Leave her alone!" My voice shook. "Tippy gave her life in exchange. It was fairly won."

"Not fairly won," the Swan King said; "only admirably cheated." He looked from me to Larkspur. "My sister would have had me punish you both for eternity, but I find myself pleased with your wit." He turned to Joe. "And as it is, you killed her. An act of bravery or stupidity; I can't choose which."

"I know I'm meant to be sorry," Joe said. "But I was scared."

"You will pay the price for it, oh, don't worry," the Swan King said. "Come home with me, Lissy. The fourteen years have passed, Larkspur. As well you know."

"Tippy gave her life!" Larkspur cried.

The Swan King only shrugged. "You cheated *me,* all those years ago, with your disobedience. Lissy is the price." He held out one hand. "Come with me, my Lissy. I can't bear to watch you fade, too, as your mother has done."

"Lissy," Connie said. "Don't go away. What's the matter with Mum and Nick?"

"Don't be an idiot!" Joe hissed.

But I was the price. Tippy's sacrifice had saved Connie and Rafe, but the Swan King still wanted me. He always would. His blood ran in my veins.

I had no choice.

I stood up, and even as I took the hand of the Swan King I felt the unbearable stretch across my back as my hawk-wings unfolded and I was no longer a girl. I was Hidden.

The world filled with feathers, and all light was gone.

46

Rafe

Dad, Miles and I climbed out of the car, our feet crunching in the gravel on the drive.

The Reach waited, alone in the moonlight, surrounded by trees. The windows glittered. Wind shifted leaves and branches, rustling, whispering. The lake shone like a sheet of foil: the Gateway.

"Why don't we just run?" I said quietly to Dad, leaning on my crutch. "Mum's car's still here. We'd be lost in the lanes before they even knew we'd gone."

If we ran, the three of us, the Gateway would still be open. We'd have time to think of a way to get Lissy home without me or Connie dying, cursed.

"The Fontevrault will know," Dad said, grimly. "They'll find us."

We had to do it. We had to trap Lissy beyond the Gateway.

Miles just stood, looking up at the house. Then he turned to Dad, and said, "I'm sorry, Adam. I started all this. I can't be without her. I can't be without Rose. I've waited long enough already."

"Don't do anything stupid, Miles," Dad said. "You know

what'll happen. You'll lose track of the years. After that, you'll never be able to come home."

"There's nothing here for me," Miles said, simply. He turned and started walking towards the lake.

I moved to follow him but Dad put a hand on my arm. "Just let him go. He's not worth it."

We watched, and probably the guys in the car watched, too, from behind their blacked-out windows.

Miles walked across the lawn, past the yew tree, right to the overgrown shore of the lake. He parted a mess of reeds and cow parsley. The water must've been in his shoes by now, but he didn't make a sound. He just carried on walking, deeper, deeper, up to the waist. Now only his head and shoulders were still above the water. Deeper.

"Miles, you idiot," Dad said, softly, as Miles's head went under. The last Gateward, gone.

He disappeared without a sound. He'd gone through the Gateway. Now we had to close it. Now he could never come back, and neither could Lissy.

Dad just turned and started walking towards the house with his bag of iron crosses. If we protected every window, every door of the Reach, the Hidden couldn't pass. Once more, the Reach would be sealed, bound by ancient prayers locking forces with iron. Words of strength, of power. The Hidden would be trapped again.

Lissy was down there somewhere. My sister. I should have known all along what she was. Maybe I did, but couldn't admit it to myself—

We were going to trap her with them. For ever.

"Rafe," Dad said. "Come on."

I couldn't believe we were doing this: that we were actually going to imprison Lissy somewhere beneath that glittering lake till the end of time. There had to be another way.

We both swung round as another car turned in at the driveway. Mum's. Whoever was driving stopped suddenly, then stalled. Badly.

"Who's that?" Dad demanded. "Who else knows we're here?" He glanced towards the black SUV where the Fontevrault Group's heavies waited for any trouble, ready in case Dad and I needed any encouragement to do what the Fontevrault had asked of us.

For the sake of the human race. It's a matter of survival—

I shook my head. I couldn't believe it. The door of Mum's car flew open and Joe stumbled out. I couldn't help smiling, even through my despair. Against all the odds, he'd survived.

"Rafe." He just stood there, staring at me. "You're all right. I thought you were dead. Listen—"

"Bad luck, mate," I said. "This is my dad. You've arrived just in time to give us a hand."

Dad barely even glanced at Joe. I wondered what he thought of Nick. "Come on." He jerked his head at the Fontevrault car. "I don't want you in any more danger, Rafe. It's time to close the Gateway."

"You can't!" Joe hissed. "The Swan King and Lissy are here."

"This is it!" I said. "Dad, we can shut the Gateway and trap them on *this* side! Surely we can deal with just one of the Hidden, the Swan King on his own without any back-up.

284

We can kill him. Joe, have you still got my knife?"

"No!" Joe was clearly panicking – the first time I'd seen him really do that since all this mess had begun. "Listen, please just listen: I don't know what to do. The Swan King is making a disease – a sickness – from Lissy's blood. He cut her. He'll do it again. It'll spread everywhere, this immortal virus that'll never die out. In days, he told us. Days. We'll all be dead." Joe stared at us. "Even if you killed him, you might not be quick enough. He might spread the disease first."

Dad and I glanced at each other. I couldn't believe what we'd almost done, the mistake Joe had only just stopped us making. Trapping the Swan King on the *wrong* side of the Gateway with an immortal pandemic.

"This changes things." Dad reached for his phone, but just as his hand moved, a wild, vicious wind blew up from nowhere, stirring the shining waters of the lake.

"He's coming," Joe said. Instinctively, we all moved closer together, Dad and Joe and I – like cornered prey. And the air filled with whirling dead leaves, even though it was only May, and feathers, so many feathers, white and brown, all twisting and turning, whipped up by that godawful wind.

And they came.

Lissy and her father the Swan King, immensely tall, his hair blacker than tar, a gold band glittering at his throat. He looked scarcely older than her, but he was her real father. It was impossible. But there they were, stepping out from nowhere into the long grass, just like Larkspur had done the first time I'd seen him. Lissy's hair had come down and was torn about in the wind, wild and red. All I could see was how

285

like the Swan King she was, trying and failing to pinpoint the moment I'd guessed the truth. How like her father she was. Those subtle differences that marked her out as alien, now I knew what to look for. Inhuman, a monster. My sister. I'd failed to save her again.

"Lissy!" I shouted, and she turned to face us. The Swan King took hold of her arm, watching us with calm amusement.

"Don't take her!" Dad's face blazed with hatred, but his expression changed the minute he focused on Lissy. "Oh, God, don't take her."

They hadn't even spoken much since the thing with Elena, a year ago now.

Lissy tried to pull away but the Swan King held onto her with no obvious effort.

I heard her cry out for Dad, shouting, "*I'm sorry, I'm sorry,*" but she turned with the Swan King. She walked with him to the water.

"Lissy!" Dad yelled, again and again. So did I. So did Joe.

We ran to the lake, all three of us, ankle deep in water. Dad would have gone in after her if we hadn't held onto him. I knew now what had really happened to Philippa de Conway's father. He wasn't a murderer in hiding. He'd gone through the Gateway to find her and had never come back.

It was Joe who finally stopped it all. "The plague," he shouted. "We've got to close the Gateway *now* before he releases it. This is our only chance of stopping him."

Dad dropped to his knees in the water. "Lissy," he said, quietly. "Oh, Lissy."

Joe and I turned to look back at the Reach. It watched

us quietly from among the trees, an ancient house: a place older than recorded history. So dangerous.

And in that moment, Joe whipped away and I realized he'd been trying to put me off guard. He ran into the water. He was going after Lissy.

"DAD!" I yelled, dragging at his arm. "Stop him. He's just a kid. He doesn't know what he's doing. He's trying to go after her."

Dad swore and struggled to his feet, but I was the one who caught Joe. Murder on my destroyed leg, dragging it along like that, agony every time my foot touched the soft mud beneath the water, sucked down, horrifying having to yank it out each time. But I caught him. The stupid, idiotic little fool.

Joe turned on me, like I'd known he would, shoving me away from him, spitting in my face, but Dad was there too by that point. Together we wrestled him to the water's edge, where he sat in the mud.

"Why did you do that?" he yelled. "Why did you do that to me? It was my choice, not yours."

"We've got to close the Gateway." Dad sounded exhausted. There were pale tracks in the grime on his face. He'd been crying, letting her go, watching her go, without even having made things up between them. I think that was worse than anything. My own father in a state like that. He turned to Joe, then to me. "We've got no choice, Rafe."

It was time to imprison Lissy.

Joe

Three days later

So she's gone.

Lissy, down in that underground nightmare. Miles too, so Rafe and his dad say. I wonder how she's being treated. If she's kept as a prisoner in one of those miserable caves, or sitting at the Swan King's side in that frozen white chamber.

Bastards. They wouldn't let me go after her. Now there's no one to make sure she's all right, see she's treated OK. I would've done that for her. For Lissy, and don't ask me why but I would have. That's all.

Connie is home from hospital, spending most of her time lying on the sofa covered with a duvet, resting her head in Miriam's lap. The rest of us move about the house like ghosts, unable to leave the last place Lissy was.

It's like we're closer to her here than we could ever be anywhere else. So we've stayed.

Miriam didn't even speak to anyone except Connie till tonight. She found Lissy's top in the tumble dryer, and at last she cried till Adam opened a bottle of wine, then another. Even Dad joined in, and he's not normally a big drinker.

They all got pissed, like it was letting off steam, all finally talking about what had happened. The Hidden. Lissy.

I couldn't say a word.

"I knew she'd been abducted," Dad kept saying, like a stuck record, *"But I never expected this."*

"How could you have?" Miriam said, and laughed. And then she just cried, on and on.

It was bad. I got up and left.

I sat on my bed, staring at the iron crosses nailed haphazardly above the window, beside the door. School started a few days ago but no one's mentioned going home.

What if the Hidden find a way of lifting the protection from their side? We've all checked every opening in the house, time and time again, to the point of obsession. *But what if they find a way? What if they get in, with the plague?*

What if all that stuff about old prayers combining with the iron was just a load of crap? Maybe we weren't protected from the Hidden at all. And the Fontevrault. They'd be back for Adam, surely? Rafe and Connie's dad. He was part of the Fontevrault, and he'd betrayed them, hiding Lissy all those years as part of his own family. A human girl with Hidden blood. A hybrid. The Fontevrault's worst nightmare. They'd be back for Adam all right. The question was when. Any day. Any how.

The door swung open, and I couldn't help jumping. It was Rafe. Still limping.

He sat down on my bed, and for a few moments neither of us spoke. Too much had happened. We'd witnessed it all.

"We've got to find a way of getting her out of there," I said at last.

But Rafe just shook his head. "Not you," he said. "You need to back off. Forget about all this. Look what happened to Miles. It's like a disease. You're infected."

"Piss off," I said. I'm not scared of him any more. Well, maybe a bit. He's still a mad bastard. Unpredictable and potentially violent, despite looking like butter wouldn't melt. "I don't know what you're talking about."

Rafe just sighed. "Don't give me that. You can't stop thinking about her. I saw. I saw the way you looked at her at the lake. You hardly know each other and you followed Lissy down into the Halls of the Hidden, you'd have followed her again if me and my dad hadn't stopped you."

"Right. I was running away from the Fontevrault the first time, in case you'd forgotten."

He shook his head. "But not the second time, Joe. Don't deny it. You'll make it worse for yourself. I know what they're like, the Hidden. How people become obsessed by them. That's what you're like with Lissy. You'd do anything for her, wouldn't you?"

I just stared out of the window at the dark water, ashamed by how obvious it was. Lissy was somewhere on the other side. I just couldn't reach her.

"Forget about my sister, Joe," Rafe said. "Even if she ever came back, she'd still be young when you were old and weak and dying. You can't have her. Walk away. Just walk away, like Miles should have done."

I still didn't speak and after a while, Rafe left. I heard him shut the door, a quiet click.

So I didn't tell Rafe, not about Larkspur. *There's still one Hidden left on our side of the fence, mate.*

The question I keep asking myself is what he will do next.

Larkspur

I sit down to rest on a wall already hot with the sun's heat, drawing the hooded blue robe closer around my body. The city sprawls out before me, a jumble of white rooftops and shadowed alleyways. I watch the people move about, smaller than insects from up here. They pulse with life, loving, laughing, weeping then dying: all so fast. The waste they cast aside heaps against the city wall, a stinking tide of human rubbish that spreads out behind me, rotting food, broken trinkets, they gather so much about them and in the end it is all discarded.

White gulls swoop and soar above the rubbish, scavenging.

Each time one gull veers from the flock my heart clenches like a fist, because I know my father will come; he will find me eventually. Somehow he will open the Gateway, or find another less well protected. There are others. Of course there are, all bound in iron or otherwise sealed somehow, long ago.

The Reach is bound by iron. Again. Lissy is not like me, or my poor mother, her throat cut by a mortal knife, or even Rose. Lissy can touch iron. My father will find a way. She'll lift the protection. When he wants something, he gets it, just like Lissy.

He'll find a way of opening the Gateway, of lifting those

iron-bound age-old prayers and curses left there by those poor church-men grieving for Tippy and her father.

The mortals have not yet started to die. I have been waiting; I have seen them suffer great plagues before now: their dead piled up in the streets, the nights thick with fear and their cries of mourning.

But that has not yet happened. Still they all seem to live and die at their usual pace.

Whatever has become of Lissy in the White Hall of the King, she has not yet helped him break through to this world. Perhaps tomorrow they will all start to die. Or the day after. Hope lives like a frail featherless bird just moments old. And while there is still hope, I must try to end this a better way, because the mortals will not let my father go unpunished. They will take their revenge.

And then we will *all* die.

But Rose is dead, though, and I will be the one who pays for that, because I was there. I chose not to stop the boy. If I could have wielded that knife myself, I would. When my father comes I will be ready. I won't be alone. He has taken Lissy, my only sister, but there was another like her. Long ago when the world was young, before the covenant in the great church at Fontevrault, far to the west where the sun was warm on our backs and sweet bitter olives hung in the trees, and the air smelt of crushed oranges. Before it was all forbidden.

And all the time, with every rumour I follow, every half-forgotten story, I am closer to finding him. I trace every step.

Together, we will fight. Together, we will destroy the Swan King for all time.

Acknowledgements

I'd like to say a big thank-you to Denise
Johnstone-Burt, Daisy Jellicoe, Ellen Holgate,
Kirsty Ridge and Catherine Clarke for all their
help with *Hidden Among Us*.

BLOODLINE

I N THE WILD LANDSCAPE
of Dark Age Britain, Essa is abandoned by
his father in a lonely marsh-village trapped
between two warring kingdoms. Destined
to become tangled in the bitter feud, Essa's part in
it is more important than he ever dreamed. But how
will Essa save those he loves and discover the secret
of his true identity when he can trust no one?

*"A rich, vivid historical fantasy and a tremendously
assured first novel."* Philip Reeve

BLOODLINE RISING

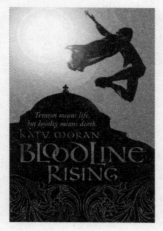

Cai, the ghost, is the fastest, most cunning young criminal in Constantinople. A perfect life, until he is captured, bound and sent to Britain – the home his barbarian parents fled long ago. When he is taken in by Wulfhere, prince of Mercia, Cai soon discovers that his Anglish master knows more about his family than he does. But war threatens and Cai finds he must choose: will he betray his new clan and save himself, or be loyal and risk his life?

"An excellent, well-written novel that makes a lasting impression." Books for Keeps

SPIRIT HUNTER

Two empires are at war.

This time, the Empress of China is sure she
will destroy the Horse Tribes for ever.

She sends a deadly weapon across the desert
with her army: Swiftarrow, her Shaolin spy.
But Swiftarrow has more than one mission to
complete. He must also find a new recruit for the
empress, a young barbarian to train as Shaolin:
swift as a shadow, more silent than death.

Out on the Steppe, a young Horse Tribe shaman
dreams of a great battle and the slaughter of
her people. She knows that war is coming.
She must stop the bloodshed. But how?

"Epic... Exciting..." Independent

Dangerous to know

Bethany + Jack

Two teenagers in love.

Why is everyone desperate to keep them apart?

"Beautifully observed." The Book Bag